Rosy is my Relative

Rosy, the elephant bequeathed to young Adrian
Rookwhistle by a reprobate relative, turned out
to be a handful: not only because of her size but
also because of her fondness for strong drink. To
Adrian she represented the chance to get away
from a City shop and a suburban lodging by
exploiting her theatrical talent and experience.
To Rosy their progress towards the gayer South
Coast resorts offered undreamed-of opportunities
for drink and destruction.

So the Monkspepper Hunt is driven to de-
lirium and Lady Fenneltree's stately home re-
duced to a shambles. In due course the constabulary caught up with the pair, whose ensuing
trial was alike a triumph of the law and of
Rosy's enormous charm. The verdict was—but
then the story has to be read to be believed, if
then.

In spite of all this the author firmly maintains
that his first novel is entirely credible, further
that it is 'an almost true story'!

GERALD DURRELL

Rosy is My Relative

Collins
FONTANA BOOKS

First published 1968
First issued in Fontana Books 1969

© Gerald Durrell 1968
Printed in Great Britain
Collins Clear-Type Press
London and Glasgow

For
NOEL COWARD
who has a passion
for pachyderms

CONTENTS

AUTHOR'S NOTE

ALTHOUGH MANY PEOPLE will not believe me, I would like to place it on record that this is an almost true story. By this I mean that Rosy and Adrian Rookwhistle really did exist. I had the privilege of meeting Rosy myself. Nearly all the adventures described in this book really happened. I have merely embroidered and polished here and there.

I am deeply indebted to Miss Eileen Molony, for it was she who first drew my attention to Rosy and Adrian Rookwhistle, and so provided the recipe for this fairy story.

I would also like to thank Lord Coutanche, Sir Robert Le Masurier, Bailiff of Jersey, and Mr. Cutland the Bailiff's Secretary for allowing me to attend the Royal Court in St. Helier in order to gather what authors normally rather pompously call atmosphere. I am also grateful to Mr. John Langin for reading the relevant portions of the book and keeping me straight on legal procedure. I would hasten to add, however, that my interpretation of the law bears absolutely no resemblance to the way that justice is dispensed in Jersey.

My thanks also to Mr. Swanson who allowed me to go behind the scenes of the Royal Opera House and who gave me many fascinating details about its history.

Mr. Douglas Matthews of the London Library went to a great deal of trouble to find me books dealing with the period. Again I would like to state that if I have gone wrong anywhere, the mistake is mine and not his.

Last, but certainly not least, I would like to thank my secretary, Miss Doreen Evans, who before coming to me was appropriately enough, secretary to a Coroner and Clerk to the justices, and gave me useful information during the writing of this book.

GERALD DURRELL

1 THE ABOMINABLE ACTION OF AN UNCLE

Unaware that doom was overtaking him, Adrian Rook-whistle, in his shirt sleeves, was occupied in making faces at himself in his looking-glass. At seven o'clock every morning Adrian would stand in his attic bedroom and commune thus with his reflection. The mirror was a large one with a wide gilt frame, and its surface was grey and pitted, like a tired iced pond at the end of a hard winter. It reflected both Adrian and his room in a sort of greyish haze, as though the whole scene was being viewed through a large cobweb. Adrian gazed at his reflection with some animosity.

"Thirty years!" he said, accusingly. "Thirty years . . . half your life gone! And what have you seen? What have you done? Nothing!"

He glared at himself in the mirror, disliking his unruly dark hair that no amount of water would flatten, his large, rather soulful dark eyes and his wide mouth. It was, he decided, a thoroughly unattractive face. He lowered his lids fractionally, moulded his mouth into the nearest approach to a sneer that it was capable of, and breathed deeply through his nose so that his nostrils flared out in the most satisfactory way.

"Sir," he snarled through clenched teeth, "unhand the lady or I will be forced to deal with you. Ignorant though you are, you cannot be unaware of the fact that I am the finest swordsman outside France."

He paused and stared at his reflection; he had to confess that, even allowing for his natural prejudice, he did not look like the finest swordsman outside France. Adventure, he had decided some time ago, was what he really craved, but it seemed that adventure so seldom came to people with his sort of face. There *had* been one occasion (and he blushed now even to think of it) when he had seized what he thought to be his great opportunity and had stopped what he assumed to be a runaway horse-drawn bus. It transpired that the bus was in fact a horse-drawn fire engine performing an errand of mercy. The broken leg he had sustained was a mere nothing compared to the reprimand that the Magistrate had given him, and the fact that the shop that was on fire had been burnt to the ground.

Adrian was the product of a union between the Reverend Sebastian Rookwhistle and Rowena Rookwhistle. His parents had conceived him—in a moment of mental aberration—during the course of a long and extremely dull married life entirely devoted to carrying out God's commands. For a long time, indeed, Adrian was under the impression that his father was the only man in the country who had direct access to the Almighty. Adrian's appearance in the world had been treated by his father with a certain embarrassment, and by his mother with an air of pleased surprise.

His upbringing, in the village of Meadowsweet, had been so placid, so blameless and so dull that Adrian had difficulty in remembering anything about it at all. Meadowsweet was one of those tiny, remote hamlets where conversation was confined to meteorological or agricultural subjects, conducted in a series of inarticulate grunts, and where the greatest excitement of the day was the earth-shattering recollection that ten years previously Farmer Raddle's cow had given birth to twin calves. Here Adrian grew up, and his only entertainments were bell-ringing, tea parties at the vicarage once a week, and visits to those sick members of the local peasantry who were too weak to fend off the ponderous patronage of the Reverend Rookwhistle.

When Adrian had reached the age of twenty, his father and mother were removed from this world in one fell swoop, the Almighty (in one of his more absent-minded moments) having failed to inform the Reverend Rookwhistle that the bridge between the villages of Meadowsweet and Hellebore had been washed away. So Adrian was deprived of mother, father and vicarage. His father's savings turned out to be so modest as to be almost non-existent, and it became obvious that Adrian would have to work for his living. So, in the brilliant summer of 1890, armed with a letter of introduction from one of his father's friends, he made his way to the great, sprawling, rattling, jingling, smoke-shrouded City, and there became a clerk in the highly respectable establishment of Bindweed, Cornelius and Chunter, purveyors of greengroceries to Ladies and Gentlemen of Quality. Here he had spent ten hardworking but uneventful years on the princely salary of fifteen shillings a week. But Adrian felt that there was more to life than being enshrined for ever in the emporium of Bindweed, Cornelius and Chunter. Recently this problem had been occupying his mind to the exclusion of practically everything else, and he talked about it to his reflection in the mirror :

"*Other* people," he muttered as he paced up and down his room, with an occasional sideways glance at the mirror to make sure he was still there, "*other* people lead exciting, interesting lives. They have extraordinary things happen to them . . . they have *adventures*. Why can't they happen to me?"

He squared up to the mirror again. His eyelids drooped. He sneered.

"I have warned you, sir," he said, his voice quivering with ill-concealed passion, "unhand that lady or 'twill be the worse for you."

He made a vague chopping motion with his hand that knocked his hair-brush on to the floor.

So occupied was he with his own thoughts that he had been unaware of the slow, strange thumping and wheezing noise which should have warned him that his landlady was making one of her infrequent sorties to the attic. A thunderous knocking on the door made him jump so badly that he dropped his imaginary sword.

"Are you there, Mr. Rookwhistle?" enquired Mrs. Lavinia Dredge in her trenchant baritone, as if it were the last place in the world that she expected to find him.

"Oh, yes, Mrs. Dredge," said Adrian, hastily glancing round the room to make sure it would meet with her approval. "Do come in."

Mrs. Dredge pushed open the door and leant against it, gasping with all the vigour of a leviathan that had just zoomed up from several hundred fathoms. She was large-boned, like one of the better varieties of Shire horse, and on this stalwart framework there hung great, soft, voluptuous rolls of avoirdupois. A buttress-work of stays, linen and rubber was required to keep this bulk under control, so Mrs. Dredge's body creaked and groaned alarmingly with each breath she took. Her black hair was piled high on her head and nailed in place with a forest of pins and round her massive neck hung a vast array of necklaces and pendants that tinkled and clattered as her massive bosom heaved.

This early morning appearance of Mrs. Dredge threw Adrian into a panic. What awful crime, he wondered, had he committed now? He distinctly remembered having wiped his boots last evening when he came in, so it could not be that. Had he forgotten to put the cat out? No, it could not be that. Had he cleaned the bath?

"Do . . . er . . . do you want to see me?" asked Adrian, thinking as he said it what a fatuous question it was. Mrs. Dredge would hardly have dragged her blubbersome body up three flights of stairs unless she *had* wanted to see him. However, such is the art of conversation in England, Mrs. Dredge admitted that, yes, she had wanted to see him. She then proceeded to wrinkle up her nose and upper lip and sniff loudly and ferociously, so that her well-developed moustache quivered.

"You 'aven't, I 'ope, Mr. Rookwhistle, been *smoking* in 'ere?" she enquired ominously.

"No, no. Good heavens, no," said Adrian, wondering if he had hidden his pipe successfully from those prying, black-currant eyes.

"I'm glad," said Mrs. Dredge, giving a great sigh that produced the most musical creakings from her scaffolding. "Mr. Dredge *never* smokes in the 'ouse."

Quite early on in his association with Mrs. Dredge, Adrian had learnt that her husband was dead (presumably smothered, Adrian imagined). But Mrs. Dredge, being a firm believer in the after-life, always referred to him as if he were still in residence. It was confusing, and one of Adrian's private nightmares was that one day he would suddenly come face to face with Mr. Dredge—perhaps neatly stuffed with horse-hair and with glass eyes—occupying a position in the hall on the landing.

"I come up to call you," Mrs. Dredge went on, "in case you 'ad slept in."

"Oh, thank you very much," said Adrian.

This sudden and unprecedented solicitude puzzled Adrian considerably.

"Also," Mrs. Dredge said, fixing her little black eyes on him accusingly, "there's a letter for you."

Of all the things that Adrian might have expected Mrs. Dredge to say, this was the least likely. Never, since the death of his mother and father, had he received a letter from anyone. What few friends he had were living in such close proximity to him that there was no need to communicate by letter.

"A letter? Are you *sure*, Mrs. Dredge?" asked Adrian, bewildered.

"Yes," said Mrs. Dredge firmly, "a letter addressed to you," and added, as if to remove any doubt, "in an envelope."

Adrian stared at her. Mrs. Dredge coloured and bridled under his glance.

"Mr. Dredge," she said haughtily, "receives any number of letters, so I 'opes I knows what one looks like."

"Oh yes, yes, I'm sure," said Adrian quickly, "but how extraordinary. I wonder who's writing to me? Thank you very much, Mrs. Dredge, for coming up to tell me. You really needn't have bothered."

"Not at all," said Mrs. Dredge regally, swivelling her

13

bulk round so that she faced more or less in the direction of the stairs. "Mr. Dredge always says you should do unto your neighbour the same as what 'e would do to you, only you're given the chance and 'e probably isn't."

With these words she creaked heavily down the stairs, and Adrian closed the door and resumed his pacing. Who on earth, he wondered, could be writing to him? As he put on his collar and tie and shrugged himself into his coat he came to the conclusion that the only people who would waste a halfpenny stamp on him were Bindweed, Cornelius and Chunter, informing him that they no longer required his services. Full of foreboding he clattered downstairs and into the kitchen. Mrs. Dredge was performing her daily all-in wrestling match with saucepans, frying-pans and various other kitchen utensils which most women seem to regard as friends but which Mrs. Dredge regarded as the serried ranks of an implacable enemy. Adrian sat down and there, next to his plate, was an envelope with his name and address clearly written in a neat, bold copperplate hand. Mrs. Dredge waddled over from the stove, clasping in one large hand a frying-pan containing the incinerated remains of three quarters of a black pudding which she shovelled on to Adrian's plate. They both coughed rather furtively over the pale blue smoke that rose from it.

"Mr. Dredge likes black pudding," said Mrs. Dredge with a faintly defensive air.

"Did he? I mean, does he?" said Adrian, stirring the charred remains on his plate with his fork. "I expect it's awfully good for one."

"Yes," said Mrs. Dredge with satisfaction, "it's what kept 'im going."

Adrian inserted a forkful of red hot, tasteless, leatherlike substance into his mouth, and tried to compose his features into an expression of delight.

"Good, eh?" said Mrs. Dredge, who was watching him like a hawk.

"Delicious!" said Adrian, who had burnt his tongue

severely. Mrs. Dredge sat down heavily, and rested her massive bosom on the table-top.

"Well," she asked, her little black eyes fixed on the letter, "aren't you going to open it?"

"Oh, yes," said Adrian, who had been overcome with reluctance to open the letter at all, "in a minute. This black pudding is really excellent, Mrs. Dredge."

But Mrs. Dredge was not going to be led aside by any gastronomic exchanges.

"It might be important," she said.

Adrian sighed and picked up the envelope. He would get no peace from Mrs. Dredge until he had read the letter and divulged its contents to her. Aware of her eyes upon him, he tore the letter open and unfolded the two sheets of paper it contained.

The very first words riveted his attention, for it began: "My dear Nephew." He dimly remembered that when he was ten years old or so, his Uncle Amos had arrived, unheralded, at the vicarage accompanied by three morose-looking Collie dogs and a green parrot, whose command over the shorter and more virulent words in the language was complete.

He remembered his uncle as being a kindly and exuberant man, whose unannounced arrival and the linguistic abilities of whose parrot had tried even the Reverend Sebastian's Christian charity to breaking point. After staying a couple of days, Uncle Amos had disappeared as mysteriously as he had arrived. His father had told him later that Uncle Amos was the black sheep of the family, "lacking in moral fibre," and as the subject was obviously painful, Adrian had never mentioned his uncle again.

He now read his uncle's letter with staring eyes and a sinking sensation that convinced him that his entire stomach, including the black pudding, had been suddenly and deftly removed.

"MY DEAR NEPHEW,

You probably will not recall the occasion when, some

years ago, I made your acquaintance at the rather repulsive vicarage which your father and mother insisted on inhabiting. Since then I have learnt of their demise—not, I must confess, with any great sorrow since, in the conversations I have had with both your parents over the years, they always gave me to understand that their one desire in life was to leave it and be enfolded in the bosom of the Lord. However, these circumstances make it appear that you are my only living relative. From what I remember of you, you seemed a nice enough boy at the time, though whether in the intervening years your parents have managed to fill your head with a lot of flim-flam and nitty-water I have no way of knowing.

Be that as it may, I am not at this juncture in a position to argue with fate. The local leech has apprised me of the fact that I have not long to live. The thought does not particularly alarm me, since I have led a full life and committed nearly all the more attractive sins. What does worry me, however, is the fate of my co-partner. She has been with me now for the last eighteen years, and together we have seen fair weather and foul. Therefore I should not like to feel that upon my demise she would be cast out friendless into the world, without a man to look after her. I say 'man' advisedly, for she does not get on with members of her own sex.

Having given the matter considerable thought I have decided that you—as my only living relative—should be the person to undertake this duty. This will not prove to be an irksome burden upon your pocket for if you go to Ammassor and Twist, Merchant Bankers of 110 Cottonwall Street in the City, you will find—lodged in your name —the sum of £500. I beg that you will use this to sustain Rosy in the style to which she is accustomed.

As death-bed scenes are always unpleasant, I am sending Rosy down to join you immediately so that she will not have to stand by and be harrowed by the sight of me drawing my last breath. She should, in fact, arrive almost simultaneously with this letter.

Whatever your father may have said of me (and it's

probably all true) this is, at least, one good act that I am performing in an otherwise satisfactorily corrupt existence. Your father was, in his rather weak-minded way, always a champion of those unfortunates who were left friendless in the world, and I can only hope that you have inherited this trait. Therefore, I beg, do what you can for Rosy. The whole thing has been a great shock to her, and I look to you to soothe her in her grief.

Your very affectionate Uncle,
AMOS ROOKWHISTLE

P.S. Rosy, unfortunately—and I feel that I am, in some small measure, to blame for this—has a certain inclination towards what your father (never at a loss for a trite phrase) frequently described as 'The Demon Drink.' I beg that you will watch her alcohol consumption, as a surfeit tends to make her intractable. But then she is, alas, not alone in this.

A.R."

2 THE INTERMINABLE WAIT

It seemed to Adrian that the whole world had become dark and gloomy; an icy trickle of water was running up and down his spine, defying the laws of gravity. Through the dull buzzing in his ears he dimly heard Mrs. Dredge's voice.

"Well?" she said, "what's it all about?"

Dear heaven, thought Adrian, I can't possibly tell her.

"It's . . . it's a letter . . . um . . . from . . . er . . . one of my father's friends," he said, prevaricating wildly. "He just thought that I would like to know how things were in the village."

"After ten years?" snorted Mrs. Dredge. " 'E's taken 'is time, 'asn't 'e?"

"Yes . . . yes, it has been a long time," said Adrian, folding the letter up and putting it in his pocket.

But Mrs. Dredge was not one of those people who could be fobbed off with a précis. Her own harrowing description of Mr. Dredge's death generally occupied an hour and a half, so this flimsy explanation of the letter's contents hardly satisfied her.

"Well, how are they all, then?" she enquired.

"Oh," said Adrian, "they appear to be enjoying good health, you know."

Mrs. Dredge waited, her black eyes fixed on him implacably.

"Several of the people I knew have got married," Adrian went on desperately, "and ... and ... several of them have had babies."

"You mean," enquired Mrs. Dredge, a hopeful gleam in her eye, "you mean the ones that 'ave got married 'ave 'ad babies, or the other ones?"

"Both," said Adrian unthinkingly. "No, no, of course I mean the ones that have got married. Anyway, they're all in great ... er ... great spirits and I must ... um ... I must write and congratulate them."

"You mean congratulate the ones that 'ave got married?" asked Mrs. Dredge, who liked to get things clear in her mind.

"Yes," said Adrian, "and the ones who have had babies, of course."

Mrs. Dredge sighed. This was not her idea of how to tell a story. If it had been *her* letter, now, she would have eked out the contents with miserly care and regaled Adrian for a week with snippets of information and speculation.

"Well," she said philosophically, surging to her feet, "it will give you something to do in the evenings, I suppose."

As rapidly as he could, his mind still reeling under the shock of his uncle's letter, Adrian shovelled the unattractive remains of the black pudding into his mouth, washed it down with some tea, and rose from the table.

"Going already?" said Mrs. Dredge in surprise.

"Yes. I thought I would just call in on Mr. Pucklehammer on my way to work," said Adrian.

"Don't you go spending too much time with '*im*, now," said Mrs. Dredge severely. "That man could be an evil influence on an upright, honest young man like yourself."

"Yes, I suppose you're right," said Adrian meekly. He numbered Mr. Pucklehammer among his closest friends, but he was not prepared to argue about it just then.

"Don't be late for your supper," said Mrs. Dredge. "I got a nice bit of 'addock."

As an inducement to punctuality, Adrian felt, this left a lot to be desired.

"No, I won't be late," he promised, and made his escape from the house before Mrs. Dredge could think up a fresh topic of conversation to delay him.

Mr. Pucklehammer was by trade a carpenter and coffin maker who owned a large yard about a quarter of a mile from Mrs. Dredge's establishment. A few years previously Adrian had gone to the yard to have some minor repairs done to his big wooden trunk. He and Mr. Pucklehammer had taken an instant liking to each other and had since become firm friends. Adrian, who did not make friends easily because of his shyness, had come to look upon Mr. Pucklehammer as his father confessor. His one thought now was to get down to the yard as quickly as possible and discuss with his friend the contents of this letter that threatened to undermine the very foundations of his quiet, orderly world. Mr. Pucklehammer, he felt sure, would know what to do.

As he hurried down the road he began to agree with his father's estimation of his Uncle Amos's character. How could anyone *do* a thing like that? Leaving aside the money (which he admitted was generous), how could anyone suddenly plant on an innocent nephew a lady of indeterminate years with an addiction to the bottle? It was surely not humane. At this point another terrible thought struck him, and he stopped so suddenly his bowler hat fell off. Dimly he remembered his father saying that his Uncle Amos had worked in circuses and fairgrounds. What if this Rosy turned out to be an acrobat, or— worse still—one of those fast, abandoned females who

19

stood on the backs of horses in spangled tights? To have a female acrobat suddenly pushed into your life was bad enough, but to have a drunken female acrobat pushed into your life was surely more than anyone could endure. How *could* his uncle have done this to him? Retrieving his bowler hat, he made Mr. Pucklehammer's yard almost at a run.

Mr. Pucklehammer was sitting on a newly completed coffin finishing his breakfast, which consisted of a pint of beer and a cheese sandwich of mammoth dimensions. He was a short, stocky little man with a face like an amiable bulldog. In his time he had been—among many other things—a champion wrestler and weightlifter. The excesses of this career had left him completely musclebound so that now, although every muscle and sinew stood out in carunculations like a melting candle, he could only move with difficulty.

"Hello, boy," he greeted Adrian, waving the sandwich at him amicably. "Want some breakfast? Spot of beer, eh?"

"No, no," said Adrian, out of breath and pale with emotion, "I want your advice."

"Ho?" said Mr. Pucklehammer, raising his shaggy brows. "What's to do? You look as if you've seen a ghost."

"Far worse, far worse," said Adrian dramatically. "I'm ruined . . . read this."

He thrust the letter at Mr. Pucklehammer, who surveyed it with interest.

"I can't read," said Mr. Pucklehammer simply. "Never seem to have had time to learn, somehow, what with one thing and another. You read it to me, boy."

In a voice trembling with emotion Adrian read him the contents of his Uncle Amos's letter. When he came to the end there was silence as Mr. Pucklehammer inserted a large section of cheese sandwich into his mouth and chewed meditatively.

"Well," said Adrian at last, "what am I to do?"

"To do?" said Mr. Pucklehammer, swallowing his sandwich in surprise. "Why, do exactly as your uncle wants you to do."

Adrian gazed at his friend in amazement, wondering if Pucklehammer had either misunderstood the letter or had taken leave of his senses.

"But how *can* I?" he said, his voice rising. "How can I take on a strange female . . . a strange, *drunken* female? Mrs. Dredge would never allow her in the house . . . then there's my job. Good Lord, if they got to know about it they'd sack me. And suppose she's one of those female acrobats, what do I do then?"

"I don't see what's wrong with that," said Mr. Pucklehammer judicially. "Saw one of them myself once. Nice fleshy piece she was too. Had sequins all over her. Lovely bit of dolly-roll."

"Oh, my God," said Adrian in agony, "I hope she's not going to arrive here all covered with sequins."

"There's no denying," said Mr. Pucklehammer musingly, "there's no denying that five hundred pounds is a very generous sum, very generous indeed. Why, with that sort of money you could give up your job . . . you've often said you wanted to."

"And what about this inebriated female?" asked Adrian sarcastically.

"Well, you two could live very comfortably on a hundred and twenty a year and in four years you could set up a little business," said Mr. Pucklehammer. "If she's one of the fair folk you want to go in for something like a Punch and Judy. I've got a nice Punch and Judy I could let you have cheap."

"I have no intention of spending the next four years with a large, sequin-covered drunk playing at Punch and Judy," said Adrian loudly and clearly. "I wish you'd be more constructive."

"I don't see what you're flapdoodling about, boy," said Mr. Pucklehammer severely. "Here you've got a nice legacy with a female thrown in. Lots of young men would give anything to be in your shoes."

"I wish they *were* in my shoes," said Adrian desperately. "If they want to spend the rest of their lives with a drunken acrobat, they're welcome."

"Your uncle didn't say she was drunk *all* the time," said Mr. Pucklehammer fairly. "She might be quite nice. Why don't you just wait and see what she's like when she turns up?"

"I can imagine what she's like, and the thought appals me," said Adrian. "Why, I don't even know her surname."

"Well, as long as you know her Christian name that's the main thing," said Mr. Pucklehammer philosophically. "Gets you on to a more intimate footing straight away."

"I *don't* want to get on an intimate footing with her," shouted Adrian, and then, smitten by a dreadful thought, "My God! What happens if she turns up while I'm at work and Mrs. Dredge meets her?"

"Ah, yes," said Mr. Pucklehammer musingly, "that's a point. You want to avoid that if you can."

Adrian paced up and down, thinking desperately, while Mr. Pucklehammer finished off the remains of his beer and wiped his mouth.

"I've got it," said Adrian at last, "it's Mrs. Dredge's Day to-day . . . you know, she goes to visit Mr. Dredge at the cemetery and spends the whole day there. She doesn't generally get back until evening. If I could send a message to work to say that I'm ill, or something, then I could hang around and wait for this Rosy person."

"Good idea," agreed Mr. Pucklehammer. "Look, I'll send young Davey round to the shop to tell 'em you're not well. Don't you worry about that. What you'd better do is to nip back smartish and keep an eye on the house. I'll be here if you want me."

So Adrian, cursing the day he said he wanted adventure, made his way back to Mrs. Dredge's establishment, and lurked furtively on the corner. Presently, to his relief, Mrs. Dredge appeared, clad in flowing black bombazine and with a large, purple hat on her head, clasping in her hand an enormous bunch of roses which were her weekly tribute to Mr. Dredge's grave. She passed down the road like a large and ominous galleon in full sail, and disappeared from sight.

Adrian paced up and down, his mind filled with wild, impracticable solutions to the problem. He would run away to sea. He rejected this almost immediately, for he felt sick on the top deck of a horse-drawn bus travelling very slowly, so he knew that he—or rather, his stomach— was not cut out for a nautical career. Should he pose as Mr. Dredge and say that he, Rookwhistle, had unfortunately just died? Intriguing though this solution was he was compelled to admit that it would require someone more skilled in the art of duplicity to achieve success.

It's no good, he thought desperately, wiping his damp hands on his handkerchief, I shall just have to be firm with her. I shall point out that I am a young man making my way in the world, and that I cannot, at this stage, accept the responsibility of a strange woman. I will let her have the five hundred pounds and she must go. But what if she bursts into tears and has hysterics or, worse still, what if she is drunk and turns belligerent? The sweat broke out on his brow at the thought. No, he must remain firm, kind but firm. Hoping that he would have the courage to be kind but firm when the moment arrived, Adrian resumed his pacing.

By midday he was in such a state of nervous tension that a leaf falling from a tree made him start uncontrollably. He had just decided that death would be preferable to this agony of waiting, when the dray turned into the road. It was an enormous dray, pulled by eight extremely exhausted-looking cart horses, and driven by a stout, choleric-looking little man in a bright yellow bowler hat and a red and yellow check waistcoat. Idly, Adrian wondered what such an enormous dray could contain. The man in the yellow bowler was obviously nearing his destination, for he had pulled a piece of paper out of his waistcoat pocket and was comparing it with the numbers of the houses as he passed. Then to Adrian's astonishment he pulled up his team of horses outside Mrs. Dredge's house. What on earth, thought Adrian, had his frugal landlady been buying? The dray was large enough to contain almost anything. He walked down the road to where the driver was mopping his face with a large handkerchief.

"Good morning," said Adrian, full of curiosity.

The man settled his bowler hat more firmly on his head and gave Adrian a withering look.

" 'Morning," he said, brusquely, "if it *is* a good morning, which I, for one, doubt."

"Are you . . . er . . . have you got something for this house?" enquired Adrian.

"Yes," said the man, consulting the piece of paper in his hand. "Leastways, I got something for a Mr. Rookwhistle."

Adrian jumped and broke out in a cold sweat.

"Rookwhistle . . . are you sure?" he asked faintly.

"Yes," said the man, "Rookwhistle. Mr. A. Rookwhistle."

"I am Mr. A. Rookwhistle," quavered Adrian. "What . . .?"

"Ah!" said the man, giving him a malevolent look, "so you're Mr. Rookwhistle, are you? Well, the sooner you collect your property, the sooner I'll be 'appy."

He stamped off round the back of the dray and Adrian, following him, found him struggling with the massive doors.

"But what have you got?" asked Adrian desperately.

By way of an answer the man threw back the great double doors and revealed to Adrian's incredulous and horrified gaze a large, wrinkled and exceptionally benign-looking elephant.

3 THE SHOCKING ARRIVAL

"There she is," said the carter, with satisfaction, "and she's all yours."

"It can't be," said Adrian faintly, "it *can't* be mine . . . I don't want an elephant."

"Now look 'ere," said the carter with some asperity, "I've travelled all night, see, to bring this ruddy animal to you. You're Mr. A. Rookwhistle, therefore she's your animal."

Adrian began to wonder if the shocks he had already received that morning had unhinged his mind. It was bad enough having to cope with an acrobat, without finding himself suddenly saddled with, of all things, an elephant. Then, suddenly, he had an awful suspicion.

"What's its name?" he asked hoarsely.

"Rosy," said the carter, "leastways, that's what they told me."

At the sound of her name the elephant swayed to and fro gently and uttered a small squeak, like the mating cry of a very tiny clarinet. She was shackled inside the dray by two chains padlocked round her front legs, and they made a musical clanking noise when she moved. She stretched out her trunk seductively towards Adrian and blew a small puff of air at him. Oh God, thought Adrian, I'd much rather it was a drunken acrobat.

"Look here," he said to the carter, "what am I going to *do* with her?"

"That," said the carter with ill-concealed satisfaction, "is your problem, mate. I was merely engaged to deliver 'er and deliver 'er I 'ave. So now, as I 'aven't 'ad any breakfast, if you'll kindly remove 'er from me van, I'll be on me way."

"But you can't just leave me in the street with an elephant," Adrian protested.

"Why not?" enquired the carter simply.

"But I can't take her in there," said Adrian wildly, gesturing at Mrs. Dredge's six foot square front garden. "She won't fit, for one thing . . . and she'd tread all the plants down."

"Ar, you should 'ave thought of that before you ordered 'er," said the carter.

"But I didn't order her. She was left to me by my uncle," said Adrian, reflecting as he said it how very unlikely the whole thing sounded.

"'E couldn't 'ave liked you very much," said the carter.

"Look, do be sensible," Adrian pleaded. "You can't just stick an elephant down in front of me and then go off and leave me."

"Now you look 'ere," said the carter in a shaking voice, his face growing purple, "I was engaged to transport an elephant. It was foolish of me, I know, but there we are. I've been on the go all night. Every pub we passed she nearly 'ad the dray over. It's the worst ruddy journey I've ever 'ad in twenty-four years' experience as a carter. And now all I want to do is to get rid of 'er as quickly as possible. So if you'll kindly remove 'er, I'll be on me way."

Even if he succeeded in getting Rosy into Mrs. Dredge's front or back garden, Adrian thought, how was he to explain the sudden appearance of an elephant? It was too much to hope that Mrs. Dredge would not notice her. But something had to be done, for the carter was adamant and growing more and more purple and restive with each passing moment. Then Adrian had an idea. Pucklehammer, he thought, Pucklehammer's yard. That would be the place to take her.

"Look," said Adrian desperately to the carter, "can you take her down the road a bit? I've got a friend who's got a yard. We can put her in there."

The carter sighed deeply. "See 'ere," he said, "I've delivered your elephant to you. I was not asked to deliver it anywhere else but 'ere."

"But it's only just down the road, and it'll be worth a sovereign to you," said Adrian.

"Well, that's different," said the carter and he slammed the doors of the dray, shutting off the sight of Rosy, who had picked up a small wisp of straw in her trunk and was daintily fanning herself with it. The carter shouted to his horses, they strained forward, and the massive dray rumbled down the road, with Adrian pacing feverishly beside it, endeavouring to persuade himself that there was nothing Mr. Pucklehammer would like better than an elephant in his yard. He left the carter in the street and went into the yard. Mr. Pucklehammer was still sitting on the coffin, consuming yet another pint of beer.

"Hello, boy," he said jovially, "got your acrobat?"

"Mr. Pucklehammer," said Adrian in a low, controlled voice, "you've got to help me. You are, indeed, the only person I can turn to in what is rapidly becoming a nightmare."

"Why, what's happened, boy?"

"She . . . it . . . has arrived," said Adrian.

"What's she like?" enquired Mr. Pucklehammer with interest.

"She . . . Rosy," said Adrian, "is an elephant."

"An *elephant*?" said Mr. Pucklehammer, and whistled. "That's a bit of a problem for you."

"You could put it that way," said Adrian coldly.

"An elephant," repeated Mr. Pucklehammer thoughtfully. "Well, well. That *is* a bit of a facer."

"I'm inclined to agree with you," said Adrian. "What I'm to do with her I just don't know, but all I do know is that the wretched man who brought her, not unnaturally wants to get rid of her. She won't fit in Mrs. Dredge's garden, so I've had to bring her here. Will you let me keep her in your yard for a bit, until I decide what to do?"

"Yes, yes, boy, of course," said Mr. Pucklehammer readily, "plenty of room here. Never had an elephant here, come to think of it. It'll make a bit of a change."

"Thank God," said Adrian fervently, "I'm most grateful to you." He went back into the road where the carter appeared to be melting steadily into his handkerchief.

"It's all right," said Adrian, "she can come in here."

The carter threw open the doors of the dray, and Rosy uttered a pleased squeal at the sight of her friends.

" 'Ere's the keys," said the carter, handing them to Adrian. "One for each padlock."

"Is she tame?" asked Adrian nervously, realising that up until that moment he had had no experience with elephants.

"I think so," said the carter. "You'll soon find out though, won't you?"

"Perhaps I ought to get it something to eat," said Adrian, "to keep it occupied. What do they eat?"

"Buns," said Mr. Pucklehammer, who was peering at Rosy with interest.

"Do be sensible," said Adrian irritably. "Where am I going to find a bun at this time of the day?"

" 'Ow about oats?" suggested the carter.

"No, no, it's buns they eat," said Mr. Pucklehammer.

"I do wish you'd stop gassing on about buns," said Adrian in exasperation, "we haven't *got* any buns."

"How about a cheese sandwich?" said Mr. Pucklehammer. "I'll go and get one and we'll try."

He returned presently with a large cheese sandwich, which he handed to Adrian. Very cautiously, holding the sandwich in front of him as though it were a weapon, Adrian approached Rosy's vast grey bulk.

"Here you are then, Rosy," he said hoarsely. "Nice cheese sandwich . . . good girl."

Rosy stopped swaying and watched his approach with twinkling eyes. When he was within range she stretched out her trunk and, with the utmost speed and delicacy, removed Adrian's bowler hat and placed it on her own massive domed head. Alarmed, Adrian jumped back, dropped the sandwich and trod heavily on the carter's foot. This did not improve the carter's already frayed temper. Picking up the sandwich Adrian approached Rosy again.

"Here you are, Rosy," he said in a trembling voice, "nice sandwich." Languidly Rosy reached out her trunk again, took the sandwich from Adrian's shaking fingers, and inserted it into her mouth which looked—to Adrian's startled gaze—the size of a large barrel. Faint grinding and slushing noises indicated that the elephant did eat cheese sandwiches. Hastily, while her mouth was full, Adrian went down on his knees, undid the padlocks and removed the shackles from Rosy's legs.

"There we are," he said, backing out of the dray. "Come along then . . . good girl."

Rosy sighed deeply, took off the bowler hat and fanned herself with it, but apart from this gave no indication that she intended to vacate the dray.

"I'm normally a patient man," said the carter untruthfully, "but I would like to point out, while you're stamping about all over me feet and stuffing that elephant on sandwiches, that I 'aven't 'ad so much as a bite to eat this morning."

"Well, I'm *trying* to get her out," said Adrian aggrievedly, "you can't *force* a thing that size."

"Would you care for a sandwich and a pint of beer?" Mr. Pucklehammer asked the carter.

"That's very obliging of you," said the carter, brightening perceptibly, "very obliging indeed."

While the carter and Adrian stood there staring at Rosy, who was now swaying to and fro and uttering heart-rending sighs, Mr. Pucklehammer went into the house and soon reappeared carrying a sandwich with a brimming pint of beer. The carter's delight at seeing these victuals was nothing compared to Rosy's enthusiasm when she saw the tankard. She uttered a loud and prolonged trumpeting that made Adrian jump, and lumbered out of the dray into the road. Mr. Pucklehammer stood rooted to the spot while Rosy, still trumpeting, seized the tankard in her trunk and proceeded to pour the contents into her cavernous mouth.

"Well, that's solved one problem," said the carter, "but what about me beer?"

"At least we know she'll eat sandwiches and drink beer," said Adrian, "though I can't see her existing for ever on that."

"I wouldn't want you to think me unfeeling," said the

carter, breathing through his nose, "but I'm more concerned with me own stomach than with 'ers."

Rosy handed the empty tankard back to Mr. Pucklehammer and followed him hopefully as he retreated into the yard. Having found an intelligent human being who appeared to recognise her needs, she was not going to let him out of her sight. She had a slow, stately, if slightly inebriated walk, and her ears flapped and cracked against the sides of her head as she moved. She uttered pleased little squeals, and as she entered the yard hot on Mr. Pucklehammer's heels, Adrian slammed the great double doors behind her, leant against them and mopped his face. That was the first step.

Although Rosy was intrigued by the drifts of curly white wood shavings, the piles of wood and the serried ranks of newly completed coffins, she still kept an eye on Mr. Pucklehammer, for he was obviously the dowser who was going to lead her to the master spring of beer. But at last they managed to creep into the house without her noticing. Once in the house Mr. Pucklehammer produced more beer and cheese sandwiches, and under the soothing influence of food and drink even the carter became almost benign.

"Funny sort of thing for your uncle to leave you," he said to Adrian.

"I wouldn't describe it as funny," said Adrian bitterly. "What I'm supposed to do with her, the Lord only knows."

"Sell 'er," advised the carter, pouring out more beer, "sell 'er to a circus. That's what *I'd* do."

"I can't," explained Adrian, "that's the awful part. I've been left five hundred pounds to look after her."

"I wonder 'ow many buns that'll buy," said the carter with interest.

"They must eat something else *besides* buns," said Adrian plaintively. "You know, cabbages and things. Anyway, we'll just have to experiment later."

"Don't you go fretting yourself, boy," said Mr. Pucklehammer. "She can stay here for two or three days until you decide what's best to be done. I'll look after her."

It was at this juncture that Rosy decided that the coffins—though fascinating in their way—were not sustaining enough. She approached the house and peered through the window. To her delight she discovered her friends gathered together in the room, consuming some of her favourite beverage. There was an air of relaxed conviviality, an air of good fellowship about the group, that Rosy found irresistible. It stimulated her. She was sure that they would want her to join them so she tapped delicately on the window with the tip of her trunk. It was a dainty, lady-like hint that she, too, would like to join in whatever celebrations were afoot. But her friends were so engrossed in their conversation that they did not notice. This, Rosy felt, was unfair. After all, she had had a long and tiring journey with only one pint of beer to sustain her, and there they were, guzzling away in the room without inviting her in. Normally, Rosy was an extremely patient elephant, but the sight of the carter pouring himself out yet another pint was too much for her. She inserted the tip of her trunk under the sash of the window and pulled. The entire window came away with a splendid crackling and tinkling noise, and Rosy, delighted with the success of her experiment, put her trunk through the window and trumpeted loudly.

"For God's sake," exclaimed Adrian, his nerves completely shattered, "give her some more beer, Mr. Pucklehammer, and shut her up."

"At this rate," said the carter helpfully, "you'll be spending most of your five 'undred quid on beer and repairs."

Mr. Pucklehammer went into the kitchen and found a large tin basin which he filled to the brim with beer. This he carried out into the yard, and Rosy's piercing squeals of delight were positively deafening. She dipped her trunk into the lovely brown liquid, sucked it up and then shot it into her mouth with a noise like a miniature waterfall. Very soon the basin was empty and Rosy, uttering small, self-satisfied belches to herself, wandered over to the shady side of the yard and lay down for a rest.

"Well, I must be on me way," said the carter. "Thanks very much for your 'ospitality."

"Not at all," said Mr. Pucklehammer.

"And you, sir," said the carter, turning to Adrian, "I wishes you the very best of luck. I 'ave a feeling with that little bundle of joy you're going to need it."

4 THE OPEN ROAD

Mr. Pucklehammer saw the carter safely out of the yard and came back into the house, where he found Adrian, his head in his hands, contemplating an empty beer mug gloomily.

"I simply can't think straight," said Adrian miserably, "I just *can't* think what to do."

"Have some more beer," suggested Mr. Pucklehammer, whose philosophy in life was simple and direct. "Stop fretting yourself . . . we'll think of something."

"It's all very well for you to keep soothing me," said Adrian irritably, "but I'm the one that's got the elephant. We don't even know what she eats yet."

"Buns," said Mr. Pucklehammer, clinging to his original premise. "You mark my words, she'll do well on buns."

"I wonder if the carter was right?" said Adrian thoughtfully. "If I could find a circus where she'd be happy and gave the owner the five hundred to look after her, I wonder if that would be legal?"

"I don't know if it would be legal," said Mr. Pucklehammer, pursing his lips thoughtfully, "but it's one solution."

"But where d'you find a circus?" said Adrian. "I haven't seen one since I was seven or eight."

"The seaside," said Mr. Pucklehammer promptly. "There's always circuses and fairs and such at the seaside."

"But we're fifty miles from the sea," said Adrian. "How would I get her there?"

"Walk her," said Mr. Pucklehammer, "the exercise will probably do her a power of good. One thing's for sure, you can't keep her here indefinitely. I don't mind having her, mind, but an elephant isn't the sort of thing you can keep in your yard without getting talk from the neighours. Nosey lot, round here."

"Well, there's nothing for it," said Adrian. "I'll have to tell Mrs. Dredge and the shop that my uncle's dying and that I have to go away for a bit. I don't think the shop will mind—I'm due for a holiday, anyway. How long do you think it will take me to get her down to the coast?"

"Rather depends," said Mr. Pucklehammer.

"Depends on what?" asked Adrian. "How many miles a day an elephant can walk?"

"No, I wasn't thinking about that," said Mr. Pucklehammer, "I was thinking about the number of pubs you might have to pass on the way."

"Yes," Adrian groaned, "I'd forgotten about that."

"Tell you what," suggested Mr. Pucklehammer. "You know that little old pony trap I've got in the shed out there? Well, if we did that up and made a sort of harness thing, Rosy could pull it. You could put all your clothes and some beer and stuff in the back . . ."

"Not beer," said Adrian hastily. "I'm not having any beer next to that creature."

"Well, food then," said Mr. Pucklehammer, "and then when you're all loaded up, off you go, eh?"

In spite of his anxiety Adrian felt a faint stirring of enthusiasm in his heart. He had always craved for adventure, hadn't he? Well, what could be more adventurous than setting off on a journey accompanied by an elephant? For the first time since receiving his uncle's letter he began to feel that things were not quite as bad as he thought. He was almost excited at the prospect of walking Rosy down to the coast.

"If I can make the coast in three days," he said thoughtfully, "it'll take me another couple of days to find a circus, I should think. Well, let's say ten days to a fortnight, to be on the safe side."

"Yes," agreed Mr. Pucklehammer, "you should be able to do it in that time, if all goes well."

"Right!" said Adrian, leaping to his feet and becoming once again (for a brief moment) the best swordsman outside France. "I'll do it!"

"Good lad!" said Mr. Pucklehammer. "I'd come with you, only I can't leave the yard. I bet you'll have a rare old time. Now, let's get organised. I'll get the trap out and give it a wash down and a lick of paint and it'll be all ready for you to-morrow."

Adrian went and peered through the window. Rosy was lying peacefully asleep, her ears twitching occasionally and her stomach rumbling with a sound like distant thunder.

"She'll need something to eat," he said worriedly. "Just listen to the poor thing's stomach."

"Now stop fussing," said Mr. Pucklehammer. "*I'll* attend to that."

He and Adrian went out into the yard and, careful not to wake Rosy, pulled the somewhat dilapidated pony trap from inside the shed.

"There you are," said Mr. Pucklehammer, gazing at it admiringly. "With a lick of paint she'll be as good as new. Now, you give her a wash down, boy, while I go and get some food for Rosy."

Adrian went and fetched a couple of buckets of warm water and a scrubbing brush, and was soon hard at work washing the trap down, whistling softly to himself. He was so absorbed in his work that it gave him a shock when a warm, grey trunk smelling strongly of beer suddenly curled round his neck in an affectionate manner. He was not yet used to the fact that elephants, for all their bulk, can move when they want to with considerably less noise than a house mouse. Rosy was standing behind him, staring down at him benignly. She blew a thoughtful blast of beer-laden breath into his ear and uttered a tiny squeak of greeting.

"Now look," said Adrian sharply, unwinding her trunk

from his neck, "you've got to stop messing about. You've been enough trouble already, heaven knows. You just go on back over there and sleep it off, there's a good girl."

By way of an answer, Rosy dipped her trunk into one of the buckets and noisily sucked up a good supply. Then, taking careful aim, she squirted the water over the sides of the pony trap. She refilled her trunk and repeated the process, while Adrian watched her in amazement.

"Well," he said at last, "if you're going to be *helpful*, that's different."

He soon found that if he indicated the area of the trap he wanted cleaned, Rosy would stand there and squirt water on it until further notice. All he had to do was keep replenishing the buckets. The force with which she could expel the water from her trunk greatly aided the cleaning process, and in next to no time the grime and cobwebs were washed away and the pony trap was beginning to look quite different. At this point Mr. Pucklehammer returned, carrying a bulging sack on his back.

"I couldn't get any buns," he said, obviously disappointed that he was not going to be able to prove his point, "but I managed to get some stale bread."

They opened the sack and extracted two large brown loaves, Adrian held them out towards Rosy, not at all convinced that she would accept this somewhat worn largesse, but Rosy uttered a squeal of pleasure and engulfed both loaves, devouring them with a speed and enthusiasm that had to be seen to be believed.

"There you are," said Adrian, "that's the feeding problem solved." He tipped the rest of the bread out of the sack and Rosy fell to like a glutton.

"My word," said Mr. Pucklehammer admiringly, "you have made a difference to that trap."

"It was mainly Rosy's work," said Adrian.

"Rosy?" asked Mr. Pucklehammer. "How d'you mean?"

"Well, she helped me. She squirted water over it . . . we had it clean in half the time."

"Would you believe it!" said Mr. Pucklehammer. "I wonder if she knows any more tricks?"

"I don't think we ought to start her off on tricks now," said Adrian hastily. "For one thing, I'd better go down to the bank and fix up about the money, hadn't I?"

"Right you are," said Mr. Pucklehammer. "You leave Rosy and me here. We'll be all right. I'll paint the trap while you're gone."

When Adrian returned to the yard some hours later, he was greeted by the sound of Mr. Pucklehammer's voice raised in song, accompanied by a periodical friendly squeal from Rosy. He went into the yard and there he found Rosy lying down, with Mr. Pucklehammer leaning against her shoulder, singing a serenade in her left ear. They were both bedaubed with splashes of paint, and an empty basin with traces of froth at the bottom and a pint tankard told Adrian that Mr. Pucklehammer and Rosy had cemented their friendship in no uncertain manner. Rather to his surprise—considering the condition of the two workers— the trap looked magnificent. Mr. Pucklehammer had obviously allowed all his latent artistic genius to come to the fore. The body of the trap was a bright clean daffodil yellow, and the shafts a brave scarlet. The spokes of the wheels had been cunningly picked out in blue and gold, and the whole thing shone like a jewel.

"Hi, boy!" said Mr. Pucklehammer, straightening up unsteadily. "Just been having a little sing-song with Rosy . . . she likes a good song. What d'you think of the cart, eh?"

"It's wonderful," said Adrian enthusiastically. "You've done it beautifully."

"Always thought I should've taken up art," said Mr. Pucklehammer gloomily, "but there's not much call for it nowadays. Did you get the money?"

"Yes, I got it," said Adrian. "There were lots of papers and things to sign . . . that's why I was so long."

"Well, if I were you," said Mr. Pucklehammer, pulling out his watch and peering at it blearily, "I'd cut off home and break the news to that Dredge woman."

"Yes, I suppose I'd better," sighed Adrian. "In the mean-

36

time don't go and give Rosy too much to drink, will you? You know what my uncle said in his letter."

"A drop of beer," said Mr. Pucklehammer severely, "never hurt no one."

Adrian stepped up to his vast, slumbering protégée and patted her domed head.

"Good night, Rosy old girl," he said.

Rosy opened one small, mischievous eye and peered at him. She looked almost as though she was smiling, Adrian reflected, as if she knew what the plans for the next day were and thoroughly approved of them. She uttered a tiny squeak, closed her eyes and went back to sleep, while Adrian left the yard and trudged down the road towards Mrs. Dredge.

As he had anticipated, Mrs. Dredge proved difficult about the whole thing. She was not at all satisfied with Adrian's excuse of a dying uncle, and in her efforts to get to the bottom of this she muddled both herself and Adrian up to such an extent that eventually neither of them really knew what the other was talking about. Finally admitting defeat, Mrs. Dredge gave up the attack and allowed Adrian (who now had a splitting headache) to go to bed.

The following morning, his bag neatly packed, he made his way down to the yard. He had spent an uneasy night beset with dreams of enormous herds of intoxicated pachyderms crushing multi-coloured pony traps underfoot, and so was somewhat relieved, on entering the yard, to be greeted by a squeal of pleasure from Rosy, who shambled forward and curled an affectionate trunk round his neck in greeting. Rosy's natural bonhomie was strangely endearing, thought Adrian. He was beginning to feel quite fond of his giant encumbrance.

With the aid of Mr. Pucklehammer he packed the back of the trap with the things they thought he would need for the journey. There was an assortment of tinned and bottled food for Adrian, three sacks of stale bread for Rosy, blankets, a hatchet, a first-aid outfit full of mysterious and potent-looking potions that belonged to Mr. Pucklehammer, a coil of stout rope, a canvas tarpaulin which, as Mr. Pucklehammer pointed out, was big enough to cover both Adrian and Rosy should it rain, Rosy's chains, in case it became necessary to shackle her, a firkin of ale, heavily disguised so that Rosy would not know it was there, and last but not least, Adrian's banjo. This instrument he had purchased some months before, but his progress on it had been slow, for he could only practise when Mrs. Dredge was down seeing Mr. Dredge at the cemetery. But Mr. Pucklehammer had thought it a splendid idea to take it with them. There was nothing, he explained to Adrian, like music when you were marching along. With music and beer, he insisted, you could get anywhere.

At last they had the trap loaded up and, with a certain difficulty, managed to hitch it up to Rosy who was fascinated by this new game and most co-operative. Then, with Adrian holding the tip of her ear as a guide, they walked round and round the yard several times to get her used to the idea.

"Well," said Adrian at last, "I suppose we'd better be going. I can't thank you enough for all your help, Mr. Pucklehammer."

"Don't think anything of it, boy," said Mr. Pucklehammer. "Only wish I was coming too. I bet you'll have a wonderful time. Now don't forget to write and let me know how you're getting on, will you?"

"I won't," said Adrian, "and thanks once again."

Mr. Pucklehammer patted Rosy affectionately on the flank and then flung open the gates of the yard. Rosy lumbered out into the road with Adrian guiding her, the trap rattling and tinkling behind them, and Mr. Pucklehammer stood and watched them out of sight.

Although they took back streets wherever possible, they still had to traverse a section of the city before they could strike out into the country, and it was in the city that Adrian added considerably to his knowledge of elephants, and the effect they had on life. For example, he soon discovered that horses were apt to have collective nervous breakdowns when suddenly confronted with one. It did

38

not seem to matter whether they were pulling an omnibus or a hansom cab, the result, so far as Adrian could see, was identical. They would utter a piercing whinny, rear up on their hind legs and then gallop off down the road at full speed, with their terrified owners clinging desperately to the reins. Rosy was considerably mystified by this; having been used to sensible, plebeian circus horses whom she considered to be her friends, this lack of enthusiasm on the part of the city horses was puzzling and hurtful, to say the least.

Another item of information that Adrian learnt about elephants—at the cost of a sovereign—was that they eat fruit and vegetables. They had rounded a corner and come face to face with an elderly man pushing a barrow piled high with market produce, at the sight of which Rosy had uttered a gleeful trumpeting and quickened her pace. She took no notice of Adrian clinging to her ear and shouting instructions. Her one thought was for the barrow-load of food so thoughtfully provided by fate. The owner of the barrow, being suddenly confronted by an elephant pulling a multi-coloured cart and bearing down on him with considerable speed, obviously bent on his destruction, turned tail and ran with a speed and agility one would not have suspected possible in one of his years. Rosy, uttering the peculiar roaring, squeaking noise she made when excited, stood by the discarded barrow and—in spite of Adrian's protests—proceeded to stuff fruit and vegetables into her mouth and chew them with immense satisfaction. While she was thus engaged Adrian had to pursue the barrow owner, calm his shattered nerves and pay for the damage. But at any rate, he reflected, it meant that Rosy had eaten a good meal, and he hoped that this would have a soothing effect on her for the rest of the trip. In this he was right, for Rosy paced along after her meal, her stomach rumbling musically, in a passive haze of goodwill.

Eventually the houses dwindled and fell away, until, when they breasted the top of a hill, the city lay glittering and sprawling behind them, and ahead, brilliant in the spring sunshine, lay the open country, a magical carpet of woods and fields, meandering rivers and misty hills, all ringing with lark song and the drowsy call of cuckoos. Adrian took a deep breath of the clean, clover-scented air.

"Well, there it is, Rosy," he said. "The country. I think we're over the worst now, my girl."

It was only later that he realised that this was the stupidest statement he could have made.

5 THE MONKSPEPPER HOLOCAUST

The sun was hot, the sky a clear blue, and all around them the hedgerows and copses, clad in a frilly green crinoline of spring leaves, were bursting like a musical box full of birdsong. It was wonderful, he decided, to be able to walk along the narrow, leafy lanes, their high banks covered with waterfalls of butter-yellow primroses, with Rosy shuffling through the dust at his side, listening to the clatter and scrape of the pony trap's wheels, and the pleasant squeaking and jingling of the harness. Presently, he removed his coat and threw it into the back of the trap. Half an hour later his waistcoat, celluloid collar and black tie joined it, and in a fit of wild daring he rolled up the sleeves of his shirt. Now, clad in his black trousers, striped braces and with his bowler hat perched jauntily on his head, he made an arresting sight, but he did not care. He was intoxicated with the sights and sounds of the countryside, and the road to adventure lay beneath his feet.

Mr. Pucklehammer had been quite right, Adrian discovered, Rosy did like singing, so as they walked along amicably together, he regaled her with music hall ditties. Finding these appreciated, Adrian got his banjo out and accompanied himself. If his playing left a little bit to be desired, Rosy was far too well-bred an audience to mention it, and the time passed very pleasantly.

By noon they were deep in the country. After consulting the map, Adrian had worked out their route so that they travelled by small side roads, for he had no desire to attract attention. In consequence they had not seen a living soul since leaving the city. They might have been two travellers in an uninhabited continent. Now, with the unaccustomed fresh air, Adrian was beginning to feel hungry. It was all right for Rosy, he reflected, she merely snatched a snack from the hedgerows as they passed. But he felt in need of something more substantial than leaves. Soon he spotted what he wanted : a gigantic meadow that sloped, as green as velvet, all daisy-starred, down to the banks of a river. The meadow was studded with groups of enormous oak trees piled with a great shimmering cumulus of leaves like giant green Pompadour wigs, and casting pleasant blue and black shadows on the lush grass.

"This is it, Rosy, my girl," said Adrian. "We'll stop here for a bite to eat."

He steered Rosy through a convenient gap in the hedge and down to a smooth patch of green sward under the oak trees. Six paces away the river ran glinting and whispering between reedy banks. Adrian unharnessed Rosy and unpacked the food. He carefully filled two large tankards of beer from the firkin and Rosy, at the sight of it, gave a prolonged and excited trumpet. Sitting on the grass Adrian made short work of a meat pie, a large slab of cheese and half a loaf of bread. After years of Mrs. Dredge's cooking, these simple foods tasted deliciously exotic to him. Rosy, having investigated the oak trees, torn down and eaten the more accessible branches, proceeded to scratch herself vigorously against the trunks, to the obvious alarm of a pair of magpies who had a nest in the upper branches. Adrian lay on his back, his eyes half closed, staring up through the filigree of leaves to the blue sky, and a great peace stole over him. Why, he thought, this isn't going to be nearly as bad as I thought. What, in fact, could be nicer? He yawned luxuriously, closed his eyes and drifted off to sleep.

He awoke some time later with a start, and lay for a moment, straining his ears, wondering what had caused the sound that had awakened him. He could hear the magpies scolding in the distance, and a lark chiming in the sky high above, but what he had heard was an extraordinary gurgling, splashing noise. He sat up and looked around in alarm. Rosy was nowhere to be seen. The most terrible thoughts immediately filled Adrian's mind : where had she gone? Was she terrorising some unfortunate cottager? Or, and he blanched at the thought, had she found a public house? He leapt to his feet and glanced around wildly.

From the cool depths of the river rose a sudden silvery fountain of spray, and Rosy surfaced. She was lying on her side in the deep water, and her normally grey hide was now black and shiny. She lay there, wallowing in ecstasy, occasionally putting her trunk under the water and blowing a series of reverberating bubbles. Filled with relief at having located her, Adrian walked down to the edge of the river, and Rosy gave a little squeak of pleasure at seeing him.

"Well, you *are* a clever girl," said Adrian. "Are you enjoying that . . . having a lovely bath, eh?"

By way of an answer Rosy shifted from her right side to her left, creating a tidal wave, and almost disappearing beneath the surface of the water.

"D'you know, old girl, I've half a mind to join you," said Adrian. "It looks wonderful."

He looked round furtively to make sure there was no one watching, and then quickly removed his clothes, retaining only his underpants for decency's sake. Uttering a piercing yell, he raced across the grass and leapt into the river. The water was icy cold but refreshing. He rose, spluttering, splashed his way over to where Rosy lay, and climbed on to her shoulder. Rosy gave a delighted squeak and, reaching up with her trunk, gently touched his face and wet hair.

"Glorious," said Adrian, patting Rosy on the ear. "Simply glorious. What an extremely good idea of yours, Rosy. What a sagacious, what an *intelligent* creature you are!"

He got precariously to his feet and proceeded to do a dance on Rosy's recumbent form, shouting "Glorious, simply glorious!" at intervals, until his feet slipped from under him and he fell with a splash into the river. As he rose choking and laughing to the surface, Rosy, gazing at him affectionately from her tiny bright eyes, squirted him with a trunkful of water. So for the next half hour they gambolled in the stream, to the extreme alarm of the coots and moorhens, and the annoyance of a kingfisher who had a nest in the bank nearby.

"The next village we come to," said Adrian as they hauled themselves dripping out of the river and lay down on the bank, "the *very* next village we come to, I shall buy a large scrubbing brush. And then I shall scrub you, Rosy my girl, until you're a lovely clean elephant."

Tired by their activities, they lay on the bank dozing, while the sun dried them. They were lying there so quietly that the fox had crossed the whole meadow and was quite close to them before they noticed him.

"Hello," said Adrian sitting up. "You're a fine fellow."

The fox stopped, one foot raised, its ears pricked. Then Rosy flapped her ears and stretched forward an enquiring trunk. The fox, uttering a sharp yap of alarm, jumped backwards and, turning sharply, ran down the river bank, plunged into the water and swam swiftly to the opposite bank. He hauled himself out of the water, shook himself vigorously, and with a baleful glance in the direction of Adrian and Rosy, disappeared into the hedge.

"Well, he wasn't very friendly, was he, Rosy?" said Adrian. "Not a convivial sort of chap at all."

He was just about to give Rosy a short but comprehensive lecture on foxes when they heard the hunt.

"Oh, Lord," gasped Adrian, who had quite forgotten that he was only wearing his underpants. "Here . . . quick . . . I must get some clothes on."

He leapt to his feet and started running to where he

had left his clothes, draped neatly over the shafts of the trap, but he was too late. Through the one gap in the tall hedge that surrounded the field poured the hunt, a brown and white cascade of hounds, moaning and howling excitedly, closely followed by a mass of red-coated huntsmen and women on beautiful prancing horses as bright and shiny as chestnuts. As a predicament it left practically nothing to be desired, Adrian decided. To be caught by what was, presumably, the aristocracy of the district in a large meadow accompanied by an elephant and a multi-coloured pony trap was eccentric enough, but when you were only wearing your underpants the whole thing became fraught with difficulty.

To make matters worse Rosy, refreshed from her swim, suddenly became very animated at the sight of the hunt. It may be that the shrill whinnying of the hunting horn was mistaken by her for the shrill cries of another elephant, or maybe the great wave of hounds, the scarlet tunics and the general air of bustling festivity, recalled to her mind the happy days she had spent with the circus. Uttering a loud and prolonged trumpet of joy, she scrambled to her feet and shambled across the meadow to meet the hunt.

The hounds, to a dog, skidded to an astonished halt. From their expressions you could tell that they thought this was unfair. They had been asked to chase and catch a small, red animal, and there, suddenly materialising in their path, was a monstrous grey animal such as one only dreams about in nightmares when one is a very young puppy. Simultaneously, all the bright shiny horses caught sight of Rosy. The effect on them was much the same as it had been on the plodding horses that pulled hansom cabs, and in a moment the meadow looked like an exceptionally bloody battlefield. Huntsmen fell like autumn leaves and lay sprawled in their scarlet coats on the grass, while riderless horses, panic-stricken, galloped wildly to and fro, seeking a way out of the meadow through the thick hedge that surrounded it.

Rosy was delighted. She was, by now, under the firm impression that this was some sort of a circus, and that this pandemonium was all part of the act. Trumpeting excitedly, she pursued the terrified pack of hounds round and round, occasionally pausing to pat a maddened horse on the rump with her trunk. Adrian, cowering behind the trunk of a tree in his wet underpants, wished he was dead. This was far worse than anything that had gone before, and what made it worse was the fact that Rosy was so obviously enjoying herself and joining in with an exuberance that was diverting, to say the least.

In Rosy's circus days she had been wont to end her performance with a mock assault on the ringmaster, for part of her act was a pretended animosity between that exalted personage and herself. As the hounds had now disappeared through the hedge, and all the horses were gathered in the far corner of the field in a quivering, hysterical mass, Rosy came to the not unnatural conclusion that the act had ended. Searching around her with a rheumy eye her glance chanced to fall on the Master of the hunt. He was rolling about on the grass, covered with mud, endeavouring to wrench off his top hat which had been wedged firmly down over his nose by his fall. This, thought Rosy, must be the ringmaster. It was a pardonable mistake, for the Master was a fine, corpulent specimen of manhood, wearing the mud-stained remains of a brilliant coat and a top hat. Rosy shambled towards him, paused to utter a shrill trumpeting, and then curled her trunk tenderly around his body and lifted him high in the air. She paused for a moment, obviously faintly surprised that her action did not provoke the roar of applause that it normally did.

One of the female members of the hunt, the Honourable Petunia Magglebrood, had just risen shakily to her feet when she was treated to the sight of the Master, no less, being waved thoughtfully to and fro by an elephant. The feelings of horror and sacrilege that filled her were overwhelming; she felt rather as a Crusader would have felt if he had seen someone lighting a fire with a piece of the True Cross.

"Put him down, you vulgar brute!" she screamed. "Put

him down!" Then she gave a piercing, tremulous wail and fainted. Rosy, still swinging the Master to and fro like a giant cat with a scarlet mouse, looked around thoughtfully. The Honourable Petunia's scream was not much in the way of applause, she thought, but it was obviously the best she was going to get. Peering out she perceived Adrian's white face peeping round the trunk of an oak tree, and so she shambled across to him and deposited the Master at his feet with the good-natured air of a retriever bringing in the first grouse of the season. The jolt with which she deposited the Master on the grass dislodged the top hat, which fell off and rolled across the meadow. It revealed the fact that the Master possessed magnificent black side-whiskers and moustache, and that his face was congested to a shade of royal purple that gave one the impression that he was either in imminent danger of dying of apoplexy, or else was going to disappear in a large puff of black smoke. He sat there, glaring up at Adrian, and making a noise that—even by his most fervent admirers—could only be described as an inarticulate gobbling.

"Er . . . Good afternoon," said Adrian, for want of a better remark. Not altogether to his surprise the Master's face turned black. He struggled desperately with his respiratory system, and at last managed to gain some control over his strangled vocal chords.

"What d'ye mean?" he said in a muted roar, articulating with difficulty. "What d'ye mean : Good afternoon? Is that your filthy, verminous, misbegotten, shapeless animal, hey?"

He pointed a quivering finger at Rosy, who had plucked herself a bunch of long grass and daisies and was fanning herself with it to keep the flies off.

"Oh, that," said Adrian, as though the presence of an elephant had escaped his notice until that moment, "*that* . . . well, yes, in a way you could say it was mine."

"Well, what the devil d'ye mean, sir?" roared the Master. "Stampin' about in the meadows with a damn' great misbegotten elephant . . . dressed in that obscene costume

46

... frightenin' the hounds ... terrifyin' the women ... even frightenin' the *horses* ... what the devil d'ye mean by it, sir?"

"I'm terribly sorry," said Adrian contritely. "We were just having a quiet swim, you see, and we didn't know you were all coming this way."

"D'you usually," enquired the Master with deadly calm, "d'you usually travel through the countryside, swimming in other people's rivers, *frightenin' the salmon,* accompanied by a misbegotten elephant?"

"Not *usually,* no," Adrian admitted, "but I'm afraid it would take too long to explain."

"*I* can explain it," shouted the Master, getting to his feet. "You're a lunatic, sir, a criminal lunatic, that's what you are. Gallopin' around the country worryin' the hunt, frightenin' the fish and probably the birds as well ... a lunatic. I shall have you and the misshapen beast under lock and key, sir, see if I don't. I shall sue for damages and for trespass. I shall get you five years' penal servitude. The charge might even be attempted murder, sir, what d'you think of that, hey? The moment I get back to the village I shall have the law on you, mark my words."

"Look," said Adrian in a panic, "I really am most awfully sorry, but if you'd just let me explain. You see, your horses and dogs ..."

"Dogs?" hissed the Master, his face regaining its purple hue, "*dogs?* Hounds, sir, hounds."

"Well, your hounds," said Adrian, "it's just that they're not used to elephants."

The Master drew a long quivering breath and cast a fierce eye over the meadow, where huntsmen, in various stages of disarray, were climbing shakily to their feet and endeavouring to catch their terrified horses.

"Yes, I can see they're not used to elephants," said the Master, "and shall I let you into a secret, you misbegotten peasant? THEY'RE NOT SUPPOSED TO BE USED TO ELEPHANTS!"

Adrian had to admit that he had a point there. The

Master picked up the remains of his top hat and placed it on his head.

"As soon as I get back to the village I shall have you and your blasted elephant arrested, mark my words," he said, and strode off after the rest of the soiled, limping huntsmen. As the last of them mounted and trotted out of the field, Adrian turned to Rosy.

"Now look what you've done," he said bitterly, "and just when I thought everything was going along all right. You've gone and mucked everything up again . . . now we're going to be arrested. I should think you'll get about five hundred years' penal servitude."

He dressed hurriedly and hitched Rosy up to the trap once more.

"The best thing is to get as far away from the village as possible," he said, as they started down the road.

After walking for a little while they came to a crossroads, and here the signpost informed them that if they turned to the left they would reach the village of Fennel, and if they turned to the right they would come to the village of Monkspepper. Adrian was not sure what to do. He did not know which village the hunt had come from and, while he knew that he could conceal himself and possibly the trap from any pursuing minions of the law, Rosy was a different matter. Looking down the road that led to Fennel he saw the beginning of a great wood, and that decided him. He could at least make some attempt at concealing an elephant in a wood. So, gripping Rosy's ear to hurry her, they set off down the road to Fennel.

6 THE ARISTOCRATIC ENTANGLEMENT

The beech wood was tall and vast, the green trunked trees standing up to their ankles in a haze of bluebells. The trees grew so closely together that even something the size of Rosy would be completely invisible thirty yards from the road. However, Adrian was not taking any chances. The farther he removed them from the hunt the better he would feel. Presently they found a small ride which meandered off at right angles to the road and disappeared deep into the forest, and this they followed for a mile or so. High in the treetops wood-pigeons crooned huskily, rabbits flashed and scuttled all around them, and squirrels fled up the tree trunks in alarm—their tails like puffs of red smoke—and chattered indignantly at them as they passed. Adrian began to regain his confidence. Surely, he thought, in this great, cool forest no one would be able to find them.

Presently the ride led them to a large field in the middle of the wood, and in the field were the somewhat bedraggled remains of a last year's haystack. But it was warm and dry, and Adrian decided that this would be the perfect place to sleep. He unhitched the cart and, with Rosy's help, pushed it deep into the undergrowth where it would be well hidden. Then he unpacked the food and the blankets and made his way to the haystack. Rosy followed him in a preoccupied manner, but presently returned to the trap and reappeared carrying the firkin of ale carefully in her trunk. So, wrapped up warmly in blankets, on a bed of sweet-smelling hay, Adrian lay and ate his supper while Rosy stood guard beside him, swaying gently from side to side. The moon slid up into the sky and peered down at them, turning the meadow to silver, and deep in the forest the owls hooted tremulously at each other.

Adrian was woken at dawn by a vast chorus of bird-song that made the wood echo and ring. The meadow was white with dew and the morning air was chilly. They made a hasty meal and rounded it off with a pint of ale each, Adrian reflecting that he was falling into Mr. Pucklehammer's evil ways of drinking ale for breakfast. Then, the cart hitched up once more, they continued on their way in the sparkling morning light, Rosy leaving great circular footprints in the dewy grass. They had crossed three fields, seeing nothing more alarming than a cock pheasant glittering in the sun, when they came to a gap in the hedge that led them on to the road once more.

They were just about to regain the road when Adrian heard the sound of horses' hooves. Hastily shushing Rosy (who was making considerably less noise than he was) he peered cautiously round the hedge, expecting to see a whole host of mounted policemen galloping in pursuit of them. But instead he saw a very elegant black landau with gold wheels and impressive crests on the doors, being pulled at a spanking pace by a pair of magnificent greys. Reclining in the back of the landau was a man clad in a pale lavender coat and white breeches, with a top hat as shiny as a beetle tipped over his face.

Adrian was so busy watching the approach of the landau that he had stupidly let go of Rosy's ear and she, acting on the assumption that the highroad was free to all travellers (including elephants), shambled out on to the road, pulling the trap behind her. By now the effect that Rosy had on horses had ceased to surprise Adrian. The two greys skidded to a halt, reared up on their hind legs and made desperate endeavours to climb through the hedge, carrying the landau with them, while the coachman, white-faced, did his best to control them.

"What *are* you trying to do, Jenkins?" enquired the man in the lavender coat languidly.

"I'm sorry, my lord," said the coachman, "but it's this here animal!"

The man in the lavender coat tilted his shiny top hat back, revealing elegant side-whiskers and curly hair of the brightest auburn shade. He had a long, pale and rather delicate-looking face lit with enormous eyes of the most vivid violet. He seemed quite unperturbed by the fact that the landau was in imminent danger of turning over. He felt thoughtfully in his waistcoat pocket, produced a monocle and proceeded to arrange it carefully in his right eye. By now the horses had succeeded in getting their heads through the hedge, and the landau was rocking and bouncing like a ship in a heavy sea.

"By Jove!" said the man in the lavender coat, surveying Rosy, "an elephant . . . a veritable elephant. 'Pon my soul, what an extraordinary thing."

Adrian was pushing at Rosy's head in a desperate endeavour to get her to go into reverse, but she was being singularly stubborn.

"You there," said the man in the lavender coat, "is that your elephant?"

"Yes, I'm afraid so . . . in a sort of a way," said Adrian, still pushing at Rosy.

"What an extraordinary thing," said the man musingly. "I suppose you aren't by any chance the person who upset the Monkspepper Hunt? I suppose you must be . . . there can't be more than one elephant in the district, surely?"

"I'm afraid so," said Adrian, "but it was all a horrible mistake, really. We didn't mean any harm, but you can see the effect she has on horses."

"Yes," agreed the man, "she does appear to have a detrimental effect on them, I will admit. Would it be asking too much, my dear fellow, for you to move her a trifle so that we can get past?"

"Certainly," said Adrian. "I'll do the best I can."

But Rosy, having gained the road, saw no valid reason for returning to the field. The struggle lasted some time and then Adrian had an idea. He ran round to the back of the trap and filled Rosy's tankard with beer. Using this as a bribe he managed to entice her back behind the hedge. Now she was out of view the coachman could get the greys under some sort of control. The man in the lavender coat had watched the whole performance with rapt attention, and when Adrian reappeared he screwed his monocle more firmly into his eye and leant forward.

"Tell me, my dear chap," he enquired, "does she drink the beer or just bathe in it?"

"She drinks it," said Adrian bitterly.

"Quite remarkable," said the man, "a beer-drinking elephant."

"I'm terribly sorry we upset your horses," said Adrian. "Rosy doesn't mean any harm, really."

"Not at all, my dear fellow," said the man, waving a slender hand. "Don't mention it, pray. Most diverting experience. Tell me, does she drink anything else besides beer?"

"Yes," said Adrian succinctly, "everything."

"Fascinating!" said the man, and then added with a gleam of humour in his violet eyes, "If that's the effect she has on my greys, I'd love to have seen what she did to the hunt."

"I must say it was quite spectacular," Adrian admitted, grinning. "I've never seen so many huntsmen fall off at once."

The man in the landau gave a crow of laughter, and then, taking off his top hat, he held out a slender hand. "I'm Lord Fenneltree, by the by, and I'm delighted to meet you."

"Thank you, sir," stammered Adrian. "My name's Rookwhistle, Adrian Rookwhistle, and that's Rosy."

"Charming names," said his lordship vaguely, and then fell into a reverie, staring into space. Adrian, never having met a lord before, was uncertain what to do. He was not at all sure that he had not been dismissed. He was just about to raise his hat and say good-bye, when his lordship woke up with a start, screwed his monocle more firmly in his eye and glared at him.

"I've been thinking," said Lord Fenneltree proudly, with the air of one describing a rare phenomenon. "Are you, by any chance, free at the moment?"

"Well . . . yes," said Adrian. "I'm just making my way down to the coast."

"Capital! Capital!" said his lordship enthusiastically, "it couldn't have been a more fortunate meeting."

"Really!" said Adrian. "Why?"

"The party," said his lordship in surprise, "the party, my dear fellow, that's been occupying my waking and sleeping thoughts for the last month."

"Oh, I see," said Adrian, who did not see at all but wanted to be polite.

"Don't you think, Jenkins," said his lordship to the coachman, "that the elephant would be admirable for the party?"

"Yes, my lord," said Jenkins woodenly. "If you say so."

"It *is* so nice to be agreed with," said Lord Fenneltree, beaming at Adrian.

"Forgive me," said Adrian, "but what is it you want me to do exactly?"

"We cannot discuss it here," said his lordship firmly, "it's too fatiguing to hold an intellectual conversation in the back of a landau. If you continue down this road a mile or so you'll see my house lying on the left-hand side. Do come there, my dear fellow, and bring your elephant. Then we'll discuss the matter further over some lunch, eh?"

"That's very kind of you," said Adrian.

"Don't mention it," said his lordship. "Home, Jenkins."

The landau rattled off down the lane and a much puzzled Adrian went back into the field to retrieve Rosy.

"This is a rum do, Rosy," he said to her as he led her down the road. "First you try and kill a member of the aristocracy, and then he invites us to lunch. At least, he invited *me* to lunch, but I suppose he'll give you a cabbage or something. I wonder what this party thing is that he keeps on about? I don't see what we can do to help. Anyway, my girl, just you remember where you are and behave yourself. I don't want to be had up for killing a lord."

Presently they came to a pair of huge wrought-iron gates, hung on tall pillars, each one guarded by snarling stone

53

griffons vivid with patches of green moss and yellow lichens. Beyond them the drive curled through noble parkland, dotted with clumps of magnificent trees, and in the distance, gigantic, rosy red in the sunlight, its mullioned windows flashing, lay the residence of Lord Fenneltree. An elderly man came trotting out of the lodge, pulling his forelock, and opened the gates wide.

"Morning, sir," he said, looking somewhat apprehensively at Rosy. "His lordship said you was coming."

Adrian and Rosy, with the trap trundling behind, made their way up the long curling drive. As they got nearer to the house the green sward gave place to neatly clipped lawns, flower beds and yew hedges which had been carefully and cunningly fashioned to represent peacocks, unicorns and similar interesting beasts. His lordship was standing on the steps leading up to the front door impatiently awaiting their arrival. He was surrounded by several footmen and an elderly and almost circular butler, all in a state of ill-suppressed excitement at the sight of Rosy.

"There you are," said Lord Fenneltree. "Excellent. Now, my dear chap, come in and have some luncheon. What, by the way, does Rosy like, apart from beer?"

"Well, any sort of fruit or vegetables," said Adrian.

"Raymond," said his lordship to the butler, "show Mr. Rookwhistle and Rosy the way to the stables and then tell the gardeners to get her some fruit and vegetables."

Once Rosy was tethered in a spacious barn in the stable yard, the gardeners appeared with wheelbarrow loads of succulent fruit and vegetables that made Adrian's mouth water and produced shrill trumpetings of enthusiasm from Rosy. There were peaches and grapes, carrots, cabbage and peas, apples, pears and apricots. Leaving Rosy engulfing these delicacies, Adrian was escorted back to the house by the butler and ushered into a vast withdrawing-room, where Lord Fenneltree was reclining on a sofa, surrounded by a pack of dogs of all shapes and sizes.

"Come and sit down," said his lordship. "Presently we'll have some lunch. Rosy all safe and sound, I trust?"

"Yes," said Adrian, "she's eating her head off. It's

very good of you to be so kind when she could have been the cause of your death. I'm really most grateful."

"Well," said his lordship, "if you're feeling all *that* grateful you might be able to do me a small service."

"Anything I can," said Adrian.

"It's this damned party," explained his lordship, closing his eyes as though the mere thought was painful to him. "You see, I have a daughter who—although I say it myself—is not utterly repulsive. Very shortly it is to be her eighteenth birthday and to celebrate it we are having a party, d'you see? My dear wife, who is, I'm afraid, a headstrong and insatiable woman, insists that this party from the point of view of extravagance and originality outshine anything that has been done previously in the district. Now, I can manage the financial side of things all right, but up to now I had been quite unable to think of anything original. Then you came along."

"I see," said Adrian cautiously.

"Now, it occurs to me," his lordship went on, "that the introduction of a large, tame, beer-drinking elephant into a party of this sort would be a very original idea, don't you think?"

"Yes," said Adrian.

"Do, my dear fellow, disagree with me if you think the idea lacking in originality," said his lordship earnestly.

"No, come to think of it, it would be a very original idea," said Adrian. "My trouble is that I have got so used to having Rosy around that her originality hadn't occurred to me."

"Quite so," said his lordship. "Now what I had in mind was this: I would suggest that we bedeck Rosy in a costume befitting her eastern origins, and I will then ride her into the ballroom, suitably attired myself. I thought of something in the nature of a maharaja. How does the thought strike you?"

"Yes," said Adrian, "I think she'll do it all right."

"Capital!" exclaimed Lord Fenneltree, beaming. "We've got about a week to arrange the details. So during that time I would be glad if you and Rosy would be my guests.

55

Fortunately, my wife and daughter are up in the city buying frills and furbelows, so we can keep our secret quite easily."

"I'm sure your idea will be a success," said Adrian.

"I hope so, my dear boy," said his lordship, rising to his feet. "And now let's have some luncheon."

After what Lord Fenneltree described as a light luncheon (which consisted of asparagus soup, plaice cooked in white wine and cream, quails cooked with grapes, a haunch of venison stuffed with chestnuts, and a bowl of fresh strawberries and cream) they set about the task of getting ready for the party. His lordship, carried away by the originality of the whole idea, was determined that no expense should be spared. Three local tailors were employed to make the rich trappings for Rosy, and three carpenters to make the howdah. This had been Adrian's suggestion. He felt that to have Lord Fenneltree astride Rosy's neck and in full control of her was a shade unwise, so he tactfully suggested that a maharaja should really recline in the comfort of a howdah, while one of his menials (Adrian himself) took over the delicate task of steering Rosy. Lord Fenneltree had been delighted with the idea.

Rosy's clothes, when they were ready, were really splendid. They were of a rich, deep blue velvet, covered with hundreds of sequins and bits of coloured glass, and embroidered all over in what Lord Fenneltree fondly imagined to be Hindu writing in gold thread. It took four people to lift this magnificent apparel, and from a range of ten paces in a strong light the blaze of glass and sequins almost blinded one. The howdah was also spectacular, cunningly carved and with a fringe round the top. It was painted in scarlet, yellow and deep blue, like the pony trap which Lord Fenneltree thought was most tasteful. Again, oriental patterns in sequins decorated it. His lordship and Adrian were delighted with the whole thing.

Then came the task of preparing the costumes that his lordship and Adrian were to wear, and they both had long sessions being measured and chalked by bewildered tailors. The tailors were bewildered, principally because they had never had to construct costumes like this before, and Lord Fenneltree kept changing his mind. One of them, in fact, had to spend a day in bed after facing the terrible wrath of Lord Fenneltree when he had produced a scarlet instead of a white turban.

The finished product was really sumptuous. His lordship had insisted on designing his own costume, and as he had only the haziest notion of what a maharaja wore, the results would not, perhaps, have satisfied the sartorial eye of an eastern potentate. It consisted of long, baggy, crimson trousers, caught in at the ankle, pointed Persian slippers heavily decorated with sequins and gold thread, and a magnificent three-quarter length coat in jade green and yellow. The whole ensemble was surmounted by a snow-white turban in which quivered four peacock feathers. These feathers had been Adrian's idea, and for several days the smaller members of the gardening staff had spent all their spare time stalking and plucking the unfortunate birds in the grounds. Adrian, as the driver, could not of course outshine the maharaja, and so he had to content himself with a small scarlet waistcoat, embroidered in gold, baggy white trousers and a white turban. When the costumes were finally ready, they tried them on in the seclusion of his lordship's bedroom, and Adrian had to admit that they both looked very remarkable indeed. His lordship, however, did not seem satisfied. Surveying himself in the mirror he seemed disturbed; he stroked his side-whiskers pensively.

"You know, my boy," he said at last, "there's something wrong. I look a little bit pale for a maharaja, don't you think?"

"Perhaps," said Adrian.

"I have it," said his lordship with a flash of inspiration. "Burnt cork!"

Before Adrian could protest the butler had been dispatched to the wine cellar from whence he soon reappeared carrying a variety of corks. With the aid of two footmen and a candelabra a sufficient quantity of burnt cork was manufactured, and his lordship proceeded to make himself up with great gusto.

"There!" he said at last, turning round in triumph from the mirror. "How does that look?"

Adrian stared at him. Lord Fenneltree's face was now a rich coal-black, against which his enormous violet eyes and auburn side-whiskers looked, to say the least, arresting.

"Magnificent," said Adrian doubtfully.

"It's just the final touch that makes all the difference," said his lordship. "Now let me do you."

He had just done half of Adrian's face when the butler reappeared in the room.

"Excuse me, my lord," he said.

"What is it, Raymond, what is it?" asked his lordship testily, pausing in his work.

"I thought you ought to know, my lord, that her ladyship has just arrived."

Lord Fenneltree started violently and dropped the burnt cork.

"Great heavens!" he ejaculated in horror. "She mustn't find us like this . . . quick, quick, Raymond, go and tell her we're just having baths or something. Don't let her come up here . . . and above all, don't mention that elephant."

"Yes, my lord," said Raymond, and left the room.

"I can't think why she's come back," said his lordship, unwinding his turban frantically. "They shouldn't be back till the day after to-morrow. Look here, Rookwhistle, she must not under any circumstances find out what we're planning. She has very little sense of fun, my wife, and she'd probably put a stop to the whole thing. So, dear boy, silent as the grave, eh? Quiet as a tombstone, what?"

It was on meeting Lady Fenneltree and her daughter Jonquil that Adrian, for the first time, began to have serious qualms about introducing Rosy into the party.

Lady Fenneltree was a tall, majestic woman with quantities of still-golden hair, an exquisite profile, and eyes like those of a particularly maladjusted python. When she spoke she articulated clearly, so that her wishes should not be in doubt, in the sort of voice you would use for addressing several hundred guardsmen. She used a pair of large and beautifully fashioned lorgnettes to magnify the malignancy of her eyes when expressing her wishes, and her stare was such that it completely paralysed Adrian's vocal chords. Jonquil, on the other hand, had taken after her father. She had his slender physique, to which she had added one or two curves of her own, enormous violet eyes and long auburn hair. Her beauty was so delicate and ethereal that it had much the same effect on Adrian's vocal chords as Lady Fenneltree's enquiring stare.

When they had entered the withdrawing-room, slightly dishevelled and with traces of burnt cork still on their faces, her ladyship had raised her lorgnettes and fixed them with a glare of such ferocity that Adrian blanched.

"My very own dear, how nice to have you back," said Lord Fenneltree faintly.

"One wouldn't have thought so, from the fact that you were not down here to receive us," said Lady Fenneltree coldly. "Who is this?"

"Ah! Yes!" said his lordship. "Let me introduce you, my love. This is Adrian Rookwhistle, the son of a dear old college friend of mine. He . . . er . . . just happened to be passing by and so I asked him to stay for the party. Adrian, this is my wife and Jonquil, my daughter."

"How do you do?" enquired her ladyship, in a tone of

voice that implied that news of his imminent demise would leave her unmoved.

"Well," said his lordship, rubbing his hands, "did you have a good time in the city, eh? Buy lots of pretty pretty things, eh?"

"Rupert," said her ladyship, "you will kindly stop addressing us as though we were a pair of backward children. We had, in fact, a very fatiguing time in the city. What is more to the point, how have *you* been getting on with preparations for the party?"

His lordship started and gulped. Adrian's heart sank. After even this brief exchange with Lady Fenneltree he was convinced that she was the last woman on earth to take kindly to having an elephant, however beautifully apparelled, inserted into her party. Still, things had gone too far now, and all he could do was to sit there and leave the explanations to Lord Fenneltree.

"Preparations!" said Lord Fenneltree, clasping the lapels of his coat and endeavouring to look cunning. "Preparations . . . well, now, it wouldn't do to tell you everything, my love. Let's just say that the preparations are well in hand, *very* well in hand. It's going to be a surprise, my love. But my lips are sealed. Wild horses wouldn't drag a word from me."

In the circumstances, Adrian reflected, this was probably just as well.

"H'm!" said Lady Fenneltree, compressing into that one exclamation more suspicion and foreboding than a hanging judge. "Well, if you must be childish. It's nice to know that you have not been entirely inactive during our absence."

"No, no!" protested his lordship earnestly. "'Pon my soul, my love, we've been working like beavers, veritable beavers. The success of the party is assured, I give you my word."

The next two days Adrian spent in an agony of apprehension. His effort to get his lordship to tell Lady Fenneltree were unavailing. Having come up with an original idea for the first time in his life, Lord Fenneltree was not going to relinquish it, and he knew that her ladyship would certainly put a stop to the whole thing if she got wind of it. But once it had been a triumphant success even Lady Fenneltree could not complain.

The difficulties of concealing the presence of an elephant in the stables from one as omniscient as Lady Fenneltree were enormous. The first thing she discovered was a complete dearth of fruit on the dining-table, and this was explained by Lord Fenneltree (in a wild flash of inspiration) as due to a new and virulent form of beetle, an explanation which—since Lady Fenneltree was no naturalist—satisfied her. She merely sacked the head gardener. Then she discovered that half the peacocks in the park were wandering around forlornly without tails. Lord Fenneltree's explanation that they were moulting was treated with scorn, for even Lady Fenneltree knew when peacocks moulted. The gamekeepers were gathered together and given a Boadicea-like harangue by her ladyship, and set to prowl the perimeter of the park in search of peacock tail poachers, with orders to shoot on sight.

During this time Adrian's overwrought nerves were not helped by the fact that he had to get up at midnight in order to exercise Rosy up and down the drive, an occupation made hazardous by the number of armed gamekeepers about. Rosy herself did not help matters. Thoroughly spoilt on her rich diet, she had taken to trumpeting loudly and shrilly if her supply of peaches ran out. Both Lord Fenneltree and Adrian were in a constant state of panic in case Lady Fenneltree heard the noise and decided to investigate. On the afternoon before the party they did, in fact, come within an ace of discovery. They were all playing a gentle game of croquet on the smooth green lawn at the back of the house when suddenly the sound of shrill and indignant trumpetings was wafted to them from the direction of the stables. Her ladyship, just about to play a shot, stiffened and stared at Lord Fenneltree who, in a desperate endeavour to drown Rosy, had burst into loud and tuneless song.

"What is that noise?" enquired her ladyship ominously.

61

"Noise?" said his lordship, hitting a croquet ball with unnecessary violence. "Noise? D'you mean my singing, my love?"

"I do not," said her ladyship grimly.

"I heard nothing," said his lordship, "did you, Adrian?"

"No," said Adrian, wishing he were somewhere else. "Not a thing."

"It sounded," said her ladyship, "not unlike a trumpet or a cornet or one of those vulgar instruments they play in bands."

Again the shrill sound of Rosy's displeasure floated to them on the breeze.

"There!" said her ladyship. "*That's the noise.*"

"Ah! That," said Adrian desperately. "I think that's the local hunt."

Lady Fenneltree was not convinced. She stood listening with her head on one side, while Adrian and Lord Fenneltree held their breath. But there was blessed silence. Presumably the supply-train of peaches had arrived.

"Talking of the local hunt," said her ladyship suddenly, "did you hear, Rupert, about that disgraceful occurrence? Some man, who could only have been deranged, attacked the hunt viciously with a large and uncontrollable elephant."

Adrian dropped his croquet mallet heavily on his foot.

"Yes," said Lord Fenneltree, trying to look severe. "Disgraceful!"

"The *worst* part of it was," hissed her ladyship, hitting her croquet ball with such vigour that it shot effortlessly through three hoops, "that the man was *stark naked!*"

"Really?" said Lord Fenneltree, his attention caught. He glanced at Adrian, who had kept this part of the story from him.

"Positively disgusting," said her ladyship.

"Stark naked, eh?" repeated Lord Fenneltree, obviously fascinated. "But why would he be stark naked with an elephant?"

"The lower classes," said Lady Fenneltree, "sometimes

do the most peculiar things, particularly when they are under the influence of alcohol."

Throughout this conversation Jonquil had been standing staring into space. Now she fixed Adrian with a melting stare.

"I have never seen a naked man," she said.

"Jonquil!" said Lord Fenneltree, greatly shocked. "I should hope you have not. There will be plenty of time for that."

The Conversation successfully diverted Lady Fenneltree's attention from Rosy's trumpeting, but it left Adrian feeling acutely embarrassed.

He was now convinced that Lord Fenneltree's idea was doomed to failure. Apart from anything else Lady Fenneltree was clearly not the sort of woman to greet with enthusiasm the revelation that for the last few days she had been entertaining in her midst the young man who, stark naked, had attacked the local hunt. He endeavoured once again to put his point of view to Lord Fenneltree, but his lordship was adamant.

"Just let me go quietly away with Rosy," Adrian pleaded. "I assure you that when your wife finds out she's going to go off like a volcano."

"Nonsense!" said his lordship airily. "Why, when she sees our splendid entrance into the ballroom she'll be so captivated she'll be speechless."

Adrian could not conceive of any set of circumstances that would render Lady Fenneltree speechless.

"But when she finds out who I am," he protested, "and when she finds out about Rosy . . . and . . . and . . . when she finds out about the fruit and the peacocks' tails . . ." His voice trailed away. He was overcome by the mental image of Lady Fenneltree finding out all these things simultaneously.

"Dear boy," said his lordship, "don't worry. You are a natural worrier. I've noticed it before. It's terribly fatiguing for the nerves. Why, when that elephant enters the ballroom my wife—who is, as you will have noticed, perceptive to a degree—will realise instantly that no other ball in the district has ever had an elephant. I tell you, dear boy, it will make her evening."

It did make Lady Fenneltree's evening, but not quite in the way that he had intended.

So the great day dawned and the whole house hummed with activity. The ballroom into which Rosy was to make her entrance was a hundred and fifty feet long and fifty feet wide. At one end were two massive carved oak doors that led out on to the stone flagged terrace. It was through these that Rosy was to appear. Above the doors, like a swallow's nest on the wall, was the gallery in which the musicians were to foregather. The whole setting was lit by twenty-four gigantic chandeliers that hung in two rows down the length of the ballroom, shimmering and glittering like upside-down Christmas trees. The floor of the ballroom had been polished and waxed so that it gleamed like a brown lake, and at the end of the room, opposite the great doors, there were long trestle tables covered with snow-white cloths. On them were great silver bowls of fruit; haunches of cold venison; lobster tails in aspic, gleaming like gigantic red flies in amber; enormous cold pies with autumn coloured crusts, stuffed with grouse, pheasant and quail; smoked eels crouching on beds of parsley and watercress; gigantic smoked salmon, each wearing a carefully embossed coat of mayonnaise studded with black pearls of caviar; and in the centre, the *pièce de résistance*, a whole roast pig, beautifully decorated, with a rosy apple in its mouth. Surrounding these snacks were great glass bowls of punch, silver buckets full of champagne, stately rows of claret and port to keep the gentlemen happy, and fresh orange juice, lemon juice, peach juice and pink and white ice-creams with which to revive the ladies after the rigours of the waltz or the valeta. As the day wore on the activity grew more and more feverish, and Adrian spent his time either in the stables, lecturing Rosy on the part she was to play, or wandering into the ballroom and gazing at the vast expanse of shining parquet with a feeling of dread in the pit of his stomach.

Presently, up the moonlit drive, clopped and tinkled the first of the carriages, carrying bevies of handsome, be-whiskered men and great colourful scented clouds of women. The band had taken up its position in the minstrels' gallery and was playing soft, soothing arrival music. Adrian, morosely drinking punch, was mentally cursing his uncle, Lord Fenneltree and Rosy for having inveigled him into this situation. But his second glass had a warming effect, and so he had a third. He had just made up his mind to go and ask Jonquil to dance when a large, be-whiskered individual came striding up, calling loudly for a drink. For a moment Adrian did not recognise him in his finery and then, suddenly, went cold all over. The man standing next to him was the Master of the Monkspepper Hunt—fortunately too preoccupied in swilling down punch to take much notice of his surroundings. Adrian, with a handkerchief held over his face, crept out of the ballroom undetected and started to search frantically for Lord Fenneltree. Eventually he managed to find him and, with some difficulty, prise him away from his guests.

"What is it . . . what's the matter?" asked his lordship irritably.

"Look here," hissed Adrian frantically, "You've got to call this off. D'you realise who's here?"

"Who?" asked his lordship.

"The Master of the Monkspepper Hunt, that's who," said Adrian.

"Well, I knew *that*," said his lordship, surprised. "I invited him."

"You invited him?" asked Adrian incredulously. "But what do you think he's going to say when he sees Rosy?"

"Ha, ha," said his lordship. "That's why I invited him, dear boy, to see what he *would* say."

"You must be mad," said Adrian desperately. "Don't you realise that the last time he met Rosy she picked him up in her trunk and hurled him to the ground? What d'you think he's going to say when he sees her here?"

"I think it will be very diverting," said his lordship.

"But he threatened to imprison me," said Adrian.

"Oh, don't you worry about old Darcey," said his lordship airily, "I'll soon smooth *him* down."

Having seen his lordship's complete inability to smooth Lady Fenneltree down, Adrian could imagine how effective his intervention with the Master of the Hunt would be.

"Now, now, my dear boy," said his lordship, "you're starting to worry again. Desist, I implore you. We shall need cool heads for the job ahead of us, cool, sober heads. I'll call you in half an hour and we'll get changed. I can hardly wait to see the effect."

He drifted away before Adrian, panic-stricken and incoherent, could stop him.

The party was in full swing now, and the ballroom looked like a great, moving flowerbed as the couples danced to and fro over its gleaming surface. The wine and the punch were flowing freely, so that many of those gentlemen who had arrived with pale, uninteresting complexions were now flushed and rosy, and those who had arrived flushed and rosy were now congested to a phenomenal degree. Ladies drooped exhausted in corners, fanning themselves vigorously and calling plaintively, like baby birds, for ice-creams or lemon squash. Moodily Adrian sent a footman for champagne, and spent the next half hour endeavouring to forget what was about to take place. But the champagne settled in his stomach like a cold, leaden bolt of doom. He was just wondering whether to try the punch again, when Lord Fenneltree materialised unnervingly at his elbow.

"The hour has come," said his lordship. "Now is our great moment of triumph!"

"I wish I could agree with you," said Adrian bitterly, as he followed Lord Fenneltree up the stairs.

In his lordship's bedroom their costumes lay resplendent on the four-poster bed, and the butler and a footman, twittering with excitement, were ready to help them on with their things. Half an hour later Lord Fenneltree, looking as Asiatic as he was ever likely to look with auburn side-whiskers and violet eyes, crept down the back stairs followed by Adrian. They reached the stable yard where all

Rosy's accoutrements were laid out, gleaming in the light of the oil lamps.

"Now," said Lord Fenneltree excited, "now to dress our star and then to make our grand entrance. I can't wait to see their faces."

8 THE PARTY

Adrian went to the great barn and threw open the doors. He noticed, as he did so, that mingling with the sweet smell of hay there was another, more pungent scent. He frowned and wrinkled his nose : the smell was very familiar, but he could not place it.

"Rosy?" he called. There was silence in the darkened barn. He was not greeted by the shrill squeal of pleasure that Rosy always gave at the sound of his voice.

"Rosy?" he called again anxiously. "Rosy, are you there?"

The silence was suddenly broken by a loud but extremely dignified hiccup. A terrible suspicion entered Adrian's mind, and at the same moment he realised what the fragrant odour was : it was rum. Picking up a lantern he hurried into the barn, and there he found Rosy. She was leaning elegantly against the wall, hiccupping gently to herself and pensively rolling a small but empty bottle to and fro with her foot. Adrian stared at her aghast. How she had obtained the rum he could not think, but while gaiety and conviviality were reigning in the house, Rosy in her lonely barn had undoubtedly been consoling herself with a quiet nip. To say that she was in no condition to appear in public would have been an understatement. She was as satisfactorily drunk as any human being Adrian had ever seen. As he watched her she picked up a wisp of hay and, after one or two abortive attempts, managed to stuff it into her mouth. She chewed meditatively, and then uttered a small lady-like belch. Suddenly a great feeling of relief flooded over Adrian. Of course! This was the answer! Dear, kind, sweet Rosy—Rosy the inimitable —had saved him at the eleventh hour! If it had occurred to him, he thought, he would have given her the rum himself. He hurried out of the barn to where Lord Fenneltree was waiting.

"You'll have to give it up now," said Adrian in triumph. "She's tight."

"Tight?" said his lordship, bewildered. "What d'you mean, tight?"

"Tight . . . drunk . . . pickled . . . stewed," said Adrian. "She's got a bottle of rum from somewhere and she's drunk the lot."

"My dear chap," gasped his lordship, "what a catastrophe. You mean she can't appear?"

"No," said Adrian bluntly. "She can't even stand."

"Ruination, ruination, after all our hard work," moaned his lordship. "Couldn't we sort of prop her up a bit, if I got the gardeners on each side of her?"

"No," said Adrian. "I tell you she can't even *walk*."

At that moment Rosy lumbered casually out of the barn, kicking the bottle in front of her.

"By Jove!" said his lordship, "she's recovered!"

Rosy was undergoing one of those strange, momentary flashes of semi-sobriety that come to people who are deep in their cups, but Adrian found it impossible to persuade Lord Fenneltree of this. While they were arguing acrimoniously Rosy spotted her costume and with a pleased—if slightly off-key—squeak shambled over to it and lay down to be dressed.

"There you are," said his lordship triumphantly. "What did I tell you? She's perfectly all right. I told you, dear boy, you worry too much."

"I tell you," Adrian said savagely, "she's as tight as a tick. If you take her into that ballroom I won't be responsible."

Lord Fenneltree approached Rosy and patted her affectionately on the head.

"Good old Rosy," he said. "You'll do it, won't you?"

Rosy hiccupped in reply. In spite of Adrian's protests the great sequined cloth was draped over Rosy's back, and the howdah hauled up and fastened in position. Then his lordship climbed up the ladder and settled himself comfortably inside.

"Come on, dear boy, don't dawdle," he said to Adrian. "This is the great moment."

Feeling as if he were mounting the scaffold, Adrian took up his position on Rosy's neck. There was just the faintest chance, he thought, that he might be able to steer Rosy rapidly in and out of the ballroom, thus satisfying his lordship and removing Rosy from the scene with the utmost dispatch. It was fortunate that Rosy was a good-natured drunk. In response to Adrian's cries of encouragement she clambered heavily to her feet and stood swaying pensively for a moment or so. Then they set off down the drive that led round the house to the terrace outside the ballroom. Rosy's tendency to stagger created havoc in several flowerbeds as she passed, but they eventually reached the great doors where the butler and the footman waited, their hands on the latches.

"Now, my lord?" enquired the butler in a hushed voice.

"Now," said Lord Fenneltree, adjusting his turban and lying back regally in the howdah. The butler and the footman pushed open the doors and, at this signal, the band stopped playing. The couples, who had been waltzing merrily around, came to a standstill. Looking down the great room they saw, framed in the doorway, a splendid, if slightly inebriated, spectacle of eastern pomp. With admiring cries they left the floor and formed two lines along the walls, clapping their hands and chattering excitedly.

"Well, go on," hissed Lord Fenneltree. "Take her in."

Offering up a brief prayer Adrian tapped Rosy smartly with his heels and awaited results. It had taken Rosy a moment or two to adjust her eyes to the glare of the huge chandeliers, but now, through a haze of rum, she saw a vast and colourful conglomeration of people who were forming what she imagined to be a ring in which she could perform. Rosy was not an old trouper for nothing. She uttered a pleased squeal, gathered herself together and entered the ballroom at a smart trot. This was her undoing.

The surface of the ballroom, polished to a mirror-like gloss, would not have offered much of a foothold to a sober elephant, let alone one in Rosy's condition. Her hind legs (not under the best of control) swept from under her and she sat down suddenly and startlingly on her bottom. All would have been well, even at this juncture, if it had not been for the speed with which she had entered the ballroom, for she proceeded to toboggan forward over the smooth parquet, while Adrian clutched at her ears and pulled frantically in a vain endeavour to stop her headlong progress. Lord Fenneltree, almost upside down in the howdah, was shouting inarticulate instructions, but there was nothing that anyone could do. The screams of the ladies and the cries of alarm from the gentlemen filled the ballroom as Rosy, glittering like a great pile of diamonds, roared with ever increasing speed down the room on her bottom and hit the long trestle tables at the far end of the room. The floor was awash with punch, champagne and eight different vintages of wine. Haunches of venison bespattered with ice-cream were scattered over the parquet, together with fruit, lobster, eels and salmon. The splintering crash of Rosy coming to a standstill shook the very house to its foundations. Then there was a long, shocked silence, only broken by Rosy, who hiccupped gently to herself.

Lady Fenneltree was indeed, for possibly the only time in her life, bereft of speech. Her husband had promised her something original, but a large, jewel-bedecked elephant sliding out of control down the ballroom accompanied by two Asiatic gentlemen was something that she had never imagined, even in her wildest dreams. The shock of Rosy's impact had snapped the lashings that secured the howdah to her back, and it had fallen to the floor. Lord Fenneltree struggled from the interior, looking rather like a brilliant butterfly emerging from a cocoon. With a sudden shock

70

Lady Fenneltree recognised him, and immediately her powers of speech came flooding back.

"Rupert!" she bellowed. "What is the meaning of this?"

It was a difficult question to answer, but Lord Fenneltree did his best.

"Surprise!" he panted, smiling nervously and waving his hands at the food and drink-encrusted chaos that surrounded him. "This is the surprise I told you about, my love."

Lady Fenneltree quivered like an overstrung harp.

"Surprise?" she said in a strangled voice.

"Yes, my love. After all, no other ball in the district has had an elephant."

"And I can fully comprehend the reason for that omission," boomed Lady Fenneltree savagely. "Will you get that animal *out of here*?"

Until now Rosy had been placidly sitting on her bottom. As far as she was concerned the slight bruising she had sustained was more than compensated for by the fact that she had apparently skidded into an elephant's paradise. On every side of her there were pools of delicious and intoxicating liquids, interspersed with various edible items such as lobster, ice-cream and game pie, which had not, hitherto, entered her experience. Happily she stretched out her trunk and sampled everything within reach, ignoring Adrian who, still perched on her neck, was making desperate endeavours to get his protégée to stand up. Presently, however, Rosy remembered her manners. These kind and generous people had arranged this delicious repast for her, and so the least she could do was to entertain them. She sucked up a trunkful of champagne to sustain her, and tried to remember all the tricks that had so delighted the crowds in her circus days. After due reflection she decided to sit up and beg.

It was an unfortunate choice. Luckily, Adrian leapt to safety at the crucial moment, for under the influence of alcohol Rosy's sense of balance had been somewhat impaired, and she fell backwards on to the floor with a resounding crash that dislodged one of the gigantic chandeliers. This dropped and burst into a thousand tinkling, glittering fragments that showered all over the ballroom. As the chandelier had contained no less than three hundred and fifty large candles the conflagration that this caused on the parquet floor was quite spectacular. The guests, now completely bewildered, were milling to and fro in an aimless fashion, uttering plaintive cries. The women kept fainting, coming to and then fainting again, with monotonous regularity, so the men were fully occupied catching them as they fell.

Rosy was faintly surprised. She could never remember her begging trick being received with such enthusiasm. She rolled over, heaved herself upright and beamed round the devastated ballroom. Everyone, it appeared, was helping her in the act. Adrian had seized a large silver bucket full of iced water and had hurled it over the pile of merrily blazing candles. This successfully put out the fire, but clouds of acrid smoke started to drift across the ballroom. Lady Fenneltree, by now almost apoplectic with rage, had seized his lordship by the lapels of his elegant coat and was shaking him to and fro, a sight so diverting that several of the ladies who had fainted recovered to watch.

As far as Rosy was concerned it was a splendid party, just as it should be, with plenty to eat and drink and everyone joining in the fun. She took a quick sip at a trickle of port that happened to pass her, and wondered whether to try her begging trick again. She decided, on reflection, that with such a good audience it was a pity to overdo things, and tried to stand on her head. This was no more successful than her begging trick, and she fell heavily on to her side. She lay there for a moment, hic-cupping gently, wondering where she had gone wrong.

It was perhaps unfortunate that the band should choose this precise moment to strike up again. They had been severely shaken by the carnage below them, but if this was the way his lordship wanted to behave, who were they to complain? But they were all old and valued family retainers, and the sight and sound of his lordship and her ladyship locked in battle, uttering phrases that should only be used in the seclusion of the bedroom, was more than they could bear. Clearly something had to be done to save the day, and so they burst forth into a gay Viennese waltz. They were not to know that in her circus days one of the highlights of Rosy's act had been her waltz. Clasping a somewhat fleshy but attractive blonde in her trunk Rosy had been wont to waltz round and round the ring with great skill and aplomb. The strains of the familiar melody floated down to where she was lying and turned her thoughts along these lines. She scrambled to her feet and peered round blearily. Again, it was unfortunate that the first person her eye happened to focus on was Lady Fenneltree.

In the middle of a complicated and derogatory exploration of Lord Fenneltree's family tree, during which she had only got as far back as the fifteenth century, she suddenly found herself lifted into the air and whirled away in what Rosy fondly imagined to be an exhilarating waltz. Lady Fenneltree's piercing screams for help, Rosy misinterpreted as cries of approbation, and so she waltzed happily on. She was pleased with herself. Never, she thought, had she danced so well. True, she fell heavily on several occasions, but she held Lady Fenneltree high so that she should come to no harm. She had accomplished one rather uneven circuit of the ballroom, followed by the rapt and horror-stricken gaze of the assembled company, when the band, realising suddenly that they were aiding and abetting rather than soothing the elephant, stopped playing. Rosy was glad. She was not as young as she used to be, the ballroom was large and Lady Fenneltree was heavy. She decided that she had done enough to entertain the guests and could now round off her act. She deposited the unconscious Lady Fenneltree on a haunch of venison, fourteen bottles of champagne and the remains of a salmon, raised her trunk proudly in the air and uttered a long and imperious trumpet. The effect of this on the company was curious and instantaneous. They decided that this monstrous beast, having tasted the blood of Lady Fenneltree, was now about to attack in earnest. For a moment they remained rooted to the spot with terror, and then all broke and ran. They scattered across the ballroom like hares and, such is the confusion that afflicts the human mind in moments of crisis, some of them, instead of running away from Rosy, actually ran towards her. Among them, putting on a pretty turn of speed for one of his corpulence, was the Master of the Monkspepper Hunt. Even in her condition Rosy recognised him. She beamed with pleasure, for was he not the kind man who had helped her with her act when she performed in the meadow? Uttering a small squeal of delight she fielded him with some dexterity with her trunk as he passed, and lifted him aloft. Adrian, fearing that the Master might meet the same fate as Lady Fenneltree, decided to intervene.

"Rosy!" he roared above the pandemonium. "Put him *down*!" Rosy was somewhat surprised, for she had not nearly finished with the Master. She had intended, as a finishing touch, to drop him into the minstrels' gallery. But she was beginning to feel tired, and if Adrian told her to drop the Master, who was she to disobey? So she uncurled her trunk and all seventeen stone of the Master of the Monkspepper Hunt hit the parquet with a resounding crash. Adrian closed his eyes and prayed for death. Then he opened them again. Lord Fenneltree was standing by him, plucking his sleeve.

"Dear boy," said his lordship, "I fear you were right. The whole thing *has* been a mistake."

Looking round at the wrecked ballroom, at the screaming, hysterical guests, at Lady Fenneltree unconscious with her head pillowed on a salmon, at the Master of the Monkspepper Hunt lying unconscious—possibly dead —on the floor, Adrian could not find it in his heart to disagree.

9 THE FLIGHT

Adrian could never remember with any clarity how he managed to get away from Fenneltree Hall unscathed. He dimly recollected that he and Lord Fenneltree had managed to get Rosy out of the wreckage of the ballroom and back to the stables. He remembered Lord Fenneltree saying that in his considered opinion it would be safer if Adrian and Rosy "slipped off" before either Lady Fenneltree or the Master, or both, regained consciousness, and the next thing he knew was that he and Rosy were walking down the moonlit road away from Fenneltree Hall, the coloured trap rattling behind them. Rosy, who was now suffering from a hangover and wanted to sleep, kept sighing lugubriously at all the untoward activity which was making her head ache. Adrian's head was also aching, but for different reasons. He had a few sharp things to say to Rosy in due course, but he wanted to put as much distance between them and Lady Fenneltree's wrath as possible, and so he kept Rosy walking at a brisk pace. Although it was a beautiful night, with the moon full and high and the sky like a dew-drenched spider's web of stars, it was cold, and the fast pace helped to keep them both warm.

After walking for three hours Adrian felt that they were reasonably safe, at least for that night. But he wanted to find a place where he and Rosy could conceal themselves the following day, for he knew Lady Fenneltree to be a woman of iron determination and he felt sure she would not rest until he and Rosy had been pursued, caught and transported back to Fenneltree Hall. And an interview with Lady Fenneltree was the last thing that Adrian wanted to face at that juncture.

The road had meandered through open fields and small copses; not the sort of country to offer the type of concealment that Adrian wanted. Now, to his dismay, he found that they were climbing up to a vast, wild piece of moorland where it would have been difficult to conceal a small dog, let alone anything the size of Rosy. Hoping that the moorland would soon end and that they would find a wood on the other side, Adrian pressed on. But the moor seemed to grow bigger and bigger until, in the cold light of dawn, it stretched away on every side as far as the eye could see, purple and brown and green, offering no place to hide at all. Then, as the sun rose, the whole moorland seemed to catch fire. At first little coiling fingers of mist started to twist up from the heather and gorse, and then these wisps merged together into gauzy curtains. Within minutes this thickened and the whole landscape disappeared into the grey haze. Rosy became quite invisible at a distance of twenty feet, but Adrian felt sure that as soon as the sun rose higher the mist would disappear, so now was the time to have a rest and something to eat. He led Rosy off the road and down into a hollow, and here he unpacked his kettle and soon had it boiling over a small fire. He made himself some tea and cut himself some bread and cheese. Then he presented Rosy with several loaves of stale bread. She viewed these with disdain, turning them over and over with her foot and sighing deeply. Then she went to the back of the trap and laid her trunk on the firkin of ale, and Adrian, for the first time in his association with Rosy, lost his temper. He leapt to his feet, ran forward and slapped Rosy's trunk as hard as he could and Rosy, astonished at this unkind act from her god, backed away uttering a squeal out of all proportion to the pain the blow had given her. She was astonished and hurt; all she had wanted was a small nip of ale to wet her dry mouth and ease her aching head, and here was Adrian going berserk.

"Keep away from that beer you . . . you . . . you bloody *elephant*, you," snarled Adrian. "That's all you damn' well think of, booze, booze, booze."

He covered the firkin up with a blanket and went and squatted morosely by his fire, glaring at Rosy.

76

"I suppose you won't really be satisfied until you've killed me," he went on sarcastically. "Not content with invading my life and disrupting it, you then frighten half the horses in the city, terrify the Monkspepper Hunt and damn' nearly *kill* the Master, and then go on to wreck one of the stately homes of England, dancing round with Lady Fenneltree in your trunk as though she was some low circus performer. They're probably offering enormous rewards for our capture even now. And look at the damages : that chandelier alone must have cost a hundred and fifty pounds. But does all this worry you? Do you feel the faintest shred of remorse? No, not *you*. All *you* think about is getting boozed up again."

He paused and poked the fire viciously. Rosy flapped her ears and waved her trunk to and fro. Although she missed the finer points of Adrian's condemnation of her actions she was a perspicacious elephant and gathered from his tone of voice that he was, for some reason that escaped her, annoyed. She was very fond of Adrian and she would have liked to do something to make him feel better. She wondered if she stood on her head whether this would take his mind off his problems. She was just about to test this out when Adrian started talking again, so she paused politely to listen.

"What I'm going to do with you, you damned animal, is to get you down to the coast by hook or by crook, and then I'm going to give you to the first person that's fool enough to want you. And I don't care *what* they do with you . . . they can do anything they *like* with you . . ." Adrian paused and searched his mind for a suitably terrible fate for Rosy. "They can put you in a *lumber yard*, for all I care. They can *stuff* you and put you in a museum. That would probably be the safest place for you. I don't care *what* happens to you as long as you get out of my life."

Adrian paused for breath and Rosy, to show him that she had been attending carefully to everything he said, flapped her ears and gave a small squeak.

"It's no good pleading," said Adrian austerely. "My

mind's quite made up. I have decided that the one thing I *don't* want in my life is an elephant, particularly one which has an infinite capacity for drink and staggers through the countryside leaving a trail of destruction behind her. As soon as we reach the coast our association is at an end. I have suffered more than any normal human being can be expected to suffer and still remain normal. So, while I still have some sanity left, you must go. Now shut up and eat your bread. It's all you're going to get."

So saying, Adrian pushed some more twigs on to the fire, rolled himself up in a blanket and tried to get half an hour's nap before the mist lifted. He was so physically and mentally exhausted that he fell into a deep sleep almost at once, and slept blissfully on for two hours. When he awoke with a start the mist had disappeared and the moorland was flooded with sunlight. He sat up and looked about him, and what he saw made him leap to his feet in alarm. Some fifty feet away, parked by the side of a small stream, was a brightly coloured if slightly battered-looking caravan, with red and white check curtains drawn tightly over its windows. Rosy was leaning against it, a look of ecstasy on her face, scratching herself so that the whole caravan shook and rocked. From inside the caravan a shrill voice was endeavouring to make itself heard above the rasp of Rosy's scratching.

"Go away, I command you," shrilled the voice. "Foul demons of the pit, desist. In the name of Nebuchadnezzar and the ten Seals of Solomon, avaunt! In the name of Erasmus and the Sacred Pentacle of Promethus . . ."

"Rosy!" shouted Adrian. "Come away from there."

Rosy sighed deeply as she left the caravan. It seemed to her that recently Adrian was always telling her not to do the things she liked doing. Adrian approached the steps that led up to the door of the caravan.

"I say!" he called. "You in there . . . I'm extremely sorry . . ."

"Avaunt!" screamed the voice. "Avaunt, you demon, in the name of . . ."

"I'm not a demon," shouted Adrian irritably. "Will you come out and let me explain?"

"No, no," screamed the voice. "You can't catch me like that . . . I'm only a poor, old woman and you're trying to lure me out so that you can snatch the soul from my body . . . avaunt, I say . . ."

"Oh, do shut up," said Adrian in exasperation. "I'm not a demon and I don't want your soul. Why don't you come out and let me explain?"

"If you're not a demon," said the voice cunningly, "how did you rock the caravan?"

"It was my elephant," explained Adrian. "She was scratching herself against the side."

"A likely story," said the voice.

"Well, if you open the door and *look* you'll see her," said Adrian.

"How would I know it was an elephant?" asked the voice. "I've never seed one."

Adrian took a deep breath and closed his eyes.

"Madam," he said at last, "I merely wanted to apologise to you for any inconvenience that my elephant may have caused by scratching herself on your caravan. If you cannot accept the apology in the Christian spirit in which it is offered, I'm sorry. And now, good day to you, I must be on my way."

"No, no, don't go, I'll come out," screamed the voice. "I never seed an elephant."

There was a long pause during which Adrian could hear various spells being muttered in the interior of the caravan, and then the door was opened a crack and a face like a walnut peered out, surrounded by straggling grey hair. It belonged to one of the tiniest old ladies that Adrian had ever seen. She looked, Adrian decided, exactly like a minute witch. She was dressed in a faded black velvet skirt, a tattered scarlet blouse and she had a thick black woollen shawl around her shoulders. She looked Adrian up and down, mumbling with her toothless gums.

"Good morning," said Adrian.

"Well, where is it?" enquired the old lady.

Adrian gestured to where Rosy was standing, endeavouring to uproot a gorse bush under the mistaken impression that it was edible.

"Eeeeeeeee!" said the old lady, expelling her breath in a long gasp of wonder. "Did you ever? The size of it ... did you ever?"

"She's quite tame," explained Adrian. "She was just scratching herself against your caravan."

"I never seed anything like it," said the old lady. "A wondrous beast ... truly wondrous."

"You wouldn't, I suppose, be wanting an elephant for your type of ... er ... work?" asked Adrian hopefully.

"Work?" said the old lady, bristling indignantly. "I don't *work*."

She stumped into the caravan and reappeared carrying a board which she hung on a hook by the door.

"That's me," she said proudly, jerking a thumb at the board. "Finest witch in these parts."

On the board was written in slightly shaky capitals the legend:

BLACK NELL THE WHITE WITCH.
SPELLS. INCANTATIONS.
THE FUTURE AND PAST FORETOLD.
WARTS CURED.

"Oh," said Adrian, surprised that the old lady had in fact turned out to be a witch. "How very interesting."

"Yes," said the old lady, "I'm on my way to the Tuttlepenny Fair. Is that where you're going?"

"No, I'm on my way down to the coast," said Adrian. "As a matter of fact I'm not altogether sure where we are at the moment. Could you tell me the best way to go?"

"Bite of breakfast?" said Black Nell. "You can't walk on an empty stomach."

"It's very kind of you," said Adrian, "but I just had some breakfast."

"Cold rabbit pie?" asked Black Nell. "Bit of cold rabbit pie, home-made bread and a mug of tea, eh?"

The thought of cold rabbit pie made Adrian's mouth water.

"Well, if you're quite sure you have enough," he said.

"Plenty," said Black Nell. "You get the fire a-going under the kettle and I'll fetch the pie."

So Adrian, Rosy and Black Nell sat down to have breakfast together. The pie was delicious, the crust melting in the mouth, the chips of rabbit meat, pink or coral, embedded in jelly as brown as amber, redolent with herbs. Adrian decided that he had never eaten anything quite so delicious in his life, not even at Fenneltree Hall. After his third piece of pie he even started to view Rosy with a less jaundiced eye. Full of pie and hot tea he grew expansive and told Black Nell all about the trials and tribulations he had had since Rosy had entered his life. To his surprise Black Nell thought it was one of the funniest things she had ever heard, and at his description of the ball she laughed until she cried, and Adrian, against his will, was forced to laugh too.

"Oh, my! Oh, my!" gasped Black Nell, holding her sides. "I wish I could have seed that."

"Looking back on it, I must admit that it was rather funny," said Adrian. "But I didn't think it was funny at the time."

Black Nell wiped her eyes, still giving shrill hoots of laughter. Then she delved in her pocket and pulled out a pack of stained and greasy cards.

"Come along, come along," she said, "I'll tell your fortune and let you know what's in store for you."

"I'm not altogether sure that I want to know," said Adrian.

"Nonsense," said Black Nell firmly, "'course you do, everyone does. Now, cut the cards and then pick out six rows of seven."

Gingerly Adrian shuffled, cut the pack and then picked out the rows of cards. Black Nell turned them face upwards and pored over them, mumbling to herself.

"Ha, ha!" said Black Nell so suddenly that Adrian jumped and the hairs on the nape of his neck prickled.

"What is it?" he asked nervously.

"Nothing," said Black Nell. "Your future's very obscure, very obscure indeed."

"Oh, well, don't bother then," said Adrian in relief.

"No, no, it's coming," said Black Nell. "I can see you going on a sea voyage."

"A sea voyage?" said Adrian incredulously. "What, with Rosy?"

"And I see danger," said Black Nell, lowering her voice to a hoarse whipser, "danger and a short, fat man. He's going to cause you a lot of trouble."

"Can't you see anything nice?" asked Adrian plaintively. "I've had quite enough trouble recently."

"Oh, yes, I can see something nice. But it's very obscure, very obscure," said Black Nell. "I'm glad all my clients don't have such obscurity in their cards or we'd never get anywhere."

She put the cards back into her pocket, took out a short black pipe and lit it.

"Tell you what," she said, puffing out clouds of grey, chest-constricting smoke, "you'd better get a move on, young fellow. You've got a tidy bit of moor to cover and it's as bald as an egg for hiding an elephant. Now, what I suggest you do is this. Go on along this road for a few miles, maybe six or seven, and you'll come to a right-hand turn. It's only a sort of rough track, really, but it goes through the dells and you've more chance of hiding there. Now, twenty miles or so along the track it crosses the railway line, see? And just after that it forks. You take the left-hand fork and presently you'll come to a pub called the *Unicorn and Harp*, run by some people called Filigree. They're the nicest people round those parts and very fond of animals. They'll probably let you stay there until the hue and cry dies down. Tell 'em Black Nell sent you."

"You're very kind," said Adrian warmly. "I'm most grateful to you."

"Well," said Black Nell philosophically, "if we what's on the road don't help each other it's a sure and certain fact that no one else will."

So Adrian hitched Rosy up to the trap again and said good-bye to Black Nell.

"Not good-bye," she said enigmatically, "I'll be seeing you again when wigs are in season."

"What?" asked Adrian bewildered.

"Joke," said Black Nell sardonically. "Cheerio."

So Adrian and Rosy set off across the brilliant moorland and by midday they had come to the turning that Black Nell had described. She had been right, for the track dipped and wound its way through gentle undulation, and offered much more chance of concealment should their pursuers catch up with them. They had their lunch by a small pond whose contents were the only liquid refreshment that Adrian allowed Rosy to have, much to her annoyance. Then they pressed on.

Presently the sun nestled down in a great bank of feathery clouds in the west and busily turned them to gold and green and red. A purplish twilight settled down over the moor, and small bats flicked and purred across the track like metronomes. The track climbed up a small rise and when they reached the top of it Adrian could see at the bottom of the valley below, the gleaming railway lines running across the track.

"There we are, Rosy," he said. "Nearly there now."

The trap tinkled and creaked its way down into the valley and when they reached the railway lines Rosy stepped across them carefully. On Adrian's instructions she drew the trap slowly after her until the wheels were resting against the lines. Then Adrian got his shoulder under the trap and heaved, at the same time telling Rosy to pull. The trap lifted, hung for a minute on the rail and bumped down. It was then that Adrian discovered that whoever had designed the rails had obviously done so with the malicious intention of entangling pony traps, for the wheels of the trap lay neatly wedged crosswise between the two lines and would neither move forward nor back. If

Rosy pulled, the shafts creaked ominously, and Adrian was frightened that they would snap off. Glancing around, Adrian saw, lying some distance away at the side of the track, the remains of an old sleeper. This, he thought, would do admirably as a lever. Telling Rosy to stay still he went to fetch it, and it was as he was returning that he heard the train.

He had been so engrossed in his efforts to get the trap off the lines that he had been oblivious to the distant sounds. But now, to judge by the harsh scream and the roar and clatter, the train was nearly upon them. Bathed suddenly in cold sweat, Adrian staggered down the line with his burden, feeling the rails throbbing and tingling with the approach of the train. He must move the trap. The roar and rattle of the train was terribly loud and frightening as he staggered up to the back of the trap and wedged the sleeper under it. He got his shoulder under it and heaved.

"Pull, Rosy, pull," he shouted, and Rosy stepped forward. The trap started to lift, teetered a moment and then bumped over the lines as the train roared round the corner like a ravening dragon. The trap was safe, thought Adrian exultantly. He turned to leap from between the lines, but the train caught him as he jumped and flung him viciously to one side. He landed in the heather covered with blood and as limp as a rag doll, while the train thundered on imperviously, flashing the golden lights from its windows and showering the countryside with glowing sparks like a meteor. It thundered away into the distance and gradually the noise of its progress faded. Adrian, bloodstained and unconscious, lay twisted in the heather, his white face staring up at the star-freckled sky.

When Adrian opened his eyes, his first impression was that he was lying on a bed composed entirely of red-hot knitting needles. His whole body ached savagely, and his right arm felt numb and bruised. Above him the stars were jerking to and fro across the sky in the most unorthodox manner and for a moment this puzzled him, until he suddenly realised that he was lying in the back of the trap which was progressing slowly along the dark road.

How, he wondered, had he got there? At length he decided that it must have been Rosy (faithful, sagacious Rosy) who had picked up his battered and unconscious body and placed it in the back of the trap. He tried to sit up, but a white-hot pain seared through him and he fainted.

When he came round, the cart was stationary, and suspended over his head in a miraculous way was a large sign on which was written *Unicorn and Harp*, and underneath it a tiny picture showing this unlikely combination. How clever of Rosy, he thought blearily, to have found the place that they were heading for. If he had been feeling himself, he would, of course, have realised that Rosy, having performed her rescue operation, had made all speed towards what her trunk told her was an old and redolent public house. With a tremendous effort, wincing with pain, Adrian managed to get down into the road. His right arm hung limply and he felt sure that it was broken. His legs had no strength in them and he staggered as though he were drunk. Rosy uttered a small pleased squeal and flapped her ears. The *Unicorn and Harp*, Adrian saw, was a long, low, timbered house with a reed roof like a great shaggy pie crust on top of it. Golden light spilled out of the mullioned windows on to the road. Weaving uncertainly to and fro like a swallow, Adrian staggered across the road and leant against the door. He was beginning to feel terrible again and he was frightened that he would faint before he could get inside, into that friendly light. He grasped the big brass knocker and beat a thunderous tattoo on the oak door, and then slumped against the jamb trying to fight down the waves of nausea that threatened to overwhelm him. He heard footsteps approaching, bolts were withdrawn from the door, and it was flung back.

There in the light stood one of the fattest men that Adrian had ever seen. He was in his shirt sleeves and trousers and wearing a pair of enormous carpet slippers richly embroidered with sunflowers, marigolds, chrysanthemums and similar brightly coloured flowers. His face was as round and as rubicund as a baby's and the top of his vast head was covered with a faint, wispy halo of pale golden hair. Under the last of his double chins, his enormous stomach swelled out in a great and noble curve that would have made a pouter pigeon look positively emaciated. He stared at Adrian's tattered, blood-stained form without any change of expression whatsoever.

"Good evening," he said, in a sweet, shrill, flute-like voice. "Is there anything you desire?"

"Accident," mumbled Adrian blearily. "I was hit by a train. Rosy's outside."

The pub and the fat man disappeared into blackness as Adrian slumped forward. The fat man, with remarkable speed, caught him as he fell, wrapped his massive arms around him, and lifted him as effortlessly as though he had been a feather. He turned and waddled into the pub carrying Adrian with him. The front door led directly into a gigantic, stone-flagged kitchen at one end of which a log fire glowed and twinkled in a huge fireplace, reflecting in the polished surfaces of the rows and rows of copper pans that hung on the walls. The fat man laid Adrian down on a large horse-hair sofa, loosened his collar, and then waddled rapidly over to the bar at the far end of the room. He poured brandy into a tumbler and went back to the sofa, lifted Adrian's head and forced a little of the liquid between his lips. Adrian coughed and spluttered and his eyes opened.

"Ah," said the fat man contentedly in his flute-like voice, "that's better. Now you just lie still while I get something to cover you."

Adrian peered myopically round the vast kitchen with its bar at one end and its huge fire at the other, and the brandy he had gulped warmed his stomach and seemed to ease some of the pains that racked his body. The fat man soon returned carrying a vast billowing eiderdown.

"I thought this would be warm," he said shrilly, tucking it carefully round Adrian. "It's genuine goose-down. Warmest thing you can have. I always wore one when I was in Tibet."

Even in his sorry condition, the mental image of the fat man wearing a goose-feathered eiderdown made Adrian grin.

"You're very kind," he said. "I'm sorry to be such a nuisance."

"Not at all," fluted the fat man. "A pleasure, my dear sir. Have some more brandy." He held Adrian's head while he gulped down the rest of the brandy.

"Wonderful thing, brandy," said the fat man unctuously. "The barges used to bring it regularly from France when I was in Egypt."

"I'm sorry to worry you still further," said Adrian, "but there's Rosy outside."

"Ah, yes," said the fat man. "I'd quite forgotten. You did mention her just before you fainted. How remiss of me; poor little thing." And so saying, he turned with extraordinary nimbleness and surged to the front door.

"It's . . ." began Adrian, but the fat man had disappeared.

There was a long pause broken only by a squeal from Rosy. It was one of her pleased squeals, but in a completely different key to the one she normally used. Adrian could only hope that this augured well. Perhaps she would think that the fat man was another elephant and take to him. Suddenly the fat man reappeared, his pink baby face wreathed in smiles. He danced across to the sofa, his hands clasped as though in supplication, his eyes shining.

"An *elephant*," he cooed shrilly. "A real, live *elephant*. My dear fellow, you *couldn't* have brought me anything I'd like better. I haven't had an elephant since I was in Nagarapore. And she likes me too. She actually put her trunk round my neck."

"Oh, yes. She's very friendly," said Adrian.

"I remember," said the fat man dreamily, "I used to have a hundred and one of them. Ah, those happy days. The tiger hunts, the pomp, the ceremony . . ."

"I'm sorry to interrupt you," said Adrian, "but I wonder if it would be possible for me to see a doctor? I rather think I have broken my arm."

"My dear fellow, *anything*," said the fat man. "But you must stay quite still and we'll bring the doctor to you. Sam will be back in a minute and then everybody will be organised. In the meantime, might I have the privilege of putting your elephant in our barn?"

"Of course," said Adrian. "It's very kind of you."

"I assure you," said the fat man earnestly, "the privilege is mine."

"Her shackles are in the back of the cart," said Adrian, "and if you could possibly give her something to eat?"

"Don't worry about a thing," said the fat man, holding up one plump finger. "I will attend to everything."

He disappeared through the front door, and Adrian heard his shrill voice talking to Rosy. Presently there was the rattling and the rumbling of the cart disappearing round the back of the pub and within ten minutes the fat man came back, dancing his way, pigeon-toed, across the great flagged kitchen, looking like an enormous pink cloud of goodwill.

"More brandy?" he fluted. "Deadens the pain." He sloshed brandy into two glasses with great abandon and handed one to Adrian.

"Your very good health, Mister, er um . . ." said Adrian.

The fat man stared, round-eyed, looking ludicrously like

a gigantic baby who has just had a safety-pin jabbed into its buttock.

"My dear sir," he shrilled, "how remiss of me. I never introduced myself. What with the excitement of the elephant and everything. Peregrine Filigree at your service." He bowed as low as his stomach would permit him.

"Adrian Rookwhistle," said Adrian, not to be outdone in courtesy, "at *your* service."

"Splendid," said Mr. Filigree, "absolutely splendid. Now all we have to do is wait for Sam. Are you, by any chance, hungry?"

"Actually, no," Adrian admitted. "I'm feeling too ghastly to eat anything."

The fat man made his way over to an outsize leather chair and wedged himself into it securely.

"Now, tell me, my dear sir," he said very solemnly, interlacing his fat fingers, "just before you fainted, you said that you had been attacked by a drain. Everything is possible in this world, I know, but I would simply adore to hear the details."

"It wasn't a drain, it was a train," said Adrian, and he went on to tell Mr. Filigree of his adventures on the railway line. He was feeling warm and drowsy and the pains in his body somehow did not seem to belong to him. He was also feeling slightly drunk, for Mr. Filigree's brandies were lavish, to say the least.

"Extraordinary," said Mr. Filigree, round-eyed as he listened to Adrian's story. "Quite extraordinary. I remember when I had to give orders to build the Great Trans-Siberian Railway, we had tremendous trouble with the wolves. Not only eating the labourers, you understand, but getting stuck on the lines as well. Huge packs of them, my dear sir."

"Fashinating," said Adrian, articulating with difficulty, "abschlutely fashinating."

"Ah!" squeaked Mr. Filigree suddenly. "Listen!"

Dimly Adrian was conscious of the clop of horse's hooves on the road outside.

"That'll be Sam," said Mr. Filigree beaming.

He leapt to his feet and danced away across the kitchen like an errant balloon. He threw open the front door.

"Sam! Sam!" he shouted into the night. "Come quickly, we've got an *elephant*." And then he danced back to Adrian and beamed down at him. "*Such* excitement," he said.

For some reason, Adrian had expected Sam to be a tall, thin and rather lugubrious individual to counteract Mr. Filigree's circular, baby-face charm; so he began to wonder whether the brandy was even more potent than he suspected when through the front door walked a slender girl of about twenty-three. Even her long skirts and the thick shawl that she had pinned around her shoulders could not disguise the slender attraction of her figure. She had a heart-shaped face and a nose with all the retroussé charm of a Pekinese, short bobbed hair the colour of burnished chestnut, and immense eyes that Adrian discovered later were leaf green flecked with gold. She paused in the doorway, looking at Adrian with astonishment, and Adrian, with a groan of pain, threw back the goose-down quilt and tried to get to his feet.

"No, no, *no*," said Mr. Filigree in shrill anguish. "You mustn't move. Sam, this poor man has been hit by a train and he's brought us the most *beautiful* elephant."

The girl drew off her gloves slowly and then moved across the kitchen towards them. To Adrian's hazy gaze she appeared to float rather than to walk, but he attributed this to the brandy.

"What on earth are you talking about, father?" she said.

"He's got an elephant," said Mr. Filigree triumphantly, as though this explained everything. "Think of *that*, Sam. A real elephant, *here*."

The girl gave a short, exasperated sigh and then turned to Adrian and held out her hand.

"I am Samantha Filigree," she said, smiling in a way that made Adrian, for no apparent reason, blush to the roots of his hair. "I'm afraid that my father's not very

90

good at explaining things. Perhaps you would care to fill in the gaps?"

Once more, his eyes fixed firmly on Mr. Filigree's excitedly heaving stomach, Adrian told about his accident. Samantha drew in her breath sharply when he had finished and then turned and surveyed her father ominously while he made vague, flapping motions with his hands and turned pink.

"And what have you done about this?" she enquired.

"Done?" said Mr. Filigree with injured innocence. "Why, everything, my dear. I've given him brandy and put the elephant in the barn."

"Really," said Samantha, "you are hopeless. Here's this poor boy lying here, mortally injured for all you know, and all you can do is prattle on about elephants."

"Well, I thought I'd leave it until you came back, my dear," said Mr. Filigree placatingly. "You always do these things so much better."

Samantha gave him a withering look and turned to Adrian.

"I'll get a doctor for you straight away," she said. "But first, let me make sure how serious it is."

Deftly she removed the quilt and examined Adrian as swiftly and as impersonally as though he had been a joint of meat. Adrian bit his lips in an effort not to cry out as she gently manipulated his right arm.

"Yes," she said at last, going over to an oak dresser, pulling open a drawer and taking out an enormous pair of scissors, "you've got a broken arm, probably a cracked rib, and a lot of minor bruises."

She walked back to the sofa twirling the scissors in her competent hands.

"I say," said Adrian, nervously eyeing the flashing blades, "don't you think we ought to wait until the doctor . . ?"

"Don't be silly," said Samantha coolly. "We've got to get that coat off you before your arm swells up any more. It will be agony taking it off the normal way, so I'm afraid you will just have to sacrifice the coat."

Skilfully, and to Adrian's surprise without causing him any pain, she cut neatly up the sleeve of his coat and then performed a similar operation on the sleeve of his shirt.

"There," she said with satisfaction. "Now, you just lie still while I go and get the doctor."

"More brandy?" suggested Mr. Filigree, determined not to be outdone in medical proficiency by his daughter. "I remember in Egypt when the slaves were dropping off the pyramids, at sometimes two a day, we always got them brandy."

"*He* can have some," said Samantha firmly, "but I want you to remain sober. I shall be back in half an hour or so." She nodded coolly to Adrian and floated out into the night.

"I do assure you," said Mr. Filigree, handing Adrian a glass of brandy, "I do positively assure you that I, my dear sir, have never been drunk." He gave a surreptitious look at the door then poured some brandy into his own glass. "Women," he fluted, "women in moments of crisis are always apt to lose their heads and say things they do not mean." He gulped the brandy down thirstily. "It's the fragility of their nature," he went on earnestly. "Samantha's a good child, but rather apt to have a sharp tongue when she loses control of a situation. Do you follow me?"

To Adrian it appeared that Samantha had the situation under considerably more control than her father, but he did not like to say so. So he nodded portentously. Mr. Filigree wedged himself once more into his arm chair and sat back beaming rosily and expansively at Adrian.

"I'm always telling Sam," he said, wagging an admonitory finger at Adrian, "I'm always telling her that if one follows the Scriptures one can't go far wrong. 'Take a little brandy to settle your stomach after a train accident.' I think you'll find it in Nebuchadnezzar, or somewhere like that, but alas, women are so frail compared to us men."

He drank thirstily from his glass, shot a quick glance at

the door and then leaned forward as far as his stomach would permit and fixed Adrian with a baleful eye.

"Do you realise," he said, with such earnestness that his voice disappeared into a falsetto squeak like that of a bat, "do you realise that women cannot *remember the past*?"

By now Adrian was enveloped in a warm rosy haze of brandy and he was not following Mr. Filigree's arguments with any great attention.

"Wash that?" he said.

"Women," repeated Mr. Filigree very solemnly, "cannot remember the past."

"All the women I've met do," said Adrian bitterly. "Generally in the most ghastly detail."

"Aha!" said Mr. Filigree, wagging his finger again, "the immediate past perhaps, but no further than that."

"Well, how far do you want them to go?" asked Adrian, leaning back and closing his eyes.

"You can go right back," squeaked Mr. Filigree, "if you try hard enough. But it's the fact that women have such limited intelligence that makes my task all the harder."

"Really?" said Adrian, half asleep.

"Yes," said Mr. Filigree firmly, pouring himself some more brandy. "Even when they do remember, it's some stupid, footling detail, like the colour that was being worn at court, or who was whose lover."

Adrian mulled this over for a minute or so while Mr. Filigree watched him anxiously.

"Do you know?" said Adrian, opening his eyes suddenly, "I haven't the least idea what you're talking about."

Mr. Filigree sighed in remorse, his double chins and his vast stomach rippling with the reverberations.

"You are not yourself," he said sorrowfully. "To-morrow, when you are better, I will explain it all to you. Now you go to sleep, the doctor should be here very soon."

"Thank you," said Adrian, and he closed his eyes and immediately sank into a deep and peaceful sleep.

Adrian lay looking at the oak-beamed ceiling, flooded with early morning sunlight, in some satisfaction. It was a week since he had arrived at the *Unicorn and Harp* and it was the first morning on which he had woken feeling really fit. The evening of his arrival Samantha had returned with Dr. Hunchmould, a short stocky little man who walked like a clockwork toy and whose breath whistled through his nostrils like bagpipes. With Samantha, coolly efficient, helping him and Mr. Filigree dancing about ineffectually, Dr. Hunchmould had stripped Adrian down, put three stitches in a long gash in his thigh, bound up his cracked ribs and encased his broken arm in plaster from wrist to elbow. The pain Adrian suffered was considerable, and by the time the doctor had finished he was exhausted. Mr. Filigree, delighted at being able to perform a useful function, had carried Adrian up the narrow stairs to a small bedroom—cuddled under the thick thatch of the roof—and put him to bed. For the next two days Adrian hardly remembered anything except that Samantha always seemed to be there, smoothing his pillow, holding his head as he vomited into a large china chamber pot covered with rosebuds, and giving him soothing, cooling drinks when his fever got high. He wondered hazily how she managed to get any sleep, for whenever he opened his eyes, either during the day or the night, she always seemed to be there, sitting patiently on a chair by his bed, concentrating on some tapestry she was making. Now that he felt better, he was overwhelmed with embarrassment at the trouble he must have caused her. He wiggled his toes into a cool part of the bed, stretched experimentally, and then wished he had not, for his body still ached and twinged.

The door opened suddenly and Samantha came in bearing a tray with his breakfast.

"Good morning," she said, smiling. "How are you feeling?"

"Much better," said Adrian, blushing as he always did when she fixed her large green eyes on him. "I think, in fact, I could get up. I'm afraid I've caused you far too much trouble as it is."

"Nonsense," said Samantha briskly, placing the tray on his lap. "You get these eggs down you. They're fresh this morning. Father went into the village for them."

"How's Rosy?" asked Adrian anxiously.

"Fine," said Samantha raising her eyebrows. "Why? Shouldn't she be?"

"She doesn't normally take to women," explained Adrian.

"Well, she's taken to me," said Samantha, "and she adores father. I think she thinks he's a kind of elephant."

She sat quietly watching him while he ate the eggs and drank the tea; then she deftly removed the tray and straightened his pillows.

"The doctor's coming to-day to take out your stitches," she said. "So you'll just stay where you are until he tells us whether you can get up."

"Look," said Adrian, "there's something I must tell you. Can you spare five minutes?"

"You're looking a bit flushed," said Samantha surveying him critically. "You sure you haven't got a temperature?"

"No, no," said Adrian, "I'm just worried."

Samantha sat down in the chair and folded her hands in her lap.

"Well?" she said interrogatively.

Stumblingly at first, and then with greater fluency, since Samantha listened with rapt attention and did not interrupt, Adrian told her how he had inherited Rosy and of the terrible trail of carnage that they had left across the countryside. Instead of the look of horror which Adrian had expected, and which indeed would have been the accepted reaction of most young ladies to such an improper tale, by the time he had finished Samantha's face was flushed with suppressed laughter, her eyes were sparkling and her lips twitching.

"So you see," concluded Adrian, "I'm probably wanted by the police. God knows what they'll do to me if they catch me, and I can't deny it. Rosy is the sort of clue that not even a policeman would overlook. So I must get down to the coast and get rid of her. While I'm in your house, I'm a danger to you. I think they call it 'aiding and abetting' or something."

Samantha gave a little crow of laughter.

"Wonderful," she said ecstatically. "Not only a wounded warrior, but a hunted criminal as well."

"It's not funny," said Adrian aggrievedly.

"No, I don't suppose it is to you," said Samantha, endeavouring to compose her features into an expression of commiseration. "But I wouldn't worry too much. Nobody knows you're here and Rosy's safely hidden in the barn. It just means that father and I will exercise her in the evening down in the meadow where nobody can see. As it is, father spends most of his time in the barn with her. At the moment he's gilding her toe-nails. No, you just lie where and don't worry. Wait and see what the doctor says."

When he arrived, Dr. Hunchmould whistled and wheezed his way round Adrian's bed, prodding and poking. He removed the stitches in Adrian's thigh and then stood surveying him and rubbing his hands crisply together.

"Well, you can get up if you want to," he said. "But take it easy. A light, nourishing diet and not too much exercise."

"When will I be able to take this plaster off?" said Adrian. "It weighs about two and a half tons."

"Not for at least four weeks," said Dr. Hunchmould.

After the doctor had gone Adrian dressed himself laboriously. His legs were wobbly and his whole body was stiff, but at length he made his way cautiously down the creaking stairs into the big kitchen where Samantha, with a brightly coloured apron on, was supervising several large copper pots from which came the most mouth-watering smells.

Adrian stood at the foot of the stairs and watched her for a moment. He had not imagined it, she really did float.

She had all the grace and nimbleness of her father. The firelight glinted on her hair, making it glow to match the copper pans.

"Hello," said Adrian. She turned and smiled at him and he felt his stomach contract into a tight knot, and the blood creeping into his face.

"Hello," she said. "How do you feel?"

"A bit shaky," admitted Adrian. "Can I help you do anything?"

"No," she said. "I remember what the doctor said. If you want to, you can go out in the barn and talk to father and Rosy."

Reluctantly, because he did not want to leave her, Adrian made his way out through the back door of the pub and across the cobbled yard to the barn. From inside came the shrill sounds of Mr. Filigree conducting a one-sided conversation with Rosy.

"And then, my dear," he fluted, "we came to this simply enormous cane brake, and there in the middle of it was the tiger. Now, the elephant I was riding was very beautiful and very brave. Not nearly, of course, as beautiful or as brave as you, but something approaching that. As the tiger sprang, she lifted her trunk and hit him in mid air, felling him to the ground."

Fascinated, Adrian made his way into the barn. Rosy was shackled in one corner and near her was a great bed of sweet-smelling hay. In front of her was an enormous wooden trough filled with carrots, apples, chopped mangolds and other delicacies, from which she was daintily feeding herself. Mr. Filigree was crouched at her feet, a pot of gold paint in one hand and brush in the other. Rosy's toe-nails gleamed golden in the dim light. She greeted Adrian's appearance in the barn with such a shrill and excited trumpet of joy that Mr. Filigree, who was not expecting it, fell backwards, upsetting the tin of gold paint.

"Hello, Mr. Filigree, hello, Rosy," said Adrian.

"Dear boy," shrilled Mr. Filigree, wallowing helplessly on his back in the pile of hay. "How nice to see you up.

Would you care to lend me a hand? There are certain postures in which I fall that make it difficult for me to rise without assistance."

Adrian stretched out a hand, clasped Mr. Filigree's chubby fingers, and hauled. With much wheezing and panting Mr. Filigree got to his feet.

"How do you think she's looking?" he asked Adrian. "Don't you think those toe-nails give her a certain glamour?"

"Definitely," said Adrian. "I haven't seen her look so elegant since we left Fenneltree Hall."

"I do wish she had tusks," said Mr. Filigree plaintively. "The ones I had *all* had tusks and we used to bore holes in them (quite painless, you know) and insert diamonds and rubies and things like that. It made all the difference."

"She does quite enough damage without having tusks," said Adrian, patting Rosy's trunk which she had curled affectionately round his neck. "You two appear to be getting on like a house on fire."

"Yes," fluted Mr. Filigree excitedly, "we have a *rapport*. It wouldn't surprise me in the slightest if she was not a reincarnation of my favourite elephant, Poo-Ting. I could tell in an instant if we only had a tiger."

"I think," said Adrian, "that life is quite complicated enough without having a tiger."

"I suppose you are right," said Mr. Filigree. "But one does like to get these loose ends tied up. It would have made a splendid chapter."

Samantha had explained to Adrian that Mr. Filigree was a devout believer in reincarnation and could, in fact, remember most of his incarnations in detail. He had been writing a book about his past lives for the last twenty years, and this already filled some forty-eight fat volumes. The chances of finishing it were slight, since practically every day he remembered some new facts which necessitated the addition of a fresh chapter.

"It would be absolutely fascinating," said Mr. Filigree wistfully, "if one could have an attested document from

Rosy to say that she was in fact a reincarnation of Poo-Ting."

"I don't think that would be possible," said Adrian.

"No, no, I suppose not," said Mr. Filigree. "But dear boy, how selfish of me to keep you talking here when you should be sitting down. Come, let's go inside and have a brandy."

He led the way back into the pub, leaving a trail of gold footprints wherever he moved.

"Samantha," he shrilled, bursting into the kitchen, "I'm convinced that Rosy is Poo-Ting." He paused with his hands held up dramatically to see the effect this news would have on his daughter.

"That's nice," said Samantha smiling at him. "Now all you need is a tiger to prove it."

"*Exactly* what I said to Adrian," said Mr. Filigree delightedly. "Didn't I say that to you, Adrian? I said 'All we need is a tiger'."

"And I said," said Adrian sinking gratefully into a chair, "I said I thought it was bad enough to have Rosy, without having a tiger as well."

Samantha came up to the chair and looked at him, her green eyes watchful and penetrating.

"Are you all right?" she said.

"Yes," said Adrian. "I'm not quite as strong as I thought I was."

She laid a cool hand on his forehead and Adrian closed his eyes and wished fervently that she would never remove it.

"Father," she said crisply, "you've been getting him over-excited. Fetch him a brandy."

"Exactly what I was going to do," said Mr. Filigree with dignity. "Isn't that so, Adrian? Didn't I say to you only just now 'Let's go in and have a brandy'?"

"Well, stop talking and get one," said Samantha. "Lunch will be ready in a minute."

Mr. Filigree poured out two large glasses of brandy, gave one to Adrian and then wedged himself into his favourite chair and beamed round with an air of innocent goodwill.

"Do you know," he said to Adrian, "I think I will write a chapter on Rosy, or rather Rosy as Poo-Ting. Of course, it can't be proved; but then, how many scientific facts can be? It is up to them really to prove it wrong, isn't it? As it says in Genesis somewhere : 'There are more things in Heaven and Earth and some of them are proved and some of them are not'."

"Yes," said Adrian politely, "I expect you're right."

"But I know it," said Mr. Filigree earnestly. "Now, you may not believe it to look at me, but I was at one time a candle maker, in the time of Richard III, and I had a cat called Tabitha. A great big, joyful creature like a snowball. Then one day, quite inadvertently, I spilt some hot candle-grease on her tail. Poor, sweet creature, she was mortified, quite naturally. When the hair grew again, it was completely black. So, there she was, a white cat with a black tail. Now, would you believe it, not long ago I was down in the village when a large cat came and started making a tremendous fuss of me and it was perfectly obvious that it was a reincarnation of Tabitha."

"Really?" said Adrian, his attention caught for the first time.

"Yes," said Mr. Filigree. "It was a beautiful big grey cat and its name, as I ascertained upon enquiry, was Henry."

"But, if it was grey and its name was Henry . . .?" began Adrian, puzzled.

"Oh, the colour was probably due to age," said Mr. Filigree, waving his hands about and diminishing such a minor discrepancy. "And you know what silly names people call things. But it was quite unmistakably my Tabitha. It was one of the most remarkable pieces of evidence that I have been vouchsafed. It was her instant recognition of me that clinched the matter."

"The fact that he was carrying a salmon and a half-barrel of oysters at the time had absolutely nothing to do with it!" said Samantha dryly, dishing the steaming stew out on to three plates, and placing them on the long trestle table. "Now, come and eat, for heaven's sake, before it gets cold."

Adrian, as he sat down, suddenly realised that he was extremely hungry. The stew smelled mouth-watering and in the heap of multi-coloured vegetables on his plate he could see small, fat dumplings, gleaming out of the gravy at him like pearls. Mr. Filigree squeaked on, explaining to Adrian how one can tell beyond a shadow of doubt when one meets a reincarnation, and Adrian nodded and said "Umm" at regular intervals, while stuffing the delicious stew into his mouth wolfishly.

When the last remnants of gravy had been eased from the plates with the aid of crusts of bread, and they were all sitting back replete and happy, there came a knock at the door.

Samantha rose from the table and went to the window where she peered round the curtain.

"Adrian," she said, "upstairs quickly. It's the police."

Adrian stumbled to his feet and looked at her aghast.

"Quickly," she cried, her eyes flashing, "and take your plate with you."

Blindly he grabbed his plate and scurried up the stairs, where he stood on the landing listening with bated breath while his heart pounded. The knocker fell on the door again and it sounded to Adrian like somebody hammering nails into his coffin.

"Just coming," he heard Samantha call in a gay, unworried tone of voice, and then he saw her opening the front door and he shrank back into the shadows and listened.

"Good morning, Miss Filigree!" said a deep, soulful voice as Samantha opened the door.

"Yes," she said.

"Sergeant Hitchbrisket," said the voice, "Moleshire Constabulary. I wonder if I might come in for a word with you?"

"Certainly," said Samantha brightly. "We have just finished lunch, but can I offer you a cup of tea?"

"That's very kind of you, miss," said Sergeant Hitchbrisket, following her into the kitchen.

He had a bony face like a ferret, and thick black hair which he had meticulously parted down the centre of his head. He nodded to Mr. Filigree who was still sitting at the table, open-mouthed, endeavouring to catch up with such rapidly moving events.

"Morning, sir," he said. "Lovely day for the time of year, isn't it?"

"Beautiful," beamed Mr. Filigree.

"Do sit down, Sergeant," said Samantha, placing a cup of tea on the table, "and tell us how we can help you."

The Sergeant unbuttoned his uniform pocket and extracted a large and somewhat battered notebook, and then a pencil. He licked the end of the pencil and then licked his thumb and flipped over the leaves of his notebook, refreshing his memory, his lips moving as he read to himself.

"Well, it's like this, miss," he said at last. "We've been told to keep a sharp lookout for a criminal and it seemed to me that you might be able to help us with our investigations."

"I doubt it," said Samantha sweetly. "We don't know very many criminals."

"That is to say," said Sergeant Hitchbrisket, reddening,

"that you might be able to give us some information leading to his apprehension."

"But, of course," said Samantha, smiling affectionately at the Sergeant. "We are always ready to help the police. Father, would you mind taking the dirty plates out into the scullery, while I talk to the Sergeant?"

"Of course, my dear," fluted Mr. Filigree, and he lumbered out of the room carrying the plates.

"My father," said Samantha in a hushed voice, "is an extremely sensitive man, and I don't want him upset."

"Ah yes. Quite, miss," said Sergeant Hitchbrisket. "As a matter of fact, it was due to your father that I came along."

"Oh," said Samantha, faintly, "why! What has he been doing!"

"Oh, nothing, nothing," said the Sergeant hastily. "It's not what he's been doing, it's what he's been talking about."

"I'm afraid I don't quite follow you," said Samantha, narrowing her green eyes at him speculatively.

"Well, miss," said the Sergeant, "it's like this. This criminal, whom I shall call Mr. X for the moment, has been going around the countryside with an elephant."

"An elephant?" said Samantha, round-eyed.

"Yes," said the Sergeant, "an elephant." He glanced again at his notebook to make sure of his facts. "He is wanted for assault and battery to the Monkspepper Hunt and wilful damage and assault at Lord Fenneltree's place."

"Good heavens!" said Samantha. "But why should he want to do that?"

"Why indeed?" said Sergeant Hitchbrisket lugubriously. "The ways of the criminal mind are very obscure, very obscure indeed. Any road, he was last seen heading in this direction, see, and then this morning your father was down in the village and was talking to Bill Plungemusket, him what keeps the poultry farm, and he happened to mention as how he got an elephant. Now it seems unlikely, miss, that there can be more than one elephant running around these parts, so I thought I'd just come up and enquire."

Although Samantha's heart sank, she managed to arrange her face in an expression of astonishment.

"My father," she said in astonishment, "said he had an elephant?"

"Yes," said Sergeant Hitchbrisket stolidly. "Leastways, that's what he told Plungemusket."

Samantha frowned. "I cannot think what he can have been talking about," she said. And then, suddenly, her brow cleared.

"Ah yes," she said, "I know."

She gave what she hoped was a gay laugh, jumped to her feet and went to the scullery door.

"Father," she called, "will you come here a minute."

Adrian, listening from the top of the stairs, almost had a heart attack. He had been so pleased when Samantha had got Mr. Filigree out of the way that to reintroduce him into the room while the minion of the law was still there struck him as being the very height of foolhardiness. Mr. Filigree, wreathed in smiles, came into the room like a chubby, benevolent cherub.

"Father," said Samantha, "Sergeant Hitchbrisket here is very interested in elephants."

"Are you, by Jove?" shrilled Mr. Filigree excitedly. "My dear chap, how nice to meet a kindred spirit. I have a positive passion for them myself. What are yours called?"

"Well, I don't actually have any," said Sergeant Hitchbrisket. "You see, it's like this, sir . . ."

"Oh, you poor man," interrupted Mr. Filigree. "Fancy having a passion for elephants, and not owning one. Now, I had a hundred and one."

"A hundred and one?" said Sergeant Hitchbrisket faintly.

"I do assure you," said Mr. Filigree waggling his fat fingers earnestly, "I do assure you, it was a hundred and one, and the best of the lot was Poo-Ting. My dear fellow, if you could only have seen her kill a tiger. It was a treat, I assure you, a real treat."

"Yes, sir, I'm sure it was," said Sergeant Hitchbrisket clearing his throat. "Tell me, when was it you had these elephants?"

"Let's see," said Mr. Filigree, screwing up his face in a determined effort at concentration. "I think it was 1470."

"1470?" croaked Sergeant Hitchbrisket, his pencil poised over his notebook.

"Or, it may have been 1471," said Mr. Filigree. "I cannot be sure."

"It was one of my father's previous incarnations," said Samantha sweetly.

"Oh, ah," said Sergeant Hitchbrisket, "incarnation, eh?"

"Yes. I was at Nagarapore," said Mr. Filigree earnestly. "It was, I assure you, a most interesting life. Quite apart from the elephants and the tiger hunts, there was the way they used to weigh me every year with gold and precious stones. Absolutely thrilling."

Sergeant Hitchbrisket folded up his notebook and stowed it away in his pocket together with his pencil.

"Most interesting, sir," he said, getting to his feet. "Most interesting. Well, I don't think I'll be troubling you any farther."

"I do assure you," said Samantha, "that should we have any news of any sort, we will get in touch with you immediately."

"Thank you, miss," said the Sergeant eyeing her.

"Not at all," she said curtly. "One should always help the police."

"Well, good day, sir. Good day, miss," said Sergeant Hitchbrisket, and he clumped his way out into the road. Samantha closed the front door and leant against it, letting her breath out in a great sigh of relief.

"It was 1471," said Mr. Filigree. "I've just remembered. Call him back."

"No, I'm sure he has got all the information he wants," said Samantha. "But really, father, you must not go down to the village and start spreading these stories about."

"They are not stories," said Mr. Filigree aggrievedly.

"No, I know they're not," said Samantha, "but it's just that people in the village don't believe in reincarnation the way you do, and so they all think the whole thing a bit queer. Now, promise me you won't go down there again and start talking about elephants and things."

"All right, my dear," sighed Mr. Filigree, "I suppose you're right."

"Of course I'm right," said Samantha. "You'll get yourself into trouble that way."

She went to the bottom of the stairs and looked up. "You can come down now, Adrian," she said. "He's gone."

Adrian came down, mopping his forehead with his handkerchief.

"You were wonderful," he said. "It took a year off my life, just to listen to you."

"I think you really have to thank father," said Samantha dryly. "It's most fortunate that India came into his reincarnation."

"But, you see, I was right," said Adrian. "What I said to you this morning. I am a danger to you here, and now you've gone and made it worse by telling lies to him."

"Rubbish," said Samantha. "Nobody's going to know you're here."

"But they're bound to find out sooner or later," said Adrian. "And when they do, you will be in it as deeply as I am, and I should hate that."

"Now, look," said Samantha, "stop being silly. You are not well enough to travel yet, and it will be another four weeks before you can take your plaster off. All you have to do is lie low here until you feel better."

"Will you promise me that I can move on as soon as I do feel better?" said Adrian. Samantha looked at him with a curious expression in her green eyes.

"When you feel better," she said, "if you want to move on, I can't stop you."

"It's, it's not a question of wanting to move on," stammered Adrian. "It's just that I don't want to get you into trouble, or your father, if it comes to that."

"Well, we shall see," said Samantha. "And since you're so anxious to be helpful, you can come and help me with the washing-up."

The next fortnight was a nightmare for poor Adrian.

Every time Mr. Filigree went down to the village to get something, he expected him to return accompanied by a group of kindly constables whom he had offered to show Rosy to. He lay awake at night visualising Samantha being arrested for aiding and abetting, and being cast into some enormous, gloomy prison to languish in a damp cell until her copper-coloured hair turned white and she died in misery and loneliness. The fact that, of all of them, it was he who was the most likely to receive a really stiff sentence did not worry him. It was the thought of Samantha in prison that would wake him up in a cold sweat. For he had fallen deeply and irretrievably in love with her. This, of course, presented another problem to his tortured mind. Even supposing he had the courage to confess his love, how could a criminal (on the run with a dangerous elephant) possibly propose to a girl like Samantha?

At length he could stand it no longer. He came downstairs early one morning and found Samantha cooking breakfast in the kitchen, her hair gleaming like a newly minted penny.

"Good morning," she smiled. "It'll be ready in a minute."

"Samantha, I must talk to you," said Adrian firmly. She turned and surveyed him quizzically. The sunlight caught her face and the little gold flecks in her green eyes glinted and winked. Adrian swallowed and began to feel his good resolutions draining away. How could he possibly leave anybody so beautiful and so desirable?

"Look here," he insisted, "I've got to talk to you."

"My, my," said Samantha mockingly, "why are we so stern this morning?"

"I've decided," said Adrian in what he hoped was a firm, masculine voice, "I have decided that I am leaving to-night."

Samantha's eyes widened. "To-night?" she said. "Well, I suppose you know best."

She turned her attention to the frying-pan where the eggs lay spluttering in rows like miniature suns.

"It's not that I want to go," said Adrian desperately,

"but the longer I stay the greater the danger of my being discovered. You must see that."

"My dear man," said Samantha coldly, her back still turned towards him as she busied herself about the fire, "it is nothing to do with me."

"You see," said Adrian miserably, "I've got to get rid of Rosy. If I can get rid of her, then they can't connect me with the Hunt and the Hall and all that, and the only chance I have of getting rid of her is to get down to the coast."

"Have you ever heard of a familiar?" enquired Samantha.

"A familiar?" said Adrian. "No. What's that?"

"Witches used to have them in the old days," said Samantha. "They were creatures that followed them about and sometimes did their dirty work for them. Cats, and things like that. Well, I think Rosy is your familiar. Witches used to be able to attach a familiar to people they disliked so that everywhere they went they saw a black dog, or small monkey, or something."

"Oh!" said Adrian. "How interesting."

"It eventually drove the person mad," said Samantha gaily. "That's why I think Rosy is your familiar. Your uncle was probably a wizard in his spare time."

"Well, this is one familiar that I'm going to get rid of," said Adrian firmly.

Samantha flung down a spoon and whirled round to face him. Her eyes were enormous and a more vivid green than he had ever seen them before, and the little gold flecks shone and glittered.

"*You*," she said, anger flushing her face, "you are despicable."

"But . . . but . . . what have I done?" said Adrian, aghast at this sudden display of rage on the part of the normally calm Samantha.

"Wasn't Rosy left you by your uncle?" enquired Samantha.

"Yes."

"Didn't he leave you money to look after her?"

"Yes."

"Wasn't your uncle your last living relative?"

"Yes."

"Well then, strictly speaking, Rosy is *your* relative, and you have absolutely no right to talk about selling her as though she were an old clock or something. You're despicable."

Adrian stood with his mouth open, staring at Samantha hazily.

"All right," she continued, taking off her apron and flinging it into a chair, "you do whatever you think is right. If *you* consider selling one of your relatives into servitude is right, then the sooner you are out of here the better, as far as I'm concerned."

She turned and ran across the great kitchen and clattered up the stairs. Adrian heard her bedroom door shut. He was still standing there in a daze when a strong odour of burnt eggs woke him with a start and he pulled the pan off the fire, burning his fingers in the process.

Mr. Filigree waddled into the house, sniffing the rank smell of burning appreciatively.

"Ah," he said, smacking his lips, "breakfast."

"I'm afraid you'll have to get your own," said Adrian curtly. "Samantha's gone and locked herself in her bedroom."

"Ah well," said Mr. Filigree philosophically, "it happens, you know, dear boy. It happens."

"What happens?" snarled Adrian.

"Oh, things," said Mr. Filigree, vaguely waving his fingers. "Piques; tantrums; arguments; furores. Upsidownsy, upsidownsy."

"Yes. Well, I'm damned if I'm going to be upsidownsied," said Adrian. "I'm leaving."

"Do you know," said Mr. Filigree, peering into the pan, "I do believe these eggs are burnt."

"Yes, and you can blame your daughter for *that*," said Adrian.

"No doubt," said Mr. Filigree. "However, there appears to be one lurking here," he said, pointing a fat finger, "that has escaped the holocaust. Would you like to share it with me?"

"No," said Adrian. "I'm going to pack."

Packing with one arm was more difficult that he had anticipated, but eventually he jumbled his clothes in somehow. He was still simmering with rage at Samantha's outburst, which he considered to be quite beyond the bounds of propriety. After all, he wanted to get rid of Rosy for *her* sake, didn't he? It was *her* he was thinking of and there she was, carrying on as though he were some sort of sadistic criminal. Well, he'd show her.

To his immense chagrin, he discovered that it was impossible for him to harness Rosy to the trap with his arm encased in plaster, and so he was forced to ask Mr. Filigree to help him.

"Do you know," said Mr. Filigree, tightening the straps that lashed the trap to Rosy's rotund form, "I wonder if you're being altogether wise, dear boy?"

"Now, don't *you* start," said Adrian. "I've had quite enough from Samantha."

"I was just thinking," said Mr. Filigree penitently, "I'm not trying to interfere in any way, but it seems to me you are going to have difficulty in hitching and unhitching Rosy."

"I'll find somebody to help," said Adrian.

When everything was ready, Adrian stood for a moment irresolute. Mr. Filigree watched him with round, anxious blue eyes.

"Well," said Adrian, with an attempt at jocularity, "here I go."

"Aren't you, um, aren't you going to say good-bye to Samantha?" squeaked Mr. Filigree.

At that moment the last thing that Adrian wanted was to see Samantha, but Mr. Filigree looked at him so plaintively, like a gigantic baby pleading for its bottle, that he had not got the heart to say no. He stamped back into the *Unicorn and Harp* and clumped his way up the stairs. He stopped outside Samantha's door and cleared his throat.

"Samantha," he called in a firm, commanding voice. "Samantha, it's me, Adrian."

"Well, I didn't think it was Rosy," came Samantha's voice from behind the door.

"I'm just off," said Adrian, making a wild gesture with his hand to indicate the extreme distance that he hoped to cover during the day. "I wanted to say good-bye."

"Good-bye," said Samantha sweetly.

"And thank you for all your trouble," said Adrian.

"Don't mention it," said Samantha. "Any time you're run over by a train and you happen to be nearby, don't hesitate to drop in."

"Yes. Well then, I'll be off," said Adrian.

There was silence from behind the door.

"The reason I'm leaving so early," he shouted, "is because we've got a long way to go."

"I do wish you wouldn't bellow through the door like that," said Samantha.

"Well, I'll be off," said Adrian.

"Yes," said Samantha in honeyed tones, "you'd better hurry, or you'll miss the slave market."

Seething with rage at the unfairness of this remark, Adrian clattered down the stairs and strode out to the barn.

"Well, good-bye, Mr. Filigree," he said. "I really am deeply grateful for all you have done for me. I hope that we will meet again some time."

"Bound to," said Mr. Filigree earnestly. "Simply cannot be avoided, dear boy. The thing is to have some sort of sign of recognition, because I mean suppose for example I was a beetle and you were the Prime Minister. Unless one had some sign of recognition, one wouldn't know, would one? A careless gesture at me as I crawled across some state papers, and you might damage me irretrievably. So, should we meet in an after life I will say 'Do you remember the *Unicorn and Harp*?' and you will say 'Yes I do'."

Adrian was about to remark that Mr. Filigree would have difficulty in saying "Do you remember the *Unicorn and Harp*?" in the unlikely event of his being a beetle crawling across state papers, but he felt that this might prolong his departure, so he nodded, took Rosy's warm leathery ear in his hand and urged her forward.

A hundred yards down the road he stopped and looked back. The *Unicorn and Harp* crouched under its thatch like a black and white tortoise under a golden shell. He thought he saw something move in the window of Samantha's room, but he could not be sure. With a sigh he took hold of Rosy's ear again, and they continued down the road.

13 THE SEA VOYAGE

The week that followed, Adrian decided, was the worst he had ever spent in his life. Travelling by night and hiding by day were bad enough, but the difficulties of hitching and unhitching Rosy from the trap were tremendous. Also, he missed Samantha terribly, and approximately once every ten minutes bitterly regretted that he had ever left the *Unicorn and Harp*.

At length he could stand his plaster cast no longer and so, leaving Rosy carefully shackled in a wood with a large supply of food all ready in front of her, he made his way to the nearest town. Here he was directed to a doctor who examined his arm.

"It's nearly four weeks," said Adrian, "and the doctor who put it on said I could take it off in four weeks."

"Well," said the doctor, "it's up to you. I can take it off if you want me to, but you will have to be very careful how you use it."

So he stripped the cast away from Adrian's arm and Adrian felt that he had been relieved of an intolerable burden. His arm was stiff, but when he moved it it caused him no pain and it was obvious the break had healed. He hurried back to the wood where he had left Rosy and that evening they continued on their way into a sunset as flamboyant as a peacock's tail.

Dawn found them following a rough track over a great headland covered with big green busbies of thrift, each one a mass of pink flowers. Then, suddenly, as they reached the peak of the headland, they came to the edge of a steep cliff and there below them was the sea, trembling and glinting in the morning light and whispering busily to itself on the shingle beach. It was not a very good place for concealing Rosy, for there was not a tree for miles, but Adrian was beginning to feel happier now; he felt he had put enough distance between himself, Fenneltree Hall and the *Unicorn and Harp*. Surely here they would be safe. As he lay dozing on the soft piles of thrift, he wondered what his next move should be. Presumably, if he made his way along the cliff far enough, he would come to a seaside town and that was where he felt certain he would find a circus or some similar institution which would accept Rosy and her legacy. He was just drifting off into a deep relaxed sleep when a shrill voice shouted "Ahoy!" and Adrian leapt to his feet as though he had been shot and wheeled around wildly. Trotting towards him through the thrift, panting and waving her hands in greeting, came Black Nell.

"Ahoy!" she crowed, beaming at him. "Well met."

"Hello," said Adrian in astonishment. "What are you doing up here?"

"A minute," panted Black Nell, "while I catch me breath."

She sat down and fanned herself vigorously for a moment or two.

"You aren't hiding Rosy very well," she said accusingly. "My caravan's right over there, and I could see her standing up against the sky. Thought she was a great rock until she moved."

"Well, I think I'm safe enough here," said Adrian glancing round anxiously.

"Where are you going to?" enquired Black Nell.

"Well, I don't really know," said Adrian. "I was going to

follow the cliffs along until I came to a town, and then see if there was a circus or something that would take Rosy off me."

"Umm," said Black Nell, pulling her pipe out of her pocket and lighting it. "Do you know these parts?"

"No," said Adrian, "I don't."

"Well," said Black Nell, pointing with the stem of her pipe, "if you take my advice, you'll go that way. That leads you to Sploshport-on-Solent. Quite a pleasant little place in its way, but from there you can catch the ferry across to the Island of Scallop."

"But what on earth do I want to go to an island for?" said Adrian. "Besides, will they take Rosy on the ferry?"

"Hush up and listen to me," said Black Nell. "The island's a favourite place for holiday-makers, see. They've got all sorts of things there, fun fairs and the like, and if there's any circus in the area, it'll be there. That's your only chance of getting shot of Rosy in this area. As for taking her on the ferry, well, how do you think the circuses get across?"

"Yes," said Adrian humbly, "I hadn't thought of that."

"Now," said Black Nell, "if you put on a steady turn of speed, you should be down at Sploshport in time to catch the evening ferry. Then, when you are across, go and see a friend of mine, Ethelbert Cleep."

"Ethelbert Cleep, *Ethelbert Cleep*?" said Adrian incredulously.

"He can't help his name," said Black Nell sharply. "After all, Rookwhistle might seem curious to some."

"True," Adrian admitted. "Well, when I see your friend what do I do?"

"Tell him your story, tell him I sent you, and act on his advice," said Black Nell.

"It is extremely kind of you," said Adrian.

"By the way, how did you get on at the *Unicorn and Harp*?" enquired Black Nell glancing at him shrewdly.

"They were wonderful to me," said Adrian, blushing slightly. "Absolutely marvellous people."

"Particularly Samantha, eh?" said Black Nell. "Or did

114

you think she was just another of those flibbertigibbet girls?"

"Flibbertigibbet," said Adrian incensed. "flibbertigibbet, Samantha, why she's, I think . . . she was . . . she is . . ."

"That's all right," said Black Nell comfortably puffing out a large cloud of smoke. "I know what you mean, but look, if you're to make that ferry you had best get a move on."

She got to her feet, patted Rosy's trunk affectionately and grinned at Adrian.

"See you again some time. Give my love to Ethelbert," she said, and stumped back over the downs like a small indomitable black mole in a great sea of green.

Hastily Adrian hitched Rosy up to the trap, then continued along the rough track over the downs until it dipped and swung down to join a proper road with houses on it. Soon more and more houses appeared and eventually Adrian and Rosy reached the middle of Sploshport-on-Solent. He immediately noticed one great difference between Sploshport and the city. Here, after many years of experience, the horses and the people had grown inured to strange processions of weird beasts passing through their midst. Nobody turned his head to look at Adrian and Rosy as they plodded through the streets, and the horses pulling the carts and carriages clopped past them as though they did not exist.

After stopping to enquire the way several times, Adrian and Rosy finally found themselves down at the docks and saw the *Sploshport Queen* wallowing at her moorings like a gigantic beetle, the spades of her paddle-wheels slapping the water as she rolled slowly and majestically in the evening sun. A great plume of black smoke from her gold and green funnel implied that she was in imminent danger of departure and people were hurrying to and fro up the gang-plank and milling about on the decks. Adrian shackled Rosy to a lamp post and made his way through the crowd until he came upon what he assumed to be a sailor who was sitting on a bollard chewing tobacco with the vacant-eyed, dispirited enthusiasm of a very ancient cow.

"Can you help me?" asked Adrian. "I want to go across on the ferry and I have got an elephant and trap. Who do I see about going?"

The sailor's jaws stopped revolving and he thought about the question for a long time.

"Not me," he said at length.

"No," said Adrian, "I didn't think it would be you. I thought you might know whom I had to see."

The sailor chewed on for a short time and then stopped once more.

"Elephants," he explained hoarsely, "is cargo."

"Yes?" said Adrian.

"Cargo is the Captain or Chief Officer," said the sailor, and apparently overcome by this brief communication with the outside world fell into another chewing trance.

Adrian fought his way up the gang-plank and on to the deck of the *Sploshport Queen*. Pushed and buffeted by enormous families of excited children, each of whom appeared to be armed with extremely sharp buckets and spades, he eventually found a ladder leading up to the bridge. He ran up this quickly and as he got to the top collided with another figure on its way down. It was perhaps unfortunate that when he had apologised and helped the figure to its feet, it turned out to be the Captain of the *Sploshport Queen*. He was a tiny, egg-shaped little man, so covered with gold braid that his uniform could be only dimly discerned beneath it. He had a spade-shaped grey beard and vibrated energy like a hive of particularly malevolent bees. He brushed himself down and surveyed Adrian from head to foot slowly and with what appeared to be cannibalistic interest.

"If this is attempted mutiny," he said in a soft reasonable voice, "then I suppose you have some slight excuse, but I would like to point out to you, young man, that to be knocked down and trampled under foot is hardly the sort of action that forms a firm basis for warm and prolonged friendship."

"I am terribly sorry," said Adrian, "but I thought you

were just leaving and I was in a hurry. You see, I've got an elephant and trap that I want to carry on your ship, if I may."

The Captain flicked a tiny scrap of dust from his uniform and surveyed Adrian again.

"I suppose," he said with a small sigh, "that I should be thankful you did not send the elephant up to see me. Where is the animal?"

"It's down there on the dock," said Adrian.

"It will cost five guineas," said the Captain.

"That's all right," said Adrian. "As long as we can go."

14 LANDFALL

Adrian, to his surprise, thoroughly enjoyed their short voyage on the *Sploshport Queen*. He had Rosy securely shackled to a massive steel bollard and felt reasonably sure that she could not get into trouble. He went below to the dining-saloon and bought them each a pint of ale, some buns for Rosy, and some sandwiches for himself and then, while they were sharing this meal, he leant on the rail and admired the sunset and the way its light seemed to smooth out the surface of the waves so that they looked like great bales of silk, unrolled across a draper's counter.

Rosy took to this new experience with her normal equanimity. She at first evinced a great interest in the sea; presumably, Adrian thought, because the sight of so much liquid forced her to the conclusion that it was drinkable and possibly intoxicating. However, finding it unobtainable from the deck, she soon gave that up and settled down to her normal rhythmic swaying from side to side, with her eyes half closed.

It was quite dark by the time they reached the Island of Scallop and, having disembarked, Rosy and Adrian made their way along the narrow cobbled streets of the town, pausing now and then to ask directions from strangers.

Eventually the road led them out of the town, over some sand-dunes, and there in the middle of the dunes like an extraordinary piece of flotsam was a small cottage constructed entirely from weather-beaten planks and bits of wood that must, at one time or another, have been cast up by the sea. Lights peered out of the windows and above the sigh of the sea Adrian could hear wafted to him the mournful sounds of a tuba in inexperienced hands, picking its way through what he, with difficulty, recognised as "My Love is Like a Red, Red Rose." The sand-dunes stretched away in every direction without a sign of any other habitation, and Adrian decided that this must be the house of Ethelbert Cleep. He and Rosy scrunched their way across the dunes and knocked on the door. The tuba uttered a discordant bellow like a bull and fell silent. After a moment, they could hear footsteps approaching the door.

"No artistry," shouted a voice from behind the door. "Bloody Philistines, banging and crashing when I'm in the middle of practice. Who is it? *Who is it?*"

Adrian cleared his throat.

"I'm Adrian Rookwhistle," he shouted.

"Adrian, did you say?" enquired a voice from behind the door. "A *boy?*"

"Yes," said Adrian, for want of a better reply.

The door was flung open and there stood a little man as tiny and as fragile as a sparrow. Adrian surveyed him incredulously. He was dressed in a long, thick, mustard-coloured cardigan which stretched almost to his knees and was done up with a series of enormous, bright gold, heavily embossed buttons; pearly grey velveteen trousers and a pair of black and white boots of weird design completed his ensemble. He had a mass of straw-coloured hair arranged in a style that made it look like an exceptionally wind-blown haystack, and he was wearing a pair of the most enormous pearl earrings that Adrian had ever seen. His thin, pale face was dominated by his eyes which were dark and shrewd and as restless as butterflies. This apparition leant provocatively against the door and surveyed Adrian.

"Darling boy," it said at last, "*what* did you say your name was?"

"Adrian, Adrian Rookwhistle. I was told to come and see you by Black Nell."

"Darling Black Nell," said the apparition. "A woman who really understands a man's needs. How *thoughtful* of her."

"You are Ethelbert Cleep, aren't you?" said Adrian.

"Yes," said Cleep archly. "My friends call me Ethel. Don't let me keep you standing here, chilling yourself to the bone. Come in, come in."

"Well, there's Rosy," said Adrian.

"Rosy?" said Cleep. "Surely you don't mean to say you have had the bad taste to bring a *woman* with you?"

"No," said Adrian gesturing at the sands outside, "this is Rosy."

Ethelbert Cleep peered out of the door and at that moment Rosy, whose manners were always impeccable, lifted up her trunk and uttered one of her falsetto trumpetings. Simultaneously Ethelbert Cleep uttered a squeak of surprise which was almost identical in timbre, and retreated into the passageway.

"What," he enqired in a hushed whisper of Adrian, "is that?"

"It's Rosy," said Adrian. "She's my elephant."

Ethelbert Cleep was holding a fragile heavily beringed hand to his chest as though in danger of suffering a heart attack.

"Is it for *me*, darling boy?" he asked. "If so, although I am overwhelmed by your generosity, I really feel I must refuse such a *lavish* present."

"No, no," said Adrian. "If you'll just let me come in a moment, I can explain everything to you."

He tied Rosy up and made his way into the Cleep establishment.

The whole cottage was one big room. At one end a staircase led up to a half-loft where, behind discreetly drawn chintz curtains, were Ethelbert's sleeping quarters. The whole room was full of chairs covered with antimacassars, tiny tables on which were precariously balanced glass domes full of decaying-looking stuffed birds and similar trinkets presumably dear to Ethelbert Cleep's heart, so that it made it almost impossible to move without knocking something over. Over the years, apparently, Ethelbert Cleep had developed a sort of bat-like system for avoiding damage to his *objets d'art*, and he flitted through the room with the greatest of ease, seated himself on a sofa and patted the cushion by his side.

"Come and sit down, darling boy, and tell me everything," he said.

Adrian picked his way carefully through the forest of bric-à-brac and lowered himself on to a chair at a convenient distance from Ethelbert Cleep.

"Well," he began, "it s like this . . ."

"Er, wait," said Cleep holding up a long forefinger. "A little refreshment."

He fluttered across the room and disappeared behind a Japanese screen covered with enormous dragons that looked as though they were in the last stages of thyroid deficiency. He reappeared carrying a decanter and two glasses, poured out a drink for Adrian, pressed it into his hand, and patted his cheek.

"Now then," he said as he seated himself on the sofa.

Adrian sniffed the wine and it seemed innocuous.

"My own, dearest heart," said Ethelbert Cleep, "I make it every year out of elderberries from the headland. *Incredibly* nourishing. Now, tell me your story. I'm sure I shall find it absolutely riveting."

So Adrian told him his adventures, and Ethelbert Cleep proved an exemplary audience. He sat with his eyes growing rounder and rounder, the glass forgotten in his hand, occasionally giving a little nervous giggle of laughter like a schoolgirl.

"Dear boy," he said when Adrian had finished, "an absolutely *fascinating* story."

"Well, it may sound like one, but it isn't when you live through it," said Adrian bitterly. "Anyway, Black Nell said I was to tell you all about it, and then to rely on your advice."

"My advice in *everything*, I hope," said Cleep archly, "but let me think, let me think."

He finished his wine, then produced from the interior of his repulsive cardigan a heavily embroidered smoking cap with a long silk tassel, wedged it firmly on his mop of hair, closed his eyes and leaned back.

"You see . . ." began Adrian.

"Hush," said Cleep without opening his eyes.

For some five minutes or so Adrian sat there finishing his wine and watching Cleep who appeared to have gone into a trance. Adrian was beginning seriously to wonder whether Black Nell had been right in sending him to this extraordinary little man. It looked as though he was more liable to get himself into further trouble than anything else.

"Got it!" said Cleep suddenly, removing his cap and putting it back in his cardigan. "Down in the town, darling boy, they have a theatre. It is, in actual fact, quite posh. You see, this place is becoming more and more of a *resort*."

He shuddered faintly at this thought and poured himself another glass of wine. "I assure you, darling boy," he continued, "that the *droves* and *droves* of hideous, purple-faced families that come flocking here are something that have to be seen to be believed."

"Yes, but what about the theatre?" said Adrian.

"Well," said Cleep, "it has only recently been built by one Emanuel S. Clattercup, a bovine and repulsive individual who, having spent the greater part of his life swindling the masses, has now decided that it is time to inflict some culture on those same unfortunate beings. Needless to say, culture at a profit."

He sipped his wine and beamed at Adrian.

"But, what has this got to do with me?" asked Adrian.

"Wait," said Cleep. "You might have thought that dear Clattercup, having gone to all the trouble of building a theatre in order to disseminate culture, would choose, as his first offering, something that a professional Thespian like myself could really get his teeth into. *Athello*, for example. My Desdemona is exquisite."

"That," said Adrian, "I can well imagine."

"Or," said Cleep, "*Romeo and Juliet*. They always said my Juliet was one of my best things, and also it used to save the company a lot of money because—not being exactly a heavy man—they didn't have to reinforce the balcony. However, this Clattercup Philistine has seen fit to start the season with, of all things, *Ali Baba and the Forty Thieves*."

"I should have thought," said Adrian, "that for a holiday resort that would have been an ideal thing to start with. After all, it would be sort of gay and bright."

"Dearest and sweetest Adrian," said Cleep closing his eyes in pain, "I may call you Adrian, mayn't I? There's a great difference between culture and gaiety. The two things are not synonymous at all."

"Well, I'm afraid I don't know very much about these things," said Adrian. "I just thought that probably the children would enjoy it. But I still don't see what it's got to do with me."

"Listen," said Cleep, "this cretinous Clattercup is about as altruistic as a brace of vultures. Now, if you could get him to include Rosy in the show and she was a success, and you *then* offered him the five hundred pounds—or what is left of it—I'm sure he would take her off your hands."

"I say," said Adrian enthusiastically, "what an excellent idea."

"I'm always having them, darling," said Cleep. "Now, what I suggest you do is to spend the night here and then to-morrow I will take you down to see Clattercup."

"Wonderful," said Adrian. "Thank you very much indeed."

"I myself," said Ethelbert reddening slightly, "am playing a minor part in the show. Not that I approve of it, you understand, but, dearest heart, one must live."

And so Adrian and Ethelbert got Rosy into the lean-to shed where Ethelbert made his elderberry wine, having first carefully removed anything that had the slightest alcoholic content. Then, going back into the house and up to the loft, Ethelbert drew back the chintz curtains displaying on one side an enormous brass double bed with a canopy over it, and at the other end an extremely uncomfortable-looking trestle bed.

"You may take your choice," he said, "but *I* always sleep in the double bed."

"Thanks," said Adrian. "Um, actually I'm a very bad sleeper, so I think I'll take the other bed."

"As you like," said Ethelbert cheerfully, "as you like."

Adrian decided, as he was dropping off to sleep, that the sight of Ethelbert Cleep in a long white nightshirt, a Japanese kimono and a night-cap with a tassel, was one that would live with him for many days to come.

The following morning when Adrian awoke, he found that Ethelbert had been up for some time and had prepared a substantial breakfast. An enormous, volcanically bubbling pot of porridge with thick cream and sugar, and a huge plate of bacon as brown and as crisp as autumn leaves and just as fragrant, almost covered with great golden fried eggs and piles of large mushrooms like strange fleshy edible umbrellas running with black juice.

"I think it always advisable to start the day with a good breakfast," said Ethelbert earnestly. "After all, one must consider one's art, and it requires a lot of both mental *and* physical energy to get inside the part that you are playing."

"Incidentally," said Adrian, with his mouth full, "what part are you playing?"

"One of the Sultan's harem," said Ethelbert without batting an eyelid. "It's a very exacting part."

Later, when they had done the washing-up, Ethelbert dressed himself in his outdoor clothes, which consisted of an Inverness and a deer stalker cap of mammoth dimensions. Then they hitched Rosy to the trap and made their way into the town.

Adrian was astonished when he saw the theatre. Although Ethelbert had told him that it was a large one, he had no idea quite how large, and the façade with its Doric columns, its flying buttresses and Gothic windows, argued that Mr. Clattercup must have acted as his own architect.

"I told you it was big," said Ethelbert in triumph, delighted at Adrian's astonishment. "Darling boy, it's something they'd be pleased to have even in the city, and I'll let you into a secret."

He paused and looked round furtively. There was nobody within earshot apart from Rosy, so he leant forward and whispered in Adrian's ear :

"It's got a revolving stage !"

He stepped back to see the effect his words would have on Adrian.

"Revolving stage?" said Adrian. "The man must be mad."

"He is, darling boy," said Cleep. "It's a deadly secret. We are going to *astonish* the audience on the first night, so don't tell a soul."

"I won't," said Adrian, "but I still think he's mad. It must have cost him a lot of money."

"This," said Cleep, waving his hand at the architectural conglomeration that confronted them, "is Clattercup's last great work. This is the monument that he has built for himself so that he will go down in history. Now, you wait here with Rosy, dear boy, while I go in and see him."

Adrian and Rosy waited patiently out in the road for half an hour or so until out of the theatre flitted Ethelbert, followed by a tubby little man dressed somewhat incongruously in a cutaway coat and striped trousers.

"Adrian," said Ethelbert, "this is Emanuel S. Clattercup, our mentor."

"Oh, aye," said the mentor. "'ow do?"

"I am very well, thank you," said Adrian, shaking hands.

"Understand you want a job," said Clattercup, peering somewhat nervously at Rosy.

"Well, yes, if it were possible," said Adrian. "I thought that since you were doing *Ali Baba* a little bit of Eastern pomp might be in keeping, and Rosy's quite used to wearing trappings and so on."

"Aye," said Clattercup, "well, she would be, wouldn't she, coming from er . . . from eh . . . coming from where she does."

"She behaves," said Adrian, colouring slightly at the falsehood, "extremely well and I'm sure that she would lend a certain something to your show."

"*Je ne sais quoi*?" suggested Ethelbert.

"What's that?" asked Clattercup suspiciously.

"It's French for I don't know what," explained Ethelbert.

"What jew mean, you don't know what?" said Clattercup.

"What I mean," said Ethelbert, "is that it's French, meaning 'I don't know what'."

Clattercup stared at him wall-eyed for a minute.

"I 'aven't the least bloody idea what you're talking about," he said at last.

Ethelbert raised his eyes to heaven.

"And some fell on stony ground," he said.

"Well, 'ow much would you want?" enquired Clattercup of Adrian. "These cultural shows take a lot of brass to get 'em on. I'm not made of brass, jew understand?"

"Well, I was just thinking in terms of a modest salary, enough to cover my own expenses and the expense of feeding Rosy," said Adrian.

"And of course you would provide the costumes," said Ethelbert.

Clattercup lit a large cigar and pondered for some minutes behind a cumulus of acrid smoke.

"Does she cost much to feed?" he said at last, jerking his thumb at Rosy.

"Er, a fair amount," said Adrian.

"Well, I'll tell you what I'll do," said Clattercup, "and I can't say fairer than this. I'll pay for her food and I'll pay for your keep until we see how you are going on. Then, if you are a success, we can discuss it further."

"Right," said Adrian, delighted, "that'll suit me perfectly."

"I shall want you for rehearsals at two o'clock this afternoon," said Clattercup.

"Fine," said Adrian, "I'll be here."

"All right," said Clattercup. "Tara."

Turning on his heel, he walked back into the theatre.

"*Darling* boy," said Ethelbert, "isn't that *wonderful*? Now we'll go back to the cottage and have a celebration, and then we'll get back here a little before two and I'll show you round the theatre."

15 THE REHEARSAL

After a celebration at Ethelbert's cottage, which consisted of apples for Rosy and a bottle of elderberry wine for Adrian and Ethelbert, the whole thing being accompanied (in a very cultural manner) by a spirited rendering by Ethelbert on his tuba of what he insisted was a fine old Irish ballad entitled "If I Were a Blackbird", they had lunch and hurried back into the town.

They tethered Rosy in a big shed outside the back of the theatre where the scenery was stored, made her comfortable with some hay and some mangolds and then Ethelbert led Adrian into the theatre.

"I have never been back stage in a theatre," said Adrian.

"Haven't you, darling boy?" said Ethelbert. "But it's such an experience. Come, I'll show you."

He danced away in the gloom and Adrian could hear the click of switches. Suddenly before him, glittering resplendent as a wedding cake, was the Sultan's palace in all its cardboard glory. Adrian looked out into the centre of the stage and gazed into the dark auditorium where he could just dimly discern the rows of seats and boxes perched around the walls. He was amazed at the great flats and sheets of scenery held on ropes and pulleys high above the proscenium arch out of sight of the audience, presumably waiting to be lowered at the appropriate moment by some minions of the theatre.

"This," said Ethelbert, joining him in front of the Sultan's palace, raising himself on tiptoe and doing a little pirouette, "is the revolving stage. We have got three scenes on it, and it goes right round when they pull those levers over there. Saves an awful lot of mucking about."

"It's really fascinating," said Adrian.

"Well, come along, darling boy," said Ethelbert, and he fluttered once more into the wings and switched off the lights, plunging the Sultan's palace into dusty gloom. He dived away through the scenery piled in corners and Adrian followed him.

Presently they came to a long narrow corridor, on either side of which was a series of doors.

"This," said Ethelbert flitting down the corridor to a door and leaning against it decoratively, "this is my dressing-room, dear boy."

He pointed to the door on which was a card that stated, rather startlingly, ETHELBERT CLEEP—CHIEF WIFE TO SULTAN. He opened the door and led Adrian into a tiny, rather dingy little room, most of one wall being taken up by a large mirror lit by gas lamps. There was a cupboard in one corner, the door hanging half open, and in it Adrian could see various exotic and eastern-looking costumes and a number of diaphanous veils.

Reclining on a horse-hair sofa on the other side of the room was an extremely large and statuesque red-head, clad (it was quite obvious) in nothing but a rather moth-eaten dressing-gown trimmed with ostrich feathers. She lay in the attitude of one who has been carved from stone and placed on top of a medieval tomb, but instead of her hands clasping to her bosom some item of ecclesiastical interest, she was holding a half-full bottle of gin. Her snores were loud and rhythmic, though lady-like in their way.

"Oh, *dear*," said Ethelbert, "she's at it again."

He flapped across the room and removed the bottle of gin from its owner's firm clasp and then started patting her cheeks daintily.

"Honoria, my dear, *Honoria*," said Ethelbert, "*do* wake up."

The lady, thus appealed to, stirred and muttered something derogatory under her breath.

"This is Honoria," said Ethelbert glancing over his shoulder at Adrian. "Honoria Loosestrife. She's our principal boy."

"Principal boy?" said Adrian.

"Yes," said Ethelbert, "she's awfully good."

Adrian sat down on a chair and studied Ethelbert carefully.

"Just let me get things straight. *You* are playing the Sultan's favourite *wife*, and *she*," he said pointing at Honoria, who was now displaying a vast expanse of pearly bosom, "*she's* playing the principal *boy*?"

"But, of course," said Ethelbert. "Silly boy, it's always like that in pantomimes."

"Oh," said Adrian. "Well, it sounds very queer to me."

"You'll soon get used to it," said Ethelbert. "It's merely a question of adjusting."

He went over to a jug and basin in the corner, wet a large flannel and proceeded to apply it to Honoria.

"Gerorf. Leavemealone," she said indistinctly.

"Now, now, dear," said Ethelbert. "You *must* be ready for rehearsals. You know what old cretinous Clattercup is like."

He squeezed about a pint of water out of the flannel all over Honoria's face and turned to Adrian.

"Such a *nice* girl," he said, "but she has, how shall I put it, a slight penchant for stimulants."

"Yes," said Adrian, "I can see that. Rosy has too."

Honoria dragged herself upright on the couch and sat looking at them blearily. Her dressing-gown had now become disarranged to a considerable degree. Adrian hastily averted his gaze.

"*There* we are then," said Ethelbert. "Feeling better?"

"No," said Honoria in a deep mournful contralto that was somehow reminiscent of the lower notes of Ethelbert's tuba, "I feel dreadful . . . dreadful."

"Well," said Ethelbert philosophically, "gin on an empty stomach is not the best way to start the day."

"*Nobody* cares about me," said Honoria lugubriously, and to Adrian's intense embarrassment and alarm large tears welled out of her eyes, trickled down her cheeks and fell on her ample bosom.

"Of *course* they do, my love," said Ethelbert. "Everybody simply *adores* you."

"They don't," sobbed Honoria. "They're jealous of me and my art."

Ethelbert sighed and raised his eyes to heaven.

"Adrian," he said, "would you be a dear and go along to the stage door and get a cup of tea for Honoria? It will make her feel better."

"Nothing," said Honoria sonorously, clasping her forehead and one breast in a dramatic gesture, "nothing, but *death* will make me feel any better."

Her gesture had succeeded in disarranging her dressing-gown still further, so Adrian fled before any more of Honoria's voluptuous figure was vouchsafed to him. He eventually found a little bewhiskered gnome of a man sitting in what looked like a glass-fronted pay box full of keys, and managed, after some argument, to extricate a large mug of tea which he carried back to the dressing-room.

To his astonishment, there was no longer an air of drunken gloom. Honoria was rolling about on the couch, giving vent to great, rich gurgles of laughter at what appeared to be some joke that Ethelbert had been telling her.

"Oh, my soul," she said sitting up and wiping her eyes. "Reely Ethelbert, you are *terrible*."

"Never a dull moment," said Ethelbert, thrusting the mug of tea into her hand.

She sipped the tea and eyed Adrian appraisingly, then she wrapped her dressing-gown closer about her and drew herself up majestically.

"Who is this?" she enquired.

"Adrian," said Ethelbert. "He has joined the show with his elephant."

"Tarrach!" said Honoria, with such ferocity that Adrian jumped. "That's all we need, an elephant in this show. Already half my best lines are killed by that ridiculous clashing of cymbals that Clattercup insists on. That orchestra *deliberately* plays off key to put me out in all my best solo numbers, and now we are to have an elephant stumping about the stage and no doubt leaving huge mounds of excrement wherever it goes."

"No, no," Ethelbert assured her earnestly. "It's a very *clean* elephant."

"As a matter of fact," said Adrian, who was beginning vaguely to grasp the method of handling Honoria's rather volatile nature, "as a matter of fact, Mr. Clattercup when he employed me said that he had got such a wonderful principal boy that nothing but the best in the way of um . . . er . . ."

"Props," prompted Ethelbert.

"Props, that's it," said Adrian, "nothing but the best of props was good enough—to give her the right background."

Honoria's eyes opened wide.

"Honest? Did he say *that*?" she asked.

"Yes," said Adrian, blushing slightly.

"Success," sighed Honoria. "Success at last. Dear boy, of course you may use your elephant." She bowed graciously to Adrian.

"Thank you," said Adrian.

"And I promise to give it every consideration on the stage," said Honoria.

"Thank you very much," said Adrian, wondering how it would be possible for even somebody as magnificently endowed with temperament as Honoria to cramp Rosy's style.

"Well, come on," said Ethelbert. "We'd better go and see

old Clattercup and find out what he wants you and Rosy to do."

The rest of the afternoon was, to say the least of it, exhausting. Mr. Clattercup, as a producer, seemed to have only the haziest notion of what could and what could not be done on a stage, and the more he ranted and raved and tore his hair, the more confused things became. Fights broke out among the Sultan's harem when it was discovered that Clattercup wanted half of them to stand behind a piece of eastern lattice-work, completely obscured from the audience. People exiting right would bump into people entering right, and, towards the end of the afternoon, everything became so confused that sometimes the principal girl (a fragile, fluffy-haired little creature who, although apparently no relative, was on fairly intimate terms with Mr. Clattercup) got positively hysterical and started singing the principal boy's songs by mistake. This produced a magnificent display of apoplexy on the part of Honoria and the stage was in such confusion that Clattercup had to allow everybody to return to their dressing-rooms for ten minutes to regain their composure.

During this brief respite Clattercup called Adrian up on to the stage.

"Now, lad," he said, "follow me. This is Sultan's palace, see."

He strode through the painted backdrops of the Sultan's palace and into the next scene which was fairly plain, dominated by a large piece of extremely unsubstantial-looking rock surrounded by a regiment of drooping palm trees. The rock was supposed to open into Ali Baba's cave, Mr. Clattercup explained.

"I'll show you how it works," he said proudly. "Ali Baba stands 'ere, jew see, and he presses this little button on the floor, jew see, and says 'Open Sesame'."

Mr. Clattercup suited action to words. The rock remained obdurate.

"Where the bloody 'ell's that props man?" shouted Mr. Clattercup. "Tell him to get this damned cave open."

A harassed props man came and, after much fiddling with wires, succeeded in getting the rock to swing open with an ominous grinding and squeaking noise and Clattercup, still breathing stertorously, stalked through the hole into the next set which was the cave. Here there were piles of artificial jewels pouring out of great wooden chests and, of course, the indispensable forty great jars in which the thieves were to be incarcerated.

"That's it," said Clattercup. "No expense spared, jew see, boy?"

"Yes," said Adrian, "it's very impressive."

"Now," said Clattercup, leading the way back to the Sultan's palace, "this is where you and that animal comes in. It's when Sultan makes his first entry. I want your elephant to come in 'ere and go across *there*, and then just stand. She'll be pulling a cart, of course, and the Sultan'll be in the cart."

"Forgive me," said Adrian, "but wouldn't it be better if he was in a howdah?"

"What's that?" enquired Clattercup suspiciously.

"Well, it's a sort of thing that is perched on the elephant's back."

Clattercup mused on this for a minute.

"No," he said at length, reluctantly. "No, it's too dangerous. That Sultan's the best baritone this side of Winklesea. If he fell off and broke his leg or something, whole show'd collapse. No, it will 'ave to be a cart."

"So I just lead Rosy from over there across the stage to *here*?" said Adrian trying to get things clear in his mind.

"No," said Clattercup, "you don't lead her, Sultan *drives* her."

"Well, I'm not altogether sure that Rosy will agree to be driven by the Sultan. You see, she's only used to me giving her orders."

"Difficulties," said Clattercup bitterly. "I've 'ad more difficulties with this bloody show than anything else I've put on. But I don't want *you* prancing all over stage. Can't you stand over there and call 'er?"

"If the rehearsal's anything to go by," said Adrian, "I don't think she would hear me."

"Bloody *'ell*," said Clattercup.

He paced up and down the stage for a minute, casting ferocious looks at the Sultan's palace, and then stopped.

"By gum, I've got it," he said triumphantly. "We'll put another gilded pillar 'ere. Sort of 'ollow, jew see, and we'll put you inside it. There'll be a little sort of peephole thing and you can shout to the animal from that. Jew understand me?"

"Er . . . yes," said Adrian doubtfully. "I suppose that would do."

He still had vivid recollections of Fenneltree Hall and was not at all certain about the success of this manoeuvre.

"Would you mind if we practised it first to make sure?"

"Of course," said Clattercup. "Rehearsals are most important. I'll get the pillar up in a jiffy and we'll 'ave a go."

Half an hour later a large and ornate pillar had been added to the Sultan's palace. Rosy, hitched to a small cart, was waiting in the wings and Adrian was inside the pillar keeping his fingers crossed and waiting for his cue. As the last chords of the opening number died away and the crowd all turned to the wings and shouted "Here comes the Sultan," just in case the audience should mistake him for a rag and bone man, Adrian hissed from inside his pillar, "Come on, Rosy."

Rosy flapped her ears, uttering a small squeak of pleasure and shambled out on to the stage. She knew where Adrian was, because she had seen him go into the pillar and could hear his voice. She shambled up to the pillar and patted it affectionately with her trunk.

"Stand still," hissed Adrian.

Rosy obeyed, flapping her ears and blinking with pleasure at the brightly-lit stage. To Adrian's astonishment the whole thing went off without a hitch, as indeed did the rest of the rehearsal, and Clattercup was so enchanted with the way Rosy had behaved that he even gave Adrian a cigar.

Jubilantly Rosy, Adrian, Ethelbert and Honoria made their way over the sand-dunes to the cottage, and having told Rosy how wonderful she was and given her a large feed and a pint of ale, they proceeded into the cottage where, with the aid of elderberry wine, gin, fresh oysters, plovers' eggs and four pints of pink, plump shrimps, they made merry. It was not until after midnight that they stumbled to bed, but *only* after Honoria, accompanied by Ethelbert, had sung for the fourth time, "I Dreamt I Dwelt in Marble Halls."

16 FIRST NIGHT

The next three days were fully occupied with rehearsal after rehearsal and Adrian's spirits rose, for, contrary to his expectations, Rosy behaved in the most exemplary fashion. In fact (owing to Mr. Clattercup's rather extraordinary methods of rehearsal) Rosy was sometimes the only one on the stage who knew what she was doing.

Honoria had formed a deep and abiding passion for Rosy who, she said in her more lachrymose moments, was the only person who really understood her, and she spent a lot of time feeding Rosy on sugar lumps and telling her about her past life.

At length the opening day arrived and the whole theatre was full of bustle and activity. Towards evening, just before the first performance, Ethelbert, Honoria and Adrian sat in the dressing-room awaiting their cues. Honoria had been imbibing fairly steadily since early morning in order, as she put it, to celebrate their first night. Ethelbert had pointed out that they had not had the first night yet, and weren't liable to if she got sloshed, at which Honoria drew herself up to her full height and said, "I know we haven't had the first night, but it's the spirit of the thing that counts."

In her bespangled garb as Ali Baba, she had draped

herself on the couch in the dressing-room, her turban slightly askew, and was making steady inroads on a new bottle of gin.

"Honoria, *darling*," said Ethelbert, "you really shouldn't. After all, it might affect your performance."

"Nothing," said Honoria stifling a small belch, "has ever affected my performance."

"And don't forget," Ethelbert continued, "you haven't got an understudy."

"Understudies," said Honoria in tones of great scorn. "True artists don't need understudies. The show must go on."

The bottle gurgled musically as she held it up to her mouth.

"I think I'd better go and see how Rosy's getting on," said Adrian. "She might be suffering from first night nerves as well."

"Darling boy, don't be *nervous*," said Ethelbert, "after all, it's all right for you—*you're* inside a pillar."

"That's true," said Adrian, "but I'm still nervous, nevertheless."

"It's getting fairly near time," said Ethelbert. "Would you be a sweetheart and stick this jewel in my navel? It tickles me so, I can't do it myself."

Solemnly Adrian attached a large, glittering false diamond to Ethelbert's navel with the aid of some spirit gum.

"There," he said, "now I must go and see Rosy."

"I'll go and see Rosy," said Honoria, rising somewhat unsteadily to her feet. "After all, she and I are the stars of this show. It's fitting that I should wish her luck on her first night."

She wandered somewhat unsteadily out of the dressing-room and closed the door behind her.

"Do you think she's going to be all right?" asked Adrian.

"Oh, yes," said Ethelbert. "If she's not unconscious by this time, she'll go on and do her stuff all right. Do you think this yashmak does things for me?"

Adrian surveyed the yashmak with care.

"What sort of things?" he asked cautiously.

Ethelbert blushed. "Well, do you think it makes me look sort of more attractive?" he said.

"Well," said Adrian, not wishing to get involved, "I'm sure it will make you look more attractive from the *audience's* point of view."

Ethelbert continued finicking with his costume, while Adrian watched him. Presently Adrian, with a start, remembered Rosy.

"Honoria's been gone a long time," he said.

"She's probably trying out her first number on Rosy," said Ethelbert, delicately adding still more mascara to an already overloaded eyelash.

"I think I'd better go and see," said Adrian. "After all, we are due on in ten minutes and I want to make sure that Rosy hasn't eaten her costume or done something silly."

Leaving Ethelbert, he made his way down the dingy, dusty corridors, and out into the great shed at the back in which Rosy was housed amid piles of faded scenery. He found Honoria sitting on a bale of hay, singing softly in her rather tremulous contralto:

"She's my elephant, she's my ele' elephant,
She's no one to go and pinch a scene,
She's the only queen, that we all know . . ."

Rosy, swaying gently from side to side, was listening enraptured to this song, clasping affectionately in her trunk the empty gin bottle.

"Honoria!" said Adrian, horror-stricken, "you haven't gone and given her *gin*?"

"Hello, Adrian," said Honoria, smiling charmingly, "is it time to go on yet?"

"Have you given Rosy gin?" barked Adrian.

"Just wet her whistle to shelebrate," said Honoria. "What the French call a soup spoon."

"But you know what drink does to her," said Adrian in anguish. "How much has she had?"

He had snatched the bottle away from Rosy and was

holding it up in front of Honoria. She fixed her eyes on it blearily.

"Just a nip," she said indistinctly, pointing a finger approximately half way down the bottle. "I must say she's a most convivi . . . conviv . . . charming drinking companion."

Adrian surveyed Rosy and she beamed back at him, whisking her ears in a skittish manner and curling and uncurling her trunk coyly. She looked all right. She didn't look anything like she had looked on the night of the terrible débâcle at Fenneltree Hall. Perhaps Honoria's intake of gin had been greater than Adrian thought, and Rosy had literally had the soup-spoonful that Honoria insisted she had given her.

"Come," said Adrian seizing Rosy's ear, and he marched her round and round the shed, watching her reactions critically. She could certainly walk straight and, apart from a roguish glint in her eye and a vague skittishness of bearing, she appeared to have suffered no ill effects.

"Honoria, you had better get into the wings," said Adrian. "You'll be on in a minute."

Dimly they could hear the sound of the orchestra (consisting of three elderly and rather decayed-looking musicians) playing a rousing march, the end of which was the signal for the rise of the curtain. Honoria, after one or two efforts, rose from the bale of hay and made her way backstage, followed by Adrian leading Rosy. In the wings he found the glittering cart that Rosy was supposed to pull, and the Sultan.

" 'Ere," said the Sultan, "where the 'ell 'ave you bin?"

"Sorry," said Adrian, hastily hitching Rosy up to the cart.

"Thought you weren't going to make it," said the Sultan.

"Proper bunch out there to-night," he added jerking his finger at the curtains, " 'arf the bloody island's 'ere."

He climbed into the back of the cart and settled himself comfortably.

137

"Are you all right?" said Adrian.

"Yus," said the Sultan. "Right as rain."

Adrian made his way out on to the stage to take up his position in the pillar. The orchestra was just coming to the end of its discordant rendering as he climbed inside it and shut the door behind him. Then, with a whoosh, the curtain rose and he could feel the wave of enthusiasm that flooded on to the stage over the footlights; the rustles, gasps coughs and little movements like sounds in a forest at night, which indicated that out in the darkness, beyond the orchestra pit, there were some four hundred people packed shoulder to shoulder and waiting.

The orchestra struck up and, to a burst of applause like a crackle of musketry, Honoria strode somewhat unsteadily on to the stage and sang her first song. At the end of this first number, it was Rosy's cue. By now Adrian had passed from being merely nervous into a state of acute panic

"Here comes the Sultan," shouted everybody just as they had done at rehearsals, and Adrian, finding that his voice had somehow turned into a falsetto squeak like that of a very tiny bat, shouted, "Come on, Rosy!"

To his astonishment, Rosy ambled on to the stage and up to the pillar as beautifully as she had done at rehearsals There was an immense and immediate reaction from the audience. An "Ahh" like the sound of a huge wave was wafted over the footlights. Rosy, enchanted by this adulation, lifted her trunk and gave a short, shrill trumpet.

"Good girl," said Adrian. "Stand still."

Rosy stood there throughout the scene that ensued occasionally swaying gently from side to side and periodically putting her trunk up to Adrian's peep-hole in the pillar and blowing a friendly, gin-laden breath at him. The climax of the scene had been reached safely and Adrian sighed with relief because now they would turn the stage to form a new scene and he could take Rosy into the wings. She did not have to reappear until the finale. He wiped the sweat from his brow. Honoria was just going into her scene changing speech . . .

"And sho my love," she said stentoriously to Mr. Clatter-

138

cup's girl friend, "I'll go and find our fortune and return to claim you as my bride."

So saying, she walked towards the right-hand side of the stage. As she did so, the stage started to revolve slowly and the moment he felt it move, Adrian knew he was doomed. It had never occurred to him to try Rosy out on the moving stage. Rosy woke out of her gin-soaked reverie to find the floor in some miraculous fashion moving backwards. She gave a small, slightly alarmed squeak and moved forward two or three paces.

"Stand still, you fool," hissed Adrian, but by now the stage was revolving quite fast and Rosy, losing her head, started to run to keep up with it. The result was that she and Honoria reached the next scene simultaneously, and half way across the set Rosy overtook her. The Sultan, panic-stricken, was clutching the sides of his vehicle and wailing "Bloody 'ell, bloody 'ell, bloody 'ell," in a mournful monotone that sounded like some curious form of prayer. The little man in charge of the massive levers that operated the stage completely lost his head at the sight of Rosy apparently running berserk, and threw the levers into reverse. The stage started to revolve in the opposite direction and Rosy, not to be outdone, turned adroitly to run with it. The result was that the shafts of the Sultan's carriage snapped like match-sticks and the carriage performed a short but very elegant flight before it crashed down on the stage operator and the levers. Now everybody lost his head. The stage, apparently damaged by the application of the Sultan's carriage to its mechanism, started to revolve faster and faster and Rosy ran faster and faster with it. She galloped through the desert scene, knocking palm trees in all directions, she shouldered her way through the market place, wrecking the stalls, she ran through the Sultan's palace, knocking down several pieces of oriental lattice work and the pillar in which Adrian was trapped.

Honoria, who had at first attributed the movements of the stage to the quantity of drink she had consumed, now became panic-stricken and ran in the opposite direction to Rosy. The hushed and spell-bound audience were treated to three scenes in rapid succession, all of them containing Rosy and Honoria running ineffectually in opposite directions and achieving no result whatsoever. Adrian had managed to extricate himself from his pillar and started running after Rosy. The stage, living up to its maker's reputation, was by now travelling at some thirty miles an hour, and as it whirled round various looser props were whisked off. A member of the orchestra was hit by a palm tree and several bits of the Sultan's palace crashed into the front row of stalls. Adrian's pursuit of Rosy was hampered by the fact that periodically he would run full tilt into Honoria and by the time they had picked themselves up, Rosy would have got a fair lead on him.

Up to now Mr. Clattercup had been standing in the wings paralysed with rage, but the sight of his principal boy, Rosy and Adrian indulging in what appeared to be a marathon race was too much for him. He leapt on to the revolving stage and grabbed Adrian as he passed.

"Stop her!" he roared at Adrian.

"What the hell do you think I'm trying to do?" snarled Adrian, pushing him away and setting off once again in hot pursuit of Rosy. Clattercup, apoplectic with rage, seized a short, stout piece of wood that had once been part of the Sultan's palace. He ran round the stage in the opposite direction to that taken by Adrian and, as Rosy appeared, lifted his weapon and hit her on the trunk. It was, to say the least, an unwise action. Rosy had been doing her best to keep up with what had suddenly become an extremely rapidly moving world and now here was a strange man beating her over the trunk with a large lump of wood. It took a lot of concentration to keep up with the stage, and she was not in any mood to have anything extraneous interfere with her task. So she simply picked up Mr. Clattercup and threw him into the orchestra pit where his sudden arrival knocked the orchestra leader unconscious for the second time, and disastrously damaged the drum and double bass.

Meanwhile, three stage hands had been making valiant attempts to remove both the Sultan and his vehicle from the machinery that controlled the stage, and at last they succeeded. However, their manipulation of the gears, though well intended, merely had the effect of making the stage revolve still faster. Rosy was now on the outer periphery of the stage and the increased speed shot her off it like a bullet from a gun. Fortunately, she was not aiming in the general direction of the audience when she went off, but crashed into the wings, bringing down curtains, ropes, pulleys, and six spot lights. So swift and complete was Rosy's disappearance that Adrian ran twice through the remains of the Sultan's palace, the desert scene and the market scene before he realised she was no longer on the stage. He then took a flying leap that landed him in the wings, and started searching frantically for her. The thought of her rampaging about the streets of the town was too awful to contemplate, and to his relief he ran her to earth in her stable, where she was standing trembling and out of breath, hopefully holding the empty gin bottle to her mouth. Adrian sank down on the bale of hay and put his head in his hands. Everything was ruined. Dimly he could hear the screams and shouts of the audience and the clank and wheeze of the ever more rapidly revolving stage. His hopes that Rosy could join the Thespian ranks of Mr. Clattercup's company had now vanished, and not only this; he had also added one more crime to the list that he had committed since he inherited her. He wished with all his soul that Samantha were there to comfort him. Suddenly Ethelbert appeared, panting for breath, his yashmak torn and the jewel missing from his navel.

"Darling boy," he gasped, "what an *absolute tragedy*. I know it wasn't your fault *or* dear Rosy's, but I think you're going to have a very hard time persuading Clattercup of this. He's recovered consciousness, so I suggest that you both simply fly."

"What's the use?" said Adrian dully. "Where could we fly to anyway?"

By the time they reached the docks, the excitement and bustle had made the gin take a firm hold on Rosy and, uttering little squeaks of pleasure to herself, she staggered along by Adrian's side, occasionally tripping over her own feet. Adrian was beyond caring. All he wanted was to get Rosy on board the ship, and it was with considerable relief that he saw that the *Sploshport Queen* had not left.

Shackling Rosy to a bollard, he rushed on deck and was lucky enough to find the Captain almost immediately.

"Aha," said the Captain, backing away from him. "Have you come to inflict another assault upon my person?"

"No," said Adrian. "I just want you to take me and my elephant back to the mainland."

"You didn't stay here very long," said the Captain.

"No," said Adrian. "There was not really any work for us to do."

"Well, get on board," said the Captain. "We're due to leave any minute now."

Adrian retrieved Rosy and led her up the wide gangway to the forrard deck where she had travelled before. Just at that moment the Chief Officer hailed him from the dockside. Telling Rosy to stand still, Adrian ran back to pay for his and Rosy's fare. It was, it transpired, an unwise thing for him to do. Rosy had by now recovered from her panic on the revolving stage, and was feeling tired, a feeling that was aggravated by the amount of gin that she had consumed. She ambled slowly across the deck and stood looking over the rail, swaying gently, and uttering little musical squeaks to herself. Then she turned, intending to go back down the gangway in search of Adrian, but her gait was uncertain and she slipped and fell against the ship's rail which, though of strong enough construction in its way, had not been designed to withstand the weight of several tons of elephant. It promptly gave way. Adrian, hurrying up the gangway, was just in time to see Rosy, her feet in the air, disappearing over the side of the *Sploshport Queen*. She hit the water with a report like a cannon and a great column of water rose some twenty feet into the air.

Now, Adrian knew from that hideous day when they had routed the Monkspepper Hunt that Rosy liked water, but a shallow river is one thing and five fathoms of sea water something very different. He ran to the gaping hole in the rails, tearing off his coat, quite prepared to dive in and save Rosy. It was not until later that he realised what extreme difficulty he would have had rescuing Rosy if she could not swim. He peered down at the dark waters and saw that Rosy had surfaced and with her trunk aloft was making steady progress toward the open sea. This was almost worse than her drowning.

"Come back!" yelled Adrian. "Rosy, come back!"

But Rosy continued to plough onwards towards the harbour entrance. There was nothing for it, thought Adrian bitterly, he would have to go to her rescue after all. So, taking a deep breath, he jumped over the side of the *Sploshport Queen*. The oily water was unpleasantly cold. He rose spluttering to the surface and struck out in hot pursuit of Rosy. Eventually, by putting on a turn of speed that made him feel his lungs were bursting, he swam alongside.

"You fool," he gasped at her. "You're swimming the wrong way."

Rosy was delighted to see him. She uttered a small gurgling squeak of recognition and wrapped her trunk affectionately around Adrian's neck, thus successfully plunging him beneath the water. He uncurled her trunk and rose gasping and spluttering.

"You bloody elephant," he gasped. He seized the edge of her ear and, feeling not unlike a very small tug in charge of a gigantic ocean liner, succeeded in turning her so that she aimed in the general direction of shore.

Some two or three minutes later they made landfall at a series of shallow steps that led up from the water to the dockside, and up these, with a certain amount of effort, they made their way. The docks had been comparatively deserted when they had arrived, but now a large crowd had assembled in the miraculous way that crowds do assemble when any accident happens. Included in the crowd was a very large and belligerent-looking policeman. As Adrian, still clinging to Rosy's ear, staggered up to the dockside and started to wring the water out of his hair, the policeman approached him, his hands behind his back, his buttons glinting in the lamplight.

"Good evening, sir," he said.

"Good evening," said Adrian, wondering what was good about it.

"Would that be your elephant, sir?" said the constable, "or were you rescuing it, like, on behalf of somebody else?"

"No," said Adrian, "it's mine."

"Ah," said the constable.

He extracted a notebook from his pocket and turned the leaves slowly, licking his forefinger copiously as he turned each page.

"You wouldn't, I suppose, by any chance, sir, be Mr. Adrian Rookwhistle, would you?" he enquired.

"That is my name," said Adrian resignedly.

"Ah," said the constable beaming at him paternally, "then perhaps you could spare the time, sir, just to step down to the station with me. One or two little matters that need to be sorted out. I understand that elephant of yours has been having quite an exciting career."

"Look, officer," said Adrian, "I can explain everything."

"Don't say a word," barked a trenchant voice suddenly from the depths of the crowd.

Adrian looked round startled and saw that the advice had been offered to him by a short, circular little man like a dumpling. He was wearing a faded, dusty looking cut-away coat, a top hat that looked as though it had been run over by a very heavy horse and cart, baggy trousers and an enormous pair of elastic-sided boots so ancient that the toes pointed skywards. Under his coat, spreading over his paunch, was a moleskin waistcoat. He had a great beak of a nose, as scarlet and as pitted as a strawberry, and fierce blue eyes under shaggy white snowdrifts of eyebrow. He was so short that he came within a hair's breadth of being a dwarf and his corpulence made him appear shorter still, but he strutted up to the constable in such a belligerent manner that the minion of the law immediately took a step backwards and touched his helmet.

"Not one word," said this little man, turning to Adrian and holding up an admonishing forefinger. So imposing was the little man's demeanour that the crowd, which had been shuffling and laughing among itself, fell silent. The little man rearranged his top hat and sniffed prodigiously. He was obviously conscious of the fact that he had made this impact and was extracting every last exquisite moment from it.

Having rearranged his battered headgear to his satisfaction, he then inserted his fingers carefully into an ample pocket in his moleskin waistcoat and extracted from it a large and battered pewter snuff box. Rosy, under the impression that it was something edible, stretched out her trunk tentatively and sniffed.

"Desist," said the little man coldly, fixing her with a malevolent stare, and to Adrian's astonishment, Rosy curled up her trunk and looked as embarrassed as only an elephant can. It was obvious that she had fallen under the little man's spell as well as the crowd. The little man opened the snuff box, whereupon it played a few tinkling bars of "God Save the Queen." He extracted a pinch of snuff delicately and then, holding out his left hand, placed the snuff reverently on the inside of his wrist. He closed the snuff box with his right hand and returned it to his pocket, then raised his wrist to his nose and sniffed deeply. The silence was complete. Everybody, including the constable, was watching him with rapt attention. He sniffed a couple of times and then, starting at the tips of his shoes and reverberating all the way up through his whole body, he sneezed enormously and voluptuously, uttering at the same time a sort of screeching yelp that made everybody, including Rosy, retreat several paces. He then produced an enormous silk handkerchief and blew his nose into it with a trumpeting worthy of a bull elephant. He stuffed the handkerchief back into his pocket and straightened his top hat which had become disarranged by the force of his sneeze.

"Inspector," he said, raising his shaggy eyebrows and looking up at the constable, "you have just been privileged to witness a sight which many people would give ten years of their lives to have seen."

"Yes, sir," said the constable. "I am constable, actually, sir."

"It matters not," observed the little man, "how menial you are, it is a matter of appreciating great acts of heroism when you see them."

"Yes, sir," said the constable woodenly.

"It is the Bible," said the little man, waving his arms oratorically, "that teaches us we have dominion over the fowls of the air and the beasts of the field."

"If you say so, sir," said the constable.

"I do say so," said the little man. "And that includes elephants." He threw his left arm round Adrian's dripping shoulders and spread out his right hand with a gesture of one about to field a tennis ball.

"Friends," he said trenchantly, "this brave young man, prompted by the sacred words of the Bible, unhesitatingly and without a thought for his own safety, cast himself into the roaring tumult of the waves to save a beast of the field."

The fact that the harbour was oily calm in no way detracted from this dramatic statement.

"Is there a man among you," continued the little man, addressing the crowd which consisted largely of women, "is there a man among you who would have performed such a deed of valour?"

"Excuse me, sir," said the constable, "I know that what this young man did was very brave, but you see, him and his elephant is wanted."

The little man swirled like a pouter pigeon and his eyes became as blue and as sharp as two periwinkles under ice.

"I," he said, adjusting his top hat with care, "I am Sir Magnus Ramping Fumitory. You may, no doubt, during your long association with the courts, have come across my name."

"Yes, sir," said the constable dismally, touching his helmet once more, "I have heard about you."

"Well, I demand to know," said Sir Magnus, "whether you intend to arrest this young man, this hero of the deeps?"

"Well, yes, sir," said the constable, "in a sort of way. I just want him and his elephant to come down to the station and help us with a bit of information. It's pursuant to a complaint."

Sir Magnus smiled a grim smile.

"What a masterly massacre of the tongue that Shakespeare spoke," he said. "Still, Chief Constable, I realise you have your duty to do, however erroneous it may be, so I will allow you to apprehend this heroic young man and I will, indeed, endeavour to protect you from the wrath of the crowd. For it is patently obvious to me where their sympathies lie."

The crowd, captivated but like most crowds not knowing what the whole thing was about, growled encouragingly. Sir Magnus beamed at them like a conductor beaming at an orchestra at the end of a particularly difficult passage of music, and then turned to Adrian.

"My boy," he said, "I shall personally accompany you to the police station, and if they arrest you and charge you, if indeed they are so inhuman and so callous as to arrest you and charge you, I, Sir Magnus Ramping Fumitory, will defend you."

"You are very kind," said Adrian, who was now so bewildered that he was not sure whether he was under arrest or not.

"Well, if you will just come along with me," said the

constable. "If nothing else, we will be able to give you a hot cup of tea at the station."

"Thank you," said Adrian, who was frozen to the marrow and felt that it was even worth being arrested in order to have a hot drink.

"Don't say a word," said Sir Magnus, "until we get to the station and find out what their paltry charges are."

So Adrian seized Rosy's ear once more, and with Sir Magnus strutting pigeon-toed on one side, and the constable lumbering on the other, and the crowd shuffling and whispering following behind, they made their way to the police station.

When they arrived they induced Rosy, with a certain amount of difficulty and with the aid of a bribe of several loaves of bread, to stand in the station yard. Inside the dour red-brick police station, the station sergeant, with a rich, peony-coloured face and an impressive moustache, peered at Adrian like a good-natured walrus.

"Good evening, sir," he said. "You're name is Adrian Rookwhistle?"

"Yes," said Adrian.

"And I wouldn't admit anything more than your name," hissed Sir Magnus.

"Well, sir," said the sergeant, "we've several charges against you, so I must warn you that anything you say may be taken down and used in evidence at your trial." He paused and stared at Adrian portentously. "The charges are as follows. That you did on 20th April in the County of Brockelberry cause a public nuisance in the meadows alongside the Monkspepper Road there situate by releasing a large wild animal, and furthermore that you allowed it to commit grievous bodily harm to Hubert Darcey, Master of the Monkspepper Hunt and that on the night of 5th June you did commit a public nuisance by allowing a large wild animal loose in a public place, to wit the Alhambra Theatre and allowed it to commit grievous bodily harm to Mr. Emanuel S. Clattercup, the theatre manager." The sergeant paused, looked down at his notes and then looked up at Adrian and beamed affably.

"That seems to be all for the moment, sir," he said.

"Ridiculous trumped-up charges," said Sir Magnus, taking off his top hat and banging it on the sergeant's desk. "Don't worry, my dear chap, I will soon have you free of this noxious web which these bovine illiterates are endeavouring to weave around you and that noble creature of yours."

"I am afraid, sir," said the sergeant, unmoved by Sir Magnus's oratory, "that I shall have to detain you in custody so that you can appear before the magistrates tomorrow morning."

"Well, that's all very well," protested Adrian, "but what about Rosy?"

"Your elephant, sir?" enquired the sergeant. "Umm, that does present a bit of a problem. You see our cells are somewhat on the small side."

"Well, she'd be all right out in the yard," said Adrian, "if she was given something to eat."

"I will attend to that, sir," said the sergeant. He picked up a clean piece of paper, licked his pencil and looked at Adrian interrogatively. "Now, what does she eat, sir?"

"Well," said Adrian, "if you get half a sack of mangolds or turnips (but she prefers mangolds), a bale of hay, half a sack of apples, half a sack of carrots, half a sack of bread . . ."

The station sergeant's face grew grim.

"You wouldn't by any chance be gammoning me?"

"No, no," said Adrian earnestly. "Really, she's got a colossal appetite."

"Well," said the sergeant, "I'll see what I can do, sir. Now, I'd be glad if you would just turn out your pockets, sir, and check the contents with me. They'll all be returned to you in due course."

Adrian emptied his pockets and the station sergeant put all his possessions in a large brown envelope and locked it away in a cabinet.

"Now, sir," he said, sounding exactly like the hall porter at a sumptuous hotel, "if you'll just come this way, I'll show you your accommodation."

Sir Magnus stretched out his hand to Adrian.

"Don't worry, my boy," he said. "I shall be here first thing in the morning to make sure that you get fair play. Just look upon this as an unpleasant—but rapidly passing —dream."

"It's beginning to feel like it," said Adrian gloomily.

He followed the sergeant down a brick-lined passage way until they came to the doorways of several tiny cells, most of which, judging by the noises and the all-pervading smell of alcohol, contained people whom Rosy would have been honoured to number among her friends. The sergeant unlocked one of the cell doors and ushered Adrian into a tiny whitewashed room with a wooden bunk, a small chest of drawers and, perched on top of it, rather incongruously, a large china bowl and ewer decorated in pink and blue flowers.

"Here we are, sir," said the sergeant. "Now you get a good night's rest and we'll see you in the morning."

He closed the door and the bolt clicked into place. Slowly Adrian peeled off his sodden clothes, climbed into the hard, narrow bed and lay there staring at the ceiling. He was convinced that he was going to get at least a year's penal servitude for his crimes, but strangely enough this didn't worry him. What did worry him was what was going to happen to Rosy, coupled with the fact that if he was imprisoned for a year, it would be a year before he would see Samantha again. By which time, of course, she might have moved and he would not be able to trace her, or, worse still, might have married some uncouth ruffian who would not appreciate her finer points.

Alone in his little cell, Adrian could visualise it all so clearly that he broke out in a cold sweat. Rosy being condemned to death by the magistrates, the clatter of boots as the army platoon detailed to carry out the sentence marched into the prison yard, the crackle of guns, the great thud as Rosy's body hit the cobbles, bleeding from a dozen wounds, and meanwhile Samantha irretrievably married to a great, coarse, hairy plough-boy who would beat her regularly every Saturday night so that, if and when Adrian ever discovered her again, she would be a gaunt shadow of her former self, and even the gold flecks in her eyes would have ceased to glitter. With Adrian's fertile imagination at work, it was not altogether surprising that he got little sleep that night.

In the morning a large constable made his appearance carrying a mug of tea and a hunk of black bread, and Adrian discovered that not only was he hungry, but his throat was so parched he could only talk in a croaking whisper.

"How's Rosy?" he asked the constable.

"Don't you go fretting about her, sir," said the constable comfortably. "She can look after herself, that elephant can. The station sergeant's nearly gone mad keeping up with her appetite. It's a wonderful beast, sir."

"In some ways I suppose she is," said Adrian.

"You seem to have got up to some tricks with her," said the constable.

"Yes," said Adrian shortly, not wishing to have to tell his story all over again. "What time do we go to the magistrates' court?"

"Ten o'clock, sir," said the constable.

"I wonder," said Adrian, "if you could possibly lend me a razor? Mine got left behind in the rush."

"Surely, sir," said the constable, and went out, locking the door behind him. Presently he reappeared with a large razor, and stayed there watching while Adrian washed and shaved, then he retrieved the razor and disappeared.

Now, thought Adrian, I must work out my defence. He paced feverishly up and down the cell, occasionally pausing to gesture wildly at the walls as he endeavoured to persuade an implacable imaginary judge that he and Rosy were innocent of any crime whatsoever. At the end of it, however, he was bound to admit that his defence, if it could be called that, was slender in the extreme. It was obvious that he must pin his faith on Sir Magnus. He was evidently well-known to the police, judging by the looks of ill-concealed loathing that they gave him, presumably because of his successes in court. But in this case, Adrian felt, even the most brilliant of lawyers would be hard-pressed to prove his innocence.

At ten o'clock the constable reappeared jangling a rather ominous pair of handcuffs.

"We're off now, sir," he said cheerfully. "It's only a step down the road, but if you don't mind, sir, it's just a formality, sir. If you'll just slip these on."

Adrian allowed him to fasten the handcuff to his left wrist and then the constable attached the other end to his own wrist.

"There we are," he said paternally, "snug as a bug in a rug."

"Does Rosy have to come too?" enquired Adrian.

"No, sir," said the constable. "That's not necessary. She's more in the nature of an exhibit, as you might say. We won't want 'er until your trial."

In the charge room Sir Magnus awaited them. In the daylight his coat and hat and his extraordinary shoes looked even more decrepit than they had done the previous night and it was obvious that several moths who had had the courage to get on the wrong side of Sir Magnus had wrought havoc with various parts of his moleskin waistcoat.

"My dear Adrian," he said, waving his walking-stick amicably, "I trust you had a good night's rest, although I fear in these places the accommodation is a little limited."

"Oh, it was comfortable enough," said Adrian, "but I didn't get much sleep."

Sir Magnus cast him a ferocious look from under his white eyebrows.

"Don't you trust me?" he asked fiercely.

"Why, yes, of course," said Adrian startled.

"Well, then, stop getting yourself into a turmoil," said Sir Magnus. He picked up his top hat and set it at a jaunty angle on his head with a loving pat.

"Come," he said, waving his cane, "let us take the air."

He led the way out of the police station as though he were leading a parade and the constable and Adrian, clanking musically, followed behind. For the first time Adrian began to realise what Rosy must have felt like when she was shackled. As people in the streets turned to stare, Adrian felt himself getting redder and redder and shrivelling up inside. It was an immense relief when they finally turned into a doorway to the magistrates' court.

For some obscure reason, Adrian had imagined that he would be tried by the magistrates' court, condemned, and carried out from there loaded down with chains, but to his astonishment justice did not appear to work in this swift and exemplary fashion. The magistrate, who looked, Adrian thought, an exceedingly good example of the criminal type, listened patiently while the constable who had arrested Adrian began his evidence. The constable, who was basso profundo in the police choir, read from his notebook slowly and ponderously, annunciating each word with relish.

"Police Constable Emanuel Dray, 124, Island of Scallop Constabulary. Sir, on the evening of the 5th June I was proceeding along the dockside at Scallop when my attention was drawn to a crowd that had gathered and was staring into the harbour and appeared greatly excited. Proceeding to the edge of the docks, I perceived the accused disporting himself in the waters with a large and unidentified object, which later, on closer inspection, proved to be an elephant.

"Having previously been informed that a man in possession of an elephant was wanted for questioning in connection with certain disturbances which had taken place in the County of Brockelberry I came to the conclusion that this must be the gentleman in question. When he and the elephant landed on the docks, I approached him and asked if the elephant was his."

At this point the magistrate raised his eyebrows and cleared his throat with a dry rustle like a small lizard wriggling between two tightly wedged stones.

"Constable," he said, "why did you ask him whether it was his elephant? I would have thought that if you find somebody disporting themselves in the harbour with an elephant it is fairly obvious that the elephant is his?"

The constable, slightly thrown off course by this interruption, shuffled his feet.

"Well, sir," he said reddening, "I thought as how it might be somebody else's elephant what he was looking after."

The magistrate gave a tiny sigh.

"An extremely unlikely hypothesis," he said. "Do continue."

It took Constable Dray a moment or so with the aid of a stubby finger to find his place in his notes, and then he cleared his throat, threw back his head like a choirboy and proceeded.

"The accused said, 'It is mine'. I then asked him if his name was Adrian Rookwhistle, to which he replied, 'That is my name'. I then asked him if he would step down to the station with me to help us in our enquiries, to which he replied, 'Look officer, I can explain everything'."

Here Constable Dray paused and beamed at the magistrate. This was, as far as he was concerned, a clear confession of guilt.

"Well?" said the magistrate coldly.

"Well, sir," said Constable Dray, his moment of glory shattered, "I then took him down to the station where he was cautioned and later charged."

"I see," said the magistrate. "Thank you, Constable."

Constable Dray shuffled out of the witness box with the ponderous care of a Shire horse and the magistrate flipped through some papers and then looked up.

The police inspector rose to his feet.

"I ask, sir," he said, "that the prisoner be remanded in custody to appear before the magistrates in a week's time."

The magistrate looked enquiringly at Sir Magnus Ramping Fumitory who, throughout the procedure, had been sitting there apparently sound asleep. Sir Magnus rose to his feet.

"Sir," he said, fishing out his snuff box and tapping it gently with his forefinger. "Sir, my client has been charged by my friends the police" (a faint growl from the inspector was quelled by a look from the magistrate) "with these paltry trumped-up charges."

Sir Magnus threw out his arms.

"Sir Magnus," interrupted the magistrate, "we are all not only conscious, but envious, of your powers of oratory. However, I would like to point out to you that at *this* precise moment your client is not on trial."

"Sir," said Sir Magnus, "this noble young stripling who, as you kindly pointed out, is *not* on trial, against whom, as yet, no proof of guilt has been offered, is, should my friends the police have their way, to be incarcerated, cut off from friends and family, cut off from the gay hurly-burly of life, cut off indeed from that magnificent dumb creature who, in times of stress, is his only consolation, cut off I might say . . ."

"Sir Magnus," said the magistrate sharply, "I would be grateful if you would get to the point. What is it you wish?"

"Bail, sir," said Sir Magnus profoundly. He made a grandiloquent gesture which inadvertently scattered half an ounce of snuff over the table in front of him.

"My client, sir," he said, "is not a vagrant, a vagabond, a gypsy, a tramp, nor is he a mountebank . . ."

The magistrate was by now beginning to lose his temper.

"Sir Magnus," he said, "we are not gathered here to construct a dictionary of synonyms."

"In short," continued Sir Magnus, not in any way put out, "I would say that my client is a man of substance, perfectly able—indeed I would say willing—to stand bail so that, for however brief a period, he may return to the outside world."

"Spare us," said the magistrate acidly. "I have grasped your point."

He sat back and surveyed Adrian briefly with a cold stare.

"It is not customary in cases like this for us to go against the recommendation of the police. However, this is a case which appears to have many unusual features, so I will grant your client bail in his own recognisance in the sum of fifty pounds."

"I am deeply grateful to you, sir," said Sir Magnus, bowing low. And then, opening his snuff box with great care, he brushed all the snuff on the table back into the box, to the accompaniment of "God Save the Queen." Adrian by now was completely confused and was, indeed, under the firm impression that by some miracle he was being discharged, having suffered no greater penalty than the loss of fifty pounds. The Clerk of the Court fixed him with a puppeteer's eye.

"Stand up, Rookwhistle," he said.

Adrian rose somewhat shakily to his feet.

"Adrian Rookwhistle, you are bound in the sum of fifty pounds, in your own recognisance, to appear before the magistrates in this court on Tuesday next. Do you understand?" the magistrate said.

"Yes, sir," Adrian replied.

Adrian left the court in a daze of delight. He was free, Rosy was free, and with a bit of luck he would be seeing Samantha very shortly. After all the ghastly experiences to which he had been subjected, this was a moment of triumph to be savoured to the full. As they reached the pavement, he seized Sir Magnus Ramping Fumitory's hand and pumped it up and down.

"My dear Sir Magnus," he said, "how can I thank you? To think that you, with your brilliant mind, should have come to my rescue in this fashion, and saved me and Rosy from what would assuredly have been a terrible fate. I cannot thank you enough."

Sir Magnus, with the long-suffering air of one extracting himself from the exuberant gambols of a puppy, disengaged his hand from Adrian's and stepped back.

"What?" he said, glowering from under his eyebrows, "are you talking about?"

"Why, the verdict," said Adrian.

"What verdict?" enquired Sir Magnus.

"But . . . they let me loose," said Adrian. "They only fined me fifty pounds."

Sir Magnus closed his eyes as though in pain and took a short walk up and down the pavement. Then he came up to Adrian and glowered into his face, tapping him on the chest with his snuff box.

"Endeavour," he said bitingly, "not to be as cretinous as the forces of law and order. I have merely got you out on bail. In a week's time you will have to appear before the magistrates and *they* will send you to the Assizes, and it's at the Assizes that you will stand or fall."

"Oh," said Adrian dismally, "I didn't realise."

His bright cloud of happiness had suddenly evaporated and he was back with his nightmares of Rosy being shot at dawn and Samantha making an unsuitable alliance.

"Well," he said dolefully, "what do I do now?"

"Do!" said Sir Magnus reddening and starting to twitch like an indignant turkey. "You will fetch Rosy and come to a tiny place I have not far from here, and there, if you show a little spirit, we will prepare your defence."

"Do you know," said Adrian helplessly, "I don't think I understand quite how the law functions."

"You can't expect to," said Sir Magnus crisply. "After all, we who administer it don't understand how it functions, so one can hardly hope you to."

"It is rather like getting on a train," said Adrian, "without knowing how to drive it."

Sir Magnus took a pinch of snuff and sniffed violently.

"I shouldn't worry," he said. "On a train journey the vital thing is to get out at the right station."

18 THE LAW

Sir Magnus's "tiny place" turned out to be a fairly newly erected mansion, done in the Tudor style, set in its own grounds up on top of the cliffs just outside the town. Rosy was installed in a large shed in the stable yard, and Adrian took up residence with Sir Magnus.

Sir Magnus was, to say the least, an exacting host. To begin with he had a deep and abiding passion for cherry brandy which he consumed (and insisted that Adrian consume) in vast quantities. With the cherry brandy he played a sort of chess game by mixing it with various other substances to see what effects he could achieve. After a couple of days Adrian's stomach was suffering from the endless permutations that Sir Magnus managed to achieve, and he had definitely decided that cherry brandy mixed with stout and milk and consumed out of a tankard was not really his drink at all.

Sir Magnus also appeared to be able to exist without any sleep. For the first three days he insisted that Adrian tell him the story of his adventures over and over again, while he paced up and down his study or stood at the table mixing a new variation on the cherry brandy theme. At two or three in the morning Adrian would stagger to bed, more dead than alive, and no sooner had his head touched the pillow than Sir Magnus—in a fascinating nightshirt constructed of *broderie anglaise*—would be standing by his bed shaking him awake to get him to repeat a certain portion of his story.

On the fourth morning Adrian dragged himself down to breakfast, his head throbbing and ringing with the chimes of cherry brandy and his eyelids glued together with lack of sleep. He found Sir Magnus, looking as perky as though he had just returned from a long and luxurious holiday, consuming a mammoth omelette.

"Now," said Sir Magnus, as though the conversation of the previous night had not ceased, "what we have got to do is this. We have got to get everybody, but *everybody* connected with this trail of carnage that you have left, as witnesses."

"I really don't see what good that is going to do," said Adrian dispiritedly.

"Think," said Sir Magnus, scattering a handful of black pepper on a forkful of omelette and shoving it into his mouth. "Think of the jury, dear boy."

Adrian, toying in a slightly nauseated fashion with a lightly boiled egg, was in no condition to think of the jury.

"What about them?" he asked.

Sir Magnus leant back in his chair, wiped his mouth with a damask napkin, pulled out his snuff box, applied snuff to his nostrils, sneezed volcanically and then blew his nose.

"The beauty of the English legal system," he said, his voice growing rich and fruity, "is that it is built up upon two completely illogical maxims. Firstly, everyone imagines that they are tried by a jury, and this of course is ridiculous. In fact, you are tried by a judge who instructs the jury. Now, let us take the jury themselves. Working on the extraordinary system that twelve men are better than two or six or four, nobody takes into consideration that twelve imbeciles might be more dangerous than two. In my experience *all* judges and *all* juries are imbeciles. Therefore the average honest-to-god criminal hasn't got a chance and the innocent man is doomed before he even steps into the dock."

Adrian was puzzled.

"I thought it was a very fair system," he said.

"It's about as fair as a particularly savage rugby match," said Sir Magnus coolly.

"I still don't see," said Adrian, "how dragging a lot of people from all over the country to this case is going to help me."

Sir Magnus took another pinch of snuff and sneezed.

"That, my dear boy, is because you don't apply your mind to the problem," he said. "Now, imagine that I am a sheep dog." He leaned forward and glared at Adrian under his eyebrows, looking if anything more like a malevolent cairn terrier than a sheep dog. However, Adrian dutifully tried to imagine him as a sheep dog.

"And imagine," continued Sir Magnus, waving a finger at him, "that the jury are a flock of sheep, and when I say a flock of sheep I am putting their collective intelligence at a much higher level than they normally display."

He paused and cast a thoughtful look at the large flagon of cherry brandy which stood on the sideboard, then glanced at his watch and sighed in a dispirited manner.

"Now," he said, "you have got me as a sheep dog, the jury as the flock of sheep and the judge as a sheep stealer." On these last words his voice sank to a hissing whisper. He got up and paced up and down the length of the breakfast table. "So," he said suddenly wheeling upon Adrian, "what is the system, eh? It is my job as sheep dog to savage the sheep stealer and herd all my little curly jury lambs into the fold of right decision. D'you take my point?"

"Well, roughly," said Adrian, "yes, but I don't think you can be so high-handed with a judge, can you?"

"Judges," said Sir Magnus coldly, "are merely inexperienced lawyers."

Adrian could not help feeling that this summary of the legal system left a certain amount to be desired, but having no experience himself, he was not in a position to argue. Sir Magnus went to the door of the dining-room, flung it open and bellowed, "Screech!"

In response to this a shrivelled, bald individual cringed and undulated his way into the room.

"Screech here," said Sir Magnus waving an airy hand at him, "will write suitable letters to all the people I want as witnesses. You will spend the morning closeted together giving him the necessary details."

"All right," said Adrian, "anything you say."

It had suddenly occurred to him, and the thought suffused his whole body in a warm glow, that he could write to Samantha and get her as a witness. Sir Magnus cast a glance at the cherry brandy decanter as though he had noticed it for the first time.

"You cannot, however," he said, "start work of this sort on an empty stomach. Have some cherry brandy."

"I don't think I will, if you don't mind," said Adrian. "If we have got to write all these letters, I'd like to keep a clear head."

"Well, please yourself," said Sir Magnus and he went across to the sideboard and mixed a liberal measure of cherry brandy with a beakerful of Irish whiskey and the juice of two lemons, tossed it down his throat and then stood shuddering for a brief moment.

"Interesting," he said softly with his eyes closed. He then turned on the unfortunate clerk.

"You know what to do, Screech," he barked. "Mr. Rookwhistle here will give you the details and I shall expect all the letters in the post by twelve o'clock."

"But of course, Sir Magnus," said Screech. "Certainly, Sir Magnus."

Sir Magnus strode out of the room and slammed the door behind him, leaving Adrian alone with Screech, who he soon discovered was a painstaking individual who wrote a beautiful copperplate hand, but whose personality was as exciting and ineffectual as cottonwool covered with glue. Finally, at ten to twelve, the last letter—the letter to Samantha—was written and as Sir Magnus came storming back into the room Screech gathered up his papers and scuttled out obsequiously.

"I have decided," said Sir Magnus, "that you are looking a little bit under the weather. I cannot have my prize client looking peaky in court."

"I think," said Adrian, stifling a yawn, "it is more lack of sleep than anything."

"Nonsense," said Sir Magnus. "It is lack of stimulation. One can do without sleep, but one cannot do without stimulation."

Adrian wondered dully what Sir Magnus would consider stimulation. He assumed it would be the fighting and killing of seventeen Spanish bulls before lunch.

"You may be right," he said peaceably.

"After lunch," said Sir Magnus rubbing his hands, "I propose you and I and Rosy take the air."

"Take the air?" said Adrian startled.

"Yes," said Sir Magnus. "We will take a walk along the sea front."

"Do you think that is a good idea . . . ?" began Adrian.

"I think it is an excellent idea," said Sir Magnus with satisfaction. "A light snack for lunch and then a brisk walk and you will find that the sea air does you a power of good."

Once they had disposed of the light snack—which consisted of a dozen oysters apiece followed by a mushroom ouffié as light and as yellow as a sunset cloud, a saddle of beef squatting regally in thick brown gravy, its melting slices as pink as coral, surrounded by all the appropriate vegetables and rounded off by a trifle whose basic ingredient appeared to be cherry brandy, aided and abetted by four or five pints of clotted cream—they went for a walk along the sea front, taking Rosy with them.

Adrian, bloated with food and dragged down by lack of sleep, could not help feeling that this exercise did his case no good in the eyes of the local inhabitants. Sir Magnus seemed completely oblivious to the effect that they were creating. He had placed his walking-stick across his shoulder and had hooked the end round Rosy's trunk and so, thus linked together, they walked along very amicably. Every time a group of children, round-eyed and excited, appeared, Sir Magnus, doffing his top hat with a regal gesture, would pull Rosy forward with the aid of his walking-stick and allow them to pat her legs and fondle her trunk. Rosy who, like most good-natured animals, was under the impression that no human being could do wrong, was delighted and with the tip of her trunk, a weapon which could be so devastating when she cared to employ it, she delicately snuffled and explored the freckled faces, the grubby hands and the pigtails.

At five o'clock, to Adrian's intense relief, after they had walked along the promenade fourteen times, they returned to Sir Magnus's house, bedded Rosy down in her stable and retired to the library where they had tea. Sir Magnus, for some obscure reason, appeared to be delighted with their outing. As Adrian munched his way through acres of brown hot toast running with butter, crisp scones shrouded in cream and strawberry jam, and great moist black slices of fruit cake as fragrant as a whole forest in mid-winter, he listened to Sir Magnus giving him a lecture on the legal system, ninety per cent of which was incomprehensible to him.

"Tell me," he interrupted at last, "why were you so pleased that we went out for a walk?"

Sir Magnus with a critical and enquiring eye added

a teaspoonful of cherry brandy to his cup of tea and stirred it thoughtfully.

"It may not have occurred to you, my dear boy," he said fulsomely, with the air of one addressing a small and rather retarded child, "that the paths of justice are never smooth. To-day we have been seen by a multitude of people, taking the air in a quiet, civilised fashion, accompanied by Rosy. Rosy, as I thought she would, behaved in an exemplary fashion, while the gawping adult populace looked on. She, with a restraint that did her credit, nuzzled and cosseted the populace's awful, snotty-nosed progeny. Do you think for one moment that Rosy's apparent adoration and gentleness with children has not been reported in the humblest hovels in the town?"

Sir Magnus paused to engulf another cream and strawberry jam encrusted scone. He wiped his mouth and, speaking somewhat indistinctly, continued.

"I don't care where they get their jury from," he said with slight smugness, "but as soon as they arrive, they will be told by somebody what a civilised creature Rosy is."

"But," said Adrian aghast, "I thought the whole point of a jury was that you could not influence them."

Sir Magnus drew himself up to his full height of four feet and looked at Adrian imperiously.

"You cannot," he said harshly, "deliberately corrupt a jury. That would be unethical."

"Yes," said Adrian, "that's what I thought."

"You can, however," said Sir Magnus smoothly, "since juries are notoriously ill-constructed mentally, tell them what to think."

He poured some cherry brandy into his empty cup and drained it with a flourish.

The next few days Adrian found extremely exhausting. Sir Magnus had insisted that he write to everybody, however remotely connected with Rosy's case, in spite of Adrian's protests. He was sure half of them would be of no value to his defence.

"You'll let me make up my mind about that, my boy," said Sir Magnus. "Now, this Filigree woman, what about her father."

"Oh, God no. You don't want him," said Adrian panic-stricken. "He does nothing but talk about his reincarnations."

"Excellent," said Sir Magnus. "Nothing like a reincarnation to create a little confusion among the jurymen. Suggest to this girl that she bring her father with her."

Adrian was in despair. He felt that Mr. Filigree in the witness box would be almost guaranteed to get him penal servitude for life. However, in due course a cold little note appeared from Samantha saying briefly that she and her father would be willing to attend as witnesses and ending "Yours sincerely" in a chilly sort of way.

Gradually the first witnesses arrived. Mr. Pucklehammer in a gay canary yellow and black check suit and a brand new brown bowler hat, delighted to see Adrian and Rosy once more. Black Nell, who had been tracked down with some difficulty, Honoria and Ethelbert, both enjoying the drama enormously, and Honoria periodically bursting into floods of gin-promoted tears at the thought of Rosy being shot and Adrian being imprisoned. Her histrionics impressed Sir Magnus tremendously as he was no mean performer himself and when the two of them got going, Adrian got the uneasy impression that it was a grand opera they were staging, and not a defence.

Then the Filigrees arrived, Samantha cool but beautiful,

shaking Adrian gravely by the hand and saying that she was delighted with this opportunity of renewing her acquaintance with Rosy, a remark which cut Adrian to the quick. Mr. Filigree was in a transport of delight for he had never seen the sea before (except in his previous incarnations) and he danced along the shore waving his fat fingers in delight like a great jelly fish. Whenever Sir Magnus wanted to question him, he would be missing and search parties would have to go down to the beach and drag him away from what had become his favourite occupation, washing Rosy down in the shallows and building sand-castles with the neighbouring children. Through them all, roaring like a bull or cooing like a dove, Sir Magnus strode gathering up the threads of their various stories.

Screech scuttled cringing at Sir Magnus's heels, his pen squeaking like a demented wren as he wrote copious notes. Adrian had made several attempts to try and see Samantha alone, but without any success. She was polite but distant, and with each passing day Adrian grew more and more miserable. By the time the trial arrived, Adrian was in the blackest depths of despair, whereas Sir Magnus, belligerent as a Christmas turkey, strode about engulfing vast quantities of cherry brandy and exuding goodwill and confidence.

After the drab school-room like appearance of the magistrates' court, Adrian had imagined that the one in which he was to stand trial would be the same, but to his astonishment it was a beautiful room. The judge's chair and desk were of heavy oak, intricately carved with oak leaves, acorns, and small dimpled cherubs dancing about. Even the front of the witness box was carved. The high ceiling was white with a blue and gold bas-relief.

The air was one of hushed reverence, but with an undercurrent of bustle and activity. Sir Magnus had discovered that Screech had left half his notes at the house, and had become so incensed that Adrian feared for the poor clerk's life. He had been occupied in trying to calm Sir Magnus down, so it was not for some minutes that he realised the court had filled up and the air of expectancy had grown even stronger.

An immensely tall, angular figure had made his appearance. His gown hung round him in long folds like the wings of a bat, and his wig was perched slightly askew over a lantern-jawed face with a blue chin, soulful spaniel-brown eyes and a turned-down mouth like a slit. But for his garb, you would have said that he was a dyspeptic undertaker in a town where nobody ever died.

"Who's that?" Adrian asked Sir Magnus.

"Him?" said Sir Magnus, peering ferociously from under his eyebrows. "That's Sir Augustus Talisman. He's the prosecuting counsel."

"I don't think I care for the look of him," said Adrian.

"What, old Gussy?" said Sir Magnus in surprise. "Oh, he's a nice enough chap in his way. But if you go through life prosecuting people, you are bound to end up looking like that."

"Who's the judge?" asked Adrian.

"Ah," said Sir Magnus with satisfaction. "We've been very lucky. We have got old Topsy."

"Topsy!" said Adrian. "That's an unusual name for a judge."

"No, no," said Sir Magnus impatiently, "he's just called Topsy. His real name is Lord Crispin Turvey."

"I don't understand," said Adrian, bewildered.

"Good heavens, boy," said Sir Magnus. "It's obvious isn't it? Turvey Topsy, Topsy Turvey. He's the best judge on this circuit. He inevitably gets the wrong end of the stick. That's why the prosecutor looks so depressed. That's why he's called Topsy."

"Do you mean to say," said Adrian in amazement, "that he doesn't know what he's doing, and he's a judge?"

"Well, what he *does* is all right," said Sir Magnus. "But he just does the opposite to any other judge. I should think he's been responsible for putting more innocent people in jail than anybody else."

"Well, I don't see how that's going to help me," said Adrian.

Sir Magnus sighed with the air of somebody who is

suffering a fool, if not gladly, with a certain amount of patience.

"Look," he said kindly, "you start off with a confused judge, you see?"

"Yes," said Adrian dutifully.

"Well, if your judge is confused before he even starts, you are half way home," said Sir Magnus. "He will then confuse the jury and I will then confuse both of them."

"I really don't see . . ." began Adrian.

"You'd be surprised," said Sir Magnus, "what you can get away with if you create enough confusion. It's like a smoke-screen in battle."

"Oh," said Adrian. "I think I see what you mean." But inwardly he was resigning himself to the fact that with Sir Magnus defending him he would have to spend at least ten years in prison.

The clerk of the court got to his feet.

"All rise," he said in a tremulous falsetto.

The court was filled with scrapings and rustlings as everyone got to their feet. A door opened and in shuffled a tiny, wizened little man, clad in red robes, who seated himself in the great carved chair and peered round, looking rather like a surprised mole. Everyone sat down and there was much throat clearing and rustling of papers. The clerk of the court rose to his feet again.

"My lord," he fluted, "the case of the Crown versus Adrian Rookwhistle. Adrian Rookwhistle," he said peering at Adrian, who had risen to his feet, "the charge against you is that on the 5th June at the Alhambra Theatre at Scallop in the County of Brockelberry you did in a public place, to wit the Alhambra Theatre at Scallop, cause a public disturbance in the aforesaid Alhambra Theatre and did thereby cause grievous bodily harm to one Emanuel S. Clattercup, using for this purpose a large wild pachyderm, to wit an elephant, to the aforesaid Clattercup in the aforesaid Alhambra Theatre. How do you plead?"

Adrian was so confused at the charge that he just stood there staring at the clerk.

"Not guilty," said Sir Magnus.

"Not guilty," said Adrian.

The clerk of the court sat down. A large and jovial constable who was sharing the dock with Adrian in a companionable fashion stuck a finger in his ribs.

"Sit down, lad," he said in a whisper.

Adrian leant over the dock.

"What happens now?" he asked Sir Magnus.

Sir Magnus took a pinch of snuff and startled the entire court with a gigantic sneeze.

"Old Gussy drones on for a bit," he said. "Just relax for a little. Doze if you feel like it."

The judge had been peering about unsteadily to try and locate the precise area of the court from which the sneeze had emanated. Eventually he managed to fix his wavering eyes upon Sir Magnus.

"Sir Magnus," he said.

"M'lord?" said Sir Magnus, rising to his feet and bowing with false obsequiousness.

"I am aware of the fact," said the judge, "that you are addicted to taking snuff. I would be very grateful if you could inform me as to whether we are going to be constantly interrupted by that extremely startling noise that you seem forced to make every time you do so."

"Beg pardon, m'lord," said Sir Magnus. "I shall stifle it next time."

"See that you do," said the judge.

He looked at the prosecuting counsel.

"Since Sir Magnus has finished clearing his nasal passages, you may proceed, Sir Augustus," he said.

Sir Augustus Talisman rose to his feet, ducked his head in the general direction of the judge and spent several moments adjusting the sleeves of his robe and fiddling with a pile of notes on the table in front of him. Then he turned and had a whispered consultation with his clerk. The clerk dived under the table and reappeared clasping five or six massive volumes, each carefully marked with long strips of pink paper, which he placed on the table next to Sir Augustus. Both Sir Magnus and the judge, having settled the matter of the snuff, appeared to have dozed off.

Sir Augustus rearranged his robe once more, cleared his throat, clasped his lapel firmly in one hand and spoke

"My lord," he said in a mellifluous voice, "the case before you is, to say the least, somewhat unusual. So unusual, in fact, that it has taken me considerable time and patience to find any precedent in the laws of this country." Here he paused and laid his hand affectionately upon the pile of calf-bound volumes on the table in front of him.

"Briefly, m'lord," he continued, "for I have no wish to waste your lordship's valuable time—nor indeed am I under the erroneous impression that your lordship prefers anything that is not succinct and to the point—I would say that this outrage (and I feel that by saying outrage I am not being in any way too harsh in my description) this outrage is one of the most extraordinary cases that I have come across in a long career at the Bar."

He paused and glanced down at his notes, tapping them thoughtfully with a forefinger. Sir Magnus appeared to be in a deep and untroubled slumber. Adrian had expected him at this point to leap up and protest, and so was somewhat disappointed.

"The defendant, Adrian Rookwhistle," continued Sir Augustus, "apparently inherited from his uncle a fully grown female elephant. The elephant's name is apparently Rosy, and so, in order to avoid confusion, and with your lordship's permission of course, I will refer to her by that name.

"On the evening of 31st May, Rookwhistle arrived in Scallop and the following day made his way to the Alhambra Theatre where he applied to Mr. Clattercup, the owner, for a job. Mr. Clattercup, feeling that the introduction of a tame, and, my lord, I stress the word, tame elephant, into his performance (which I believe was called *Ali Baba and the Forty Thieves*), would provide a strong appeal, engaged Rookwhistle and the elephant Rosy. Mr. Clattercup had spent a considerable sum of money on the production of this pantomime. On the first night, the theatre was, as would be expected, full of our ocal inhabitants who hold culture so dear to their hearts. Half of the first scene was enacted without incident, but t was then that Rookwhistle, who had, according to witnesses, been imbibing and had encouraged the elephant to mbibe as well, lost control of the animal. It ran berserk."

Adrian, shocked at this contumely, glanced at Sir Magnus, but his defending counsel still slept peacefully.

"I have here, m'lord (and I needn't worry you with the details) a list of the actual damage that was done by the aforementioned elephant, but this was damage to scenery and various stage properties. We now come to the personal damage that the animal inflicted. The violinist of the orchestra suffered numerous cuts and contusions when truck by a palm tree wielded by the elephant. The leader of the orchestra suffered severe concussion and Mr. Clatterup, the owner, not only received severe bruising, but also ustained a broken leg as a result of being hurled into the orchestra pit by the maddened and enraged creature."

At this point the judge gave a small squeak which may or may not have been laughter.

"M'lord," said Sir Augustus in the tones of one delivering a funeral oration, "I will bring evidence to show that the defendant Rookwhistle had for some considerable time been travelling the country with this animal, creating havoc wherever he passed and that, in consequence, his acceptance of this job at the Alhambra Theatre was obtained through guile and deceit, since he professed that the animal was tame while knowing that it was in fact a fierce, intractable and uncontrollable creature, a risk to life and property."

Adrian was so incensed at this twisting of the facts that he leant over the dock, seized Sir Magnus's shoulder and shook it.

"Ah," said Sir Magnus brightly, "Gussy's finished, has he? Hear what he was saying?"

"Yes," hissed Adrian, "he's twisting everything to make t look as though Rosy and I are guilty."

"Bound to," said Sir Magnus. "That's what he's paid for."

171

"But can't you say something?" said Adrian. "Can't you get up and tell the judge it isn't true?"

"Don't panic, dear boy," said Sir Magnus. "Remember that a spider spends hours weaving a web which you can destroy with a walking-stick with the flick of a wrist."

And with this Adrian had to be content. Sir Augustus was shuffling through his notes and re-settling his gown, and Adrian examined the jury.

All of them looked sour-faced, gimlet-eyed and unrelenting, and those who had not immediately gone into a trance spent their time looking surreptitiously at their watches and did not appear to be concentrating on anything in particular. They looked at Adrian as though they would be willing to condemn him there and then, either from a sense of vindictiveness or from a desire to get back to their businesses as rapidly as possible.

"I will now call my first witness," said Sir Augustus. "Sir Hubert Darcey."

"Call Sir Hubert Darcey," cried the clerk of the court.

Sir Hubert strode into the court as though on to a parade ground. He looked even more magnificently be-whiskered and terrifying than Adrian had remembered him. He stamped into the witness box and took the oath with the air of one who finds it faintly insulting that anyone should even question his truthfulness.

"You," said Sir Augustus, "are Hubert Darcey of Bangalore Manor in the village of Monkspepper?"

"Yes," replied Darcey thunderously.

"Sir Hubert," said the judge, "I wonder if you would be so good as to offer your evidence in a slightly lower tone of voice? The acoustics of this place are such that if you use the full power of your lungs, it sets up an extraordinary reverbation which runs through both my desk and my chair."

"Very good, my lord," Darcey barked.

"You are the Master of the Monkspepper Hunt, are you not?" enquired Sir Augustus.

"Yes," said Darcey. "Have been for twenty years."

"Now, do you recall the 20th April?"

"I do," said Darcey. "Vividly."

"Well, would you be so kind as to tell his lordship and the jury, in your own words, exactly what happened."

"Yes," said Darcey in his muted roar. "It was a fine mornin', mi lud, and the hounds had found in the oak woods behind Monkspepper . . ."

"Found what?" enquired the judge.

"The scent," said Darcey.

"What sort of scent?" enquired the judge with interest.

"The scent of a fox," said Darcey.

"These rural pursuits are really most interesting," said the judge musingly. "Pray continue."

"Well, the line took us through the oak woods down the Monkspepper Road and eventually led us into a meadow which abuts the river. I would like to say that there was only one entrance to this meadow and it was completely surrounded by a very thick and large bull-finch."

"Did you say bull-finch?" enquired the judge.

"Yes," said Darcey.

"I think, my lord," said Sir Augustus, feeling that at this rate he would be unable to get any evidence out of his witness at all, "I think the witness means a thick hedge. A bull-finch is a term meaning a thick hedge."

"I thought it was a term meaning a bird with a red breast."

"It is the same word, but with different connotations," said Sir Augustus.

"Thank you," said the judge.

"Well," said Darcey, "the hounds went into the meadow and we followed 'em. The first thing that caught my eye was an extremely vulgar-lookin' trap, painted in bright colours such as a gipsy might have used. Then suddenly, from behind the trees, there appeared to my astonishment an elephant. Not unnaturally, the hounds panicked, as did the horses, to such an extent in fact that even experienced riders like myself, caught unawares, were thrown. I unfortunately landed on my head and was only saved by my top hat. Before I could rid my eyes of this encumbrance, I was seized by the elephant, carried across the meadow and dashed to the ground at the feet of the accused who, to my horror, I saw was wearin' nothin' but a pair of very damp underpants."

"Why was he only in underpants?" asked the judge, obviously fascinated.

"He told me that he had been swimmin' in the river with the elephant, mi lud—frightenin' the salmon."

"Did you sustain any injury from this encounter?" enquired the judge.

"Fortunately, mi lud, just some slight bruising."

"I bring this matter up, m'lord," said Sir Augustus, "merely in order to prove my point that the defendant *did* in fact know his elephant to be a dangerous creature, as this type of assault upon people had happened prior to the affair at the Alhambra Theatre."

"I see," said the judge doubtfully.

Sir Augustus sat down and the judge, peering at the apparently unconscious Sir Magnus, said, "Would you care to join us for a brief moment, and cross-examine the witness?"

"Yes, m'lord," said Sir Magnus, rising slowly to his feet. He fixed Darcey with a penetrating eye. "You say that the only damage you suffered was slight bruising?"

"Yes."

"Was your horse a good one?" Sir Magnus enquired unexpectedly. Darcey's face grew purple.

"I breed the finest horses in the country," he barked.

"But it obviously could not have been very well trained?" enquired Sir Magnus.

"It's a perfect mount," snapped Darcey. "But horses outside circuses are not trained to cope with elephants."

"So you would say it was quite normal for your horse to panic and throw you?" said Sir Magnus.

"Of course," said Darcey.

"So your bruises were in fact sustained by falling off the horse?" enquired Sir Magnus. Darcey glared at him

"Come, come," said Sir Magnus silkily, "surely that is what you have been telling us?"

"I don't really see where this line of questioning is getting us," said the judge plaintively.

"M'lord," said Sir Magnus, "I am merely trying to point out to your lordship and to the jury" (here he cast a fierce eye which seemed to electrify the entire jury) "that the *slight* bruising, and I use the witness's own words, that he sustained, was due to the fact that he was thrown off his horse and that the bruising had nothing whatsoever to do with the elephant in question."

Sir Augustus got to his feet.

"My lord," he said, "the fact that the witness sustained the bruising through falling off his horse is not the point. He would not have fallen off his horse if it had not been threatened by the elephant."

"Did the elephant do anything to your horse?" enquired Sir Magnus of Darcey.

"No," said Darcey reluctantly. "It just trumpeted."

"Trumpeted, eh," said the judge. "Interesting. I don't think I have ever heard an elephant trumpet. What's it sound like?"

"A sort of squeaking noise, your lordship," explained Sir Magnus.

"However," he continued, glancing at the jury, "I think we have made the point that in fact the elephant in question was *not* responsible for any damage the witness sustained. Do you not agree, your lordship?"

"Yes, yes. That's very clear," said the judge and made a note.

Sir Augustus cast a baleful stare in the direction of Sir Magnus. The point, as far as he was concerned, had not been made very clear at all, but if the judge said it had, he could not very well argue the point.

"I have no more questions," said Sir Magnus, sitting down with an air of satisfaction. With the air indeed of one who has won the case. The jury were visibly impressed.

"I would perhaps like to recall this witness," said Sir Augustus, "a little later in the proceedings."

"Certainly, Sir Augustus," said the judge. He bent over his notes for a moment or so and then looked up at Sir Magnus.

"A squeaking noise, you said?" he enquired.

"Yes, my lord," said Sir Magnus. "Rather like the noise of a slate pencil magnified."

The judge carefully wrote this piece of natural history down in his notes.

"I would like to call Lady Berengaria Fenneltree."

Lady Fenneltree, clad in a deep purple velvet dress and with a black veil on her straw hat, sailed into court like a successful galleon. She took the oath, threw back her veil and nodded to the judge as much as to say "you may proceed now". In answer to Sir Augustus's questions she identified herself in her clear penetrating voice and so impressive was her demeanour that even the more absent-minded of the jurymen sat up and took interest.

"Lady Fenneltree," said Sir Augustus, "do you remember the evening of the 28th April?"

"It is an evening," said Lady Fenneltree, in a voice as brittle as the sound of icicles falling off the roof, "that is indelibly engraved upon my memory."

"Would you like to tell his lordship and the jury why?"

She half turned to the judge, pinned him to his chair with a hypnotic blue gaze, clasped her hands in front of her and began.

"On the 28th April it was my daughter's eighteenth birthday," she said.

"Does this have any bearing on the matter?" enquired the judge.

"I was asked," Lady Fenneltree said quellingly, "to tell the story in my own words."

"By all means, by all means," said the judge, and made a hasty and irrelevant note.

"It was my daughter's eighteenth birthday," recommenced Lady Fenneltree, "and we had arranged a ball in her honour. We had naturally invited a number of people. In fact,"—she allowed herself a small grim smile—"I can say that everybody who is anybody was there. I had asked my husband to think up some original entertainment, possibly of a humorous nature, for the edification of the guests. He assured me he had this matter well in hand, but wished to keep it a secret. I had been up in town shopping with my daughter, and on my return I found that" (she said gesturing disdainfully at Adrian) "installed in the house."

"With his elephant?" enquired the judge.

"Unfortunately, yes," said Lady Fenneltree.

"But how," enquired the judge giving her his full attention, and obviously deeply interested, "how did he manage to get it up and down stairs?"

"Er, my lord," said Sir Augustus getting to his feet hurriedly. "I think it should be explained that the defendant kept his elephant in the stable yard, unbeknownst to Lady Fenneltree."

"Oh," said the judge, "that's different."

He looked at Sir Magnus, convinced by now that he was an authority on elephants.

"Can elephants walk up stairs?" he asked.

"Indubitably," said Sir Magnus.

"Anyway," said Lady Fenneltree, irritated by the judge's interruption, "my husband had secreted the elephant in the stables, as Sir Augustus said, unbeknownst to me. He had worked out a ridiculous scheme which, if it had been brought to my attention, I would have put an immediate stop to. He and that Rookwhistle creature were going to dress themselves up as Indians and bring the elephant into the ballroom, sitting in a howdah."

The judge leant forward and stared at her, puzzled.

"But I always thought," he said, "that a howdah was a thing that elephants wore on their backs."

"They do," said Lady Fenneltree.

"But then, how," asked the judge plaintively, "did they manage to get the elephant into the howdah?"

Sir Augustus leapt to his feet once more, aware that Lady Fenneltree was on the verge of giving the judge a short but pungent correction.

"My lord," he said, "Lord Fenneltree and the defendant

dressed themselves in Indian costume, put a howdah on the back of the elephant and rode into the ballroom in the howdah."

The judge started to make small squeaking, snuffling noises to himself, shaking all over as though with ague. It was some seconds before the court realised that he was laughing. Presently, still trembling with mirth, he wiped his eyes and leant forward.

"What you could almost call, Sir Augustus, a pretty how da do, eh?" he said and lapsed once more into helpless laughter.

"Ha, ha," said Sir Augustus dutifully. "Extremely witty, my lord."

A ghastly silence settled over the court while the judge grappled with his sense of humour. Presently, wiping his eyes on his handkerchief and blowing his nose, he waved a hand at Lady Fenneltree. "Do please go on, madam," he said.

"My guests were all enjoying the humble but adequate entertainment that we were offering them," said Lady Fenneltree, "when suddenly the doors of the ballroom burst open and the elephant rushed in and slid to the end of the room."

"Slid?" enquired the judge.

"Slid," said Lady Fenneltree firmly.

The judge peered at Sir Augustus. "I am not altogether sure," he said, "that I understand the witness."

"It slid, my lord," said Sir Augustus, "on the parquet floor."

"Slid," said the judge musingly. He looked at Sir Magnus. "Can elephants slide?" he enquired.

"Given a suitable polished surface and sufficient impetus, I believe, my lord, that even an elephant may slide," said Sir Magnus.

"Was it meant to slide?" enquired the judge, looking at Lady Fenneltree.

"Whether it was meant to slide or not is beside the point," she said crisply. "It slid straight into all the tables containing the food and wine. My husband was in the howdah in his ridiculous outfit and he and the howdah fell off. I approached him and asked him why he had seen fit to introduce an elephant into my ballroom."

"A good question," said the judge, struck by Lady Fenneltree's penetration. "And what did he answer?"

"He said," said Lady Fenneltree, with a wormwood-like bitterness, "that it was a surprise."

"Well," said the judge judicially, "it was an honest answer. It *was* a surprise, wasn't it?"

"Since that evening," said Lady Fenneltree, "I have been searching my mind for a word which would describe the experience adequately, and 'surprise' was not one that I dredged up from my not inconsiderable knowledge of the English tongue."

"I couldn't agree with you more," said the judge with decision. "That is exactly what I think myself."

"May I continue?" enquired Lady Fenneltree. "Preferably without further interruptions?"

"Of course, of course," said the judge. "Yes, by all means. What happened next?"

He sat forward and fixed his gaze eagerly upon Lady Fenneltree like a child being told a fairy-tale.

"The food was, of course, ruined," said Lady Fenneltree. "The elephant was completely out of control, rampaging to and fro and seeking whom it could devour. I was gently remonstrating with my husband for his foolishness in introducing a wild beast into such a place, when it first pulled down a priceless chandelier, and then, rushing up to me, seized me in its trunk."

"By George!" said the judge. "What did you do, eh?"

"Being a mere woman," said Lady Fenneltree in a voice like a bugle sounding a cavalry charge, "I fainted."

"Very proper," said the judge. "It must have been a harrowing experience."

Lady Fenneltree bowed her head slightly, endeavouring, somewhat unsuccessfully, to look like a cringing and modest virgin.

"When I came to," she said, "I found myself on a salmon."

"It seems to me," said the judge in a puzzled manner, "that there are an awful lot of animals entering into this case. Were you aware, Sir Augustus, that there were so many animals in the case?"

Sir Augustus closed his eyes for a moment.

"Yes, my lord," he said, "but the salmon was dead."

"Well, it would be, in a ballroom," said the judge. "Bound to be. Unless there was a fountain or something."

"There is no fountain in our ballroom," said Lady Fenneltree.

"Well, there you are," said the judge in triumph. "It shows it must have been dead."

"It was a cold salmon," said Lady Fenneltree.

"Because it was dead?" enquired the judge.

Sir Augustus rose to his feet once again with a long-suffering air.

"For the edification of the guests, my lord," he said, "Lady Fenneltree had provided a large, cooked salmon. This had been displaced by the activities of the pachyderm and when it had finished carrying Lady Fenneltree around, it deposited her unconscious figure upon the fish."

"Fascinating," said the judge. "I cannot remember when I have enjoyed a case so much. Tell us more, Lady Fenneltree."

"When I recovered consciousness, I was on the salmon. I was just in time to see Sir Hubert Darcey being picked up by the elephant and dashed to the ground in what was obviously a deliberate attempt to kill him."

Lady Fenneltree had never been Adrian's favourite woman, and this deliberate lie he could not stomach. Since Sir Magnus was obviously not going to do anything about it, he felt he must.

"It's a lie!" he shouted, leaping to his feet. "Rosy never harmed anyone in her life. You're just a vindictive old cow."

A wave of excitement and admiration ran through the court. Lady Fenneltree cast a look of contemptuous disdain at Adrian and turned to the judge.

"My lord," she said with biting sweetness, "do you normally allow witnesses to be insulted in your court?"

"Not normally," said the judge absent-mindedly. "But tell me, what has this cow got to do with it? Seems to me there are far too many animals in this case."

Sir Augustus, looking like a very unsuccessful Horatio at the bridge, got unsteadily to his feet.

"I think, my lord," he said, "that the witness has made it quite clear that the elephant was large, malevolent, uncontrolled and, indeed, uncontrollable, and with the wild creature's natural desire to kill."

"Rubbish!" shouted Adrian.

"Will you shut up," said Sir Magnus, waking up for a brief moment. "You're doing more harm than good, ranting and raving like that. Leave the old cow to me."

"I think," said Sir Augustus, ignoring Adrian's outburst with exquisite courtesy, "I have made it plain to your lordship and to this fine body of men that make up the jury, that on two occasions this wild animal was allowed by the person who was supposed to be in charge of it, to wit Adrian Rookwhistle, to run riot. The extraordinary thing is, and indeed we have to thank a merciful providence for this, that nobody was killed."

He sat down with a faint air of satisfaction and Sir Magnus rose slowly to his feet.

"Lady Fenneltree," he said smiling at her archly, his eyebrows semaphoring up and down interrogatively, "you have given us a truthful and honest account of the events that happened on the evening of 28th April."

Lady Fenneltree bridled.

"Naturally," she said.

"From what you say," said Sir Magnus tentatively, "you must have undergone a terrible, one might almost say unhinging experience, but you displayed all the qualities of courage and determination which have made English women the envy of the world."

A slight outburst of clapping from the back of the court was immediately quelled.

"Whose side are you on?" hissed Adrian.

Sir Magnus smiled a quiet smile, took his snuff box out of his waistcoat and then, catching the judge's eye, replaced it.

"There are several things that you have not told us," said Sir Magnus, "and this displays a quality of modesty in your make-up which is, if I might be allowed to say so, utterly feminine and utterly charming."

Lady Fenneltree inclined her head regally.

"For example," said Sir Magnus looking at the jury and throwing out a hand, "you have not said anything about your lineage. You were, I believe, a Plumbdragon?"

"I was," said Lady Fenneltree. "My father was Lord Plumbdragon."

"The Plumbdragons and Fenneltrees have, I believe, been part of the aristocratic backbone of this country for something in the neighbourhood of four hundred years. Is that correct?"

"Yes," said Lady Fenneltree.

"During that time," said Sir Magnus looking at the jury, "the Plumbdragons and Fenneltrees have ruled over vast acres, cosseting and nurturing the lesser mortals who dwelt therein. They have been shining examples to the communities that lived at their gates, examples of modesty as personified by Lady Fenneltree herself, of honesty, of fair play and, above all, of truthfulness. For people like you and me (people of lesser clay) the Plumbdragons and Fenneltrees are people to be looked up to. In olden days, before the establishment of dignified, fair-minded courts like this, who was it that we, the humble, looked to for compassion and for those qualities which have made this country of ours what it is—fair play and honesty? We looked to the Plumbdragons and Fenneltrees of this world."

Sir Augustus, scenting a rat without being able to discern its shape, got to his feet.

"My lord," he interrupted, "I really don't see—fascinating though it is—what my learned friend's speech adds to the case."

"My lord," said Sir Magnus, "I know that I am appearing for the defence. Nevertheless, I do not want it to appear that I have bullied and frightened a woman in the witness box and a woman, moreover, who has all those qualities of which I have been speaking."

"But, Sir Magnus," pointed out the judge, "you have hardly as yet questioned the witness. There can be no possible reason for saying that you have bullied her."

"M'lord," said Sir Magnus, "I wish the jury to be easy in their minds."

Here he cast a glance like a blow-lamp over the jury.

"We are all trying to get at the truth. That is why we are gathered here, and all I am saying to you, my lord, and to the jury, is that from the lips of such a noble, modest and aristocratic woman, we can expect nothing but the truth."

"Well, she *is* on oath," said the judge petulantly. "I would have thought that was sufficient. I feel it would be helpful if, instead of lecturing us, Sir Magnus, you questioned the witness, endeavouring wherever possible not to bring any more animals into the case."

"As your lordship pleases," said Sir Magnus.

He turned and smiled at Lady Fenneltree caressingly.

"Your recollections of the evening of the 28th April seem remarkably clear," he said.

"They are," said Lady Fenneltree, "extremely clear."

"You forgive me for asking that question," said Sir Magnus. "To a sensitive, well brought up woman, such an experience must have been terrifying in the extreme, and so it would be understandable if your recollections of certain points were slightly blurred."

"Sir Magnus," said Lady Fenneltree crisply, "I may or may not be endowed with all the qualities that you suggest, but I have one quality which never deserts me. I am observant in the extreme."

"So observant," said Sir Magnus as though to himself, "that you overlooked the fact that an elephant had taken up residence in your stables."

Lady Fenneltree glared at him malevolently. "I do not normally," she said cuttingly, "spend my life in the stables, and my husband had concealed the fact that he had an elephant secreted there."

"Of course," said Sir Magnus, soothingly, "it is a thing that we could all overlook, isn't it?"

He glanced at the jury as though hoping that they would sympathise with Lady Fenneltree in her failing.

"However," he continued, "to return to the night of the 28th April. You say that the elephant skidded into the ballroom, upset the tables containing the food and drink and then proceeded to rampage about, to use your own words, seeking whom it might devour. Your recollection of this part of the story is quite clear, is it?"

"Quite clear," said Lady Fenneltree suspiciously.

"Later on, you say you recovered consciousness," said Sir Magnus, "in time to see the elephant deliberately endeavour to kill Sir Hubert?"

"Yes," said Lady Fenneltree.

"Your impression was that this was an unprovoked attack by a dangerous and uncontrolled wild animal?"

"Yes," said Lady Fenneltree.

"You had yourself just had an unpleasant experience by being carried by the elephant," said Sir Magnus, "and you fainted, which is of course very right and proper. When you recovered consciousness you were lying, it appears, upon a salmon?"

"Yes," said Lady Fenneltree.

"Did you sustain any bruises or contusions from this brief encounter?"

"No," said Lady Fenneltree, "but I can only attribute this to the fact that, mercifully, the animal put me down in favour of attacking Sir Hubert."

"Not an insatiable elephant," said Sir Magnus. "One would have thought that it might have finished off one victim before starting on another."

"Yet that's what happened," said Lady Fenneltree.

Sir Magnus sighed, took out his snuff-box absent-mindedly, applied snuff to his nostrils and sneezed.

"Sir Magnus," said the judge, "I hope I won't have to remind you again about sneezing in court."

"I apologise, m'lord," said Sir Magnus. "I was carried away by emotion. It is with the utmost reluctance I have to make Lady Fenneltree undergo the very unpleasant experience of being in the witness-box. To a truthful, law-abiding citizen, this can be nothing but a degrading experience."

He snapped his snuff-box shut, returned it to his pocket and turned once more to Lady Fenneltree. Somehow a subtle change seemed to have come over him. He bristled and quivered like a small, alert terrier at a rabbit hole.

"We have established then, Lady Fenneltree, have we not," he said, "that you are exceptionally perceptive and that your recollection of the evening in question is exceedingly clear, and we have established, of course, your honesty without a shadow of a doubt."

He glanced at the jury, a shiny, twinkling glance, and they all involuntarily nodded.

"Therefore," said Sir Magnus, "I need not keep you very much longer. But there is just one *small* point which I would be glad if you would clear up for the sake of the jury."

He paused and glanced down at his notes. It was perfectly obvious to everybody, including Lady Fenneltree, that he was not reading his notes. The pause was for effect, while he waited, open and gleaming like a gin trap. Lady Fenneltree realised she was being manoeuvred into something—her regal nose snuffed danger, but she could not see from which direction the danger threatened. Eventually Sir Magnus looked up and waved snow-white eyebrows at her in a disarmingly friendly fashion.

"You say that the elephant skidded down the ballroom and into the tables containing food?" he enquired.

"I have already told you that," said Lady Fenneltree. Sir Magnus shuffled his notes.

"After that," he said, "the elephant rampaged about?"

"Yes," said Lady Fenneltree.

"During the course of its destructive progress," said Sir Magnus, "you say that it pulled down the chandelier."

"Yes," said Lady Fenneltree.

"The ballroom at Fenneltree Hall, I take it," said Sir Magnus, "is fairly large?"

"It is a magnificent room," said Lady Fenneltree.

"It has, I believe, a minstrels' gallery at one end?" said Sir Magnus.

"That's where the band was situated," said Lady Fenneltree.

"One would assume then," said Sir Magnus silkily, "that since it is obviously a magnificent room, the ceiling is quite high."

"I believe," said Lady Fenneltree complacently, "that the ballroom is fifty feet high."

"Have you," enquired Sir Magnus, "ever measured an elephant's trunk?"

There was an electric silence. Everybody in court had suddenly become aware of the line that Sir Magnus was taking with the exception of the judge and the jury.

"I do not spend my spare time measuring elephants' trunks," said Lady Fenneltree with dignity.

"Well, during the last ten days, I have had this unique opportunity," said Sir Magnus, "and I have found, by experiment, that it is impossible for an elephant—however evilly disposed—to reach up and pull down a chandelier that is fifty feet above it."

He paused and straightened his wig.

"Lady Fenneltree," he said softly and sympathetically, "you underwent a ghastly experience. It is only to be expected that a woman of your fine qualities, under such circumstances, could make a mistake like this."

Lulled into a sense of false security by Sir Magnus's sudden change from harshness to sympathy, Lady Fenneltree inclined her head.

"On this one point," she said, "I may possibly be mistaken."

"It is a pity," said Sir Magnus smoothly, "because, as you say, you are so observant. It is just on this one point (and who is to blame you for it) that you made a mistake. But you tell us that the rest of your description is completely accurate, and who am I to doubt the word of a lady?"

He gave a small bow and sat down.

"What the hell was all *that* about?" asked Adrian. "I don't see that this has got anything to do with the case at all."

Sir Magnus gave him a frosty glance from under his eyebrows.

"Look at the jury," he said.

Adrian looked and saw twelve faces staring at Lady Fenneltree almost avidly. Here was a woman, an aristocrat, a person who should, by all the rules and regulations, be infallible, and Sir Magnus by some alchemy had proved her to be just as fallible as the next person. You could see the thought fermenting in their minds like yeast. Adrian was horrified.

"But look," he whispered, "Rosy *did* bring that chandelier down."

Sir Magnus produced his snuff-box and opened it carefully and then glanced up at Adrian.

"Be careful of your choice of words," he said quietly. "Lady Fenneltree wasn't. Rosy *brought* the chandelier down, she didn't *pull* it down."

"But I don't see that that makes any difference," said Adrian.

"Stop quibbling," said Sir Magnus. "I'm really not interested in the chandelier. I'm merely interested in putting what you very accurately described as a vindictive old cow into an invidious position."

Lady Fenneltree left the box, casting black looks in the direction of Sir Magnus. Sir Augustus got to his feet.

"My next witness is Lord Fenneltree," he said, with a faintly despairing air.

Lord Fenneltree ambled amiably into the witness-box as though sauntering into his favourite club, beamed and waved at Adrian, fixed his monocle carefully in his eye and took the oath. Sir Augustus, having identified beyond all shadow of doubt who Lord Fenneltree was, cleared his throat and fixed his soulful gaze upon the witness.

"On the 21st April, Lord Fenneltree," he said, "I understand that you met the defendant, Adrian Rookwhistle, in a lane some distance away from your house."

"Absolutely correct, my dear chap," said Lord Fenneltree nodding.

"You then suggested to him that he and his elephant should take up residence at Fenneltree Hall so that the elephant might take part in the birthday celebrations for your daughter?"

"Yes," said Lord Fenneltree. "Yes, you have grasped the essential facts."

"I take it," said Sir Augustus, with the air of one who has primed his witness well, "that the defendant at no time intimated to you that the animal in question might be a danger to life and property?"

"No," said Lord Fenneltree musingly, "I cannot say that he did, but then he had got no reason to, had he?"

"Lord Fenneltree," said Sir Augustus hastily, "I would be glad if you would answer just 'Yes' or 'No' to my questions. By elaborating on them you just confuse the jury."

Sir Magnus at this point opened one eye and gave a tiny snort of derision.

"When you introduced the elephant into the ballroom, what was the result?" asked Sir Augustus.

Lord Fenneltree remained silent.

"Come, sir," said Sir Augustus with some asperity, "surely you know what the result was when you introduced the elephant to the ball?"

"It is awfully difficult," said Lord Fenneltree, looking plaintively at the judge, "to answer that sort of question with either a 'yes' or a 'no'. Could I use some other word?"

"By all means," said the judge.

"Let me repeat the question," said Sir Augustus. "What was the result of your introducing the elephant to the ballroom?"

"Chaos," said his lordship, smiling happily.

"What exactly do you mean by chaos?"

"Practically everything you can think of," said his lordship. "She wrecked all the tables, she knocked down the chandelier, she did a very pretty waltz with my wife and then picked up old Darcey and dumped him on the floor. I can assure you that if it hadn't been for my wife's indignation, the whole thing would have been splendidly diverting."

"Now, my lord," said Sir Augustus, turning to the judge, "I think I have established my point that this elephant is a wild and savage animal and that Adrian Rookwhistle knew it to be. And that without any thought for persons or property, he continually allowed it to rampage throughout the county."

He cast a faintly worried look at Sir Magnus.

"Perhaps my honourable friend would like to cross-examine?" he enquired.

"No," said Sir Magnus, waving a lavish hand, "I have no wish to cross-examine at this precise moment, my lord, but I would ask permission to recall this witness later."

Sir Augustus leapt to his feet.

"I object, my lord," he said. "This is most unethical."

"It is rather unusual, Sir Magnus," said the judge.

"Yes, mi lord, I realise that," said Sir Magnus, "but I feel once you have heard the evidence of my other witnesses you will find that Lord Fenneltree has something of worth to contribute to *my* side of the case."

"Very well," said the judge. "Just this once. And now I suggest that we all adjourn. I don't know about you gentlemen, but I am beginning to feel decidedly peckish. We will resume at two o'clock."

"My lord," said Sir Magnus, "prison fare, as you know, is not of the sort that makes a gourmet tremble with delight. I would therefore ask your lordship most humbly, if it would be possible for you to release my client so that he may lunch with me?"

"You really do ask for the most unusual things, Sir Magnus," said the judge severely. "However, I suppose there can't be any harm in it. But make sure you bring him back."

"Thank you, my lord," said Sir Magnus.

The judge scrambled out of his chair while the court

stood and disappeared through the door into his chambers.

"Well," said Sir Magnus, taking a teaspoonful of snuff and inserting it up both nostrils, "a most successful morning."

He sneezed violently.

"Let us go and have some lunch, dear boy," he said to Adrian.

"I don't know what you are so pleased about," said Adrian. "As far as I can make out, everyone has talked a lot of nonsense this morning which hasn't settled anything one way or the other, and the prosecution is actually telling *lies*."

"Dear boy," said Sir Magnus, "what a charming innocent you are. However, wait until this afternoon, when *we* start telling lies."

20 FINAL SETTLEMENT

They went over the road to a small oak-beamed tavern where they sustained themselves with several flagons of ale followed by crisp, brown lamb chops, each wearing a frilly ballet skirt of paper around the bone. These were adorned with tender green asparagus shoots, awash in butter, piles of mashed potatoes mixed with cream, and a regiment of tender peas. This was followed by a cherry tart and a cheese board containing cheeses so ripe that you were aware of their presence long before they entered the room.

"Why did you say that you wanted to recall Lord Fenneltree?" asked Adrian towards the end of lunch. Sir Magnus placed a great greeny-gold lump of Stilton on a morsel of bread and thrust it into his mouth.

"Because," he said munching, "I consider him to be a better witness for the defence than for the prosecution."

"But he's a prosecution witness," said Adrian.

"He thinks he is," corrected Sir Magnus. "So does the

prosecution, but in fact if anyone's going to win this case for you, it's going to be him." He glanced at his watch. "Now, let's have another swift pint of beer," he said, "and then we'd better be getting back into court."

After lunch Sir Augustus put Mr. Clattercup in the box. From Sir Augustus's point of view he proved to be an unfortunate witness, who only succeeded in giving the impression that, at whatever cost and by whatever means, he was determined to see both Adrian and Rosy condemned. But in spite of this, the fact that his leg was encased in an enormous plaster cast and that he had to get in and out of the witness-box with the aid of two crutches and two policemen obviously impressed itself upon the jury. When Mr. Clattercup had thumped and staggered his way out of court, Sir Augustus rose to his feet and settled his gown. Then with a musing, almost affectionate air, he pulled the pile of books along the table and rested his hands upon them.

"My lord," he said, "I think you have heard sufficient evidence to persuade you that, as I said initially, this case is a very unusual one."

"Yes," said the judge, who was looking rather rosy and benign as a result of lunch. "It would be unusual even if it did not have any animals in it."

"I would like at this juncture," said Sir Augustus, "before we hear the defence, if indeed there can *be* a defence, to quote one or two parallel cases which I have succeeded in finding."

He opened one of the massive tomes in front of him and ran his forefinger along the type.

"Here, for example," he said, "you will see the case of Regina versus Pigwhistle, 1884, where the defendant was in charge of a large Shire horse which removed and ate, not only the hat, but the wig of an elderly lady in the town High Street. You will see, my lord, that it was ruled by the judge that the defendant, being in control of the Shire horse and knowing that it had a positively morbid liking for flowers, was therefore responsible by letting it come within eating distance of the hat of the lady in question.

This, I think, is a very good parallel to the case which is before us to-day."

"A good point, a good point," said the judge, "but then, Sir Augustus, if the person in question had the horse under control, and the woman of her own volition moved within striking distance of the horse, what then?"

"I think," said Sir Augustus smugly, "I can do no better than to quote the case of Regina versus Clutchpenny, 1894. The defendant in this case had a large bull . . ."

"Isn't it possible," interrupted the judge, "for you to find parallel cases which do *not* contain animals? It is really most confusing to dodge about between salmon and Shire horses and bulls and elephants."

"Unfortunately, my lord," said Sir Augustus, "it is a little difficult to find *parallel* cases that do *not* contain animals."

"I had never realised before," said the judge irritably, "that our entire legal system seems to be infested with the birds and beasts of the field. However, continue."

Sir Augustus continued. Solemnly, during the next quarter of an hour, he opened the various volumes before him and read out cases, none of which—so far as Adrian could see—bore the remotest resemblance to his case. At length and with a certain reluctance, Sir Augustus closed the last book and laid it reverently on the table.

"I think, my lord," he said, "that that should have cleared up one or two of the anomalies which might, hitherto, have been puzzling the jury."

"I shall be delighted," said the judge, "if the jury understands it. But before you sit down, Sir Augustus, just give me the details again about the man with the python."

"I don't think I've got any hope," said Adrian to Sir Magnus. This massive pile-up of legal evidence on the part of Sir Augustus had convinced him beyond a shadow of doubt that he had lost his case. Sir Magnus opened his eyes and beamed at Adrian.

"Always remember, my lad," he said, "that books are like tools. It depends how you use them. You can cut yourself on a chisel."

He leant forward and gave an affectionate pat to some-thing which Adrian had not seen earlier. Under Sir Mag-nus's table was an extremely large leather suitcase. During the lunch hour Sir Magnus must have sent Screech out for this. What it contained, Adrian could not imagine.

"Poor old Gussy," said Sir Magnus complacently, shuffling his notes into a neat pile as though he was about to deal a deck of cards, "he was really doomed before he'd even started."

"Doomed?" said Adrian, "but he's put up an almost cast-iron argument. I mean, we can't deny that Rosy did all that damage. I mean, she did it with the best possible intentions, but nevertheless, she *did* do it."

"Wait and see," said Sir Magnus as he rose majestically to his feet. He gave a little bow in the direction of the judge and smiled benignly at the jury.

"My lord," he said, "as my learned friend has so astutely pointed out, this is a very unusual case."

Here he paused and pulled the large leather suitcase from under the table, opened it and very slowly and carefully produced from it some three dozen massive volumes which, smilingly, he piled one by one into a sort of defensive rampart on the edge of his desk.

"All these books," he said, patting the pile as though it were a horse, "contain parallel examples which show conclusively that my client is innocent. But," he went on, holding up an admonishing forefinger, "as the innocence of my client is perfectly obvious to the jury, I needn't weary you with a lot of details."

He picked up all the books and returned them to the suitcase. The jury were much impressed.

"Gentlemen of the jury," Sir Magnus went on, "you have before you the defendant Adrian Rookwhistle. Now it must be obvious to anyone that he is a fine, honest, upstanding young man, who has the one special quality which we all admire and which so few of us possess. He has courage. Which one of you gentlemen would willingly dive into a threshing, storm-tossed sea in order to rescue a dumb animal? Now, as I said to you, my client's inno-

cence is obvious. You know this and I know this. The cru
of the matter, as I am sure you will all have perceived
is whether or not the elephant in question is the savage
uncontrolled and uncontrollable animal that it is mad
out to be. I would therefore like to call just a few wit
nesses to reassure you on this point.

"Mr. Pucklehammer," he called.

Mr. Pucklehammer came into the box, beamed at Adria
and made gestures of encouragement. He took the oath an
gave the closest attention to Sir Magnus.

"I believe, Mr. Pucklehammer," said Sir Magnus, "tha
you were with the defendant Rookwhistle on the day whe
he took delivery of the elephant."

"Yes, I was," said Mr. Pucklehammer. "He brought i
down to my yard."

"Your yard?" said Sir Magnus. "What is your occupa
tion exactly?"

"I am a coffin maker and carpenter," said Mr. Puckle
hammer.

"So then, your yard would presumably be full of all th
accoutrements of your trade?"

"What was that again, sir?" said Mr. Pucklehamme

"Was your yard full of coffins and similar items of car
pentry?" said Sir Magnus.

"Yes," said Mr. Pucklehammer.

"I have often wondered," said the judge, "how the
manage to make coffins that shape."

"I am sure, my lord," said Sir Magnus smoothly, "tha
Mr. Pucklehammer would be delighted to give you a prac
tical demonstration of this at the end of the proceedings.

"Most kind," said the judge.

"Now you say," Sir Magnus went on, "that the elephan
Rosy was brought into your yard. During the time sh
was there, two days I believe it to be, what was her de
meanour?"

"Bread, mostly," said Mr. Pucklehammer. "Then w
found she liked vegetables as well."

"No, no," said Sir Magnus. "What was her behaviou
like?"

"Wonderful," said Mr. Pucklehammer enthusiastically. "She's a lovely animal."

"So she didn't cause you any distress while she stayed your yard?"

"None whatsoever," said Mr. Pucklehammer. "Good as old she was. Helpful too. She helped Adrian wash the ap down."

"Wash the trap down what?" enquired the judge.

"Well, we were cleaning the trap, see, sir, and so Rosy uirted water on it with her trunk."

"Extraordinary," said the judge. "Have you ever in our experience, Sir Magnus, come across an elephant ashing down a trap?"

"No, my lord, I can't say that I have," said Sir Magnus, but I believe them to be immensely sagacious beasts."

"Extraordinary," said the judge again. "Pray continue."

"So, during the whole two days she was in your yard, he did no damage to you or to your property?" said Sir Magnus.

"None at all," said Mr. Pucklehammer determinedly. I told you, she's as timid as a mouse. Rosy'd never hurt nybody deliberately."

"Thank you," said Sir Magnus. He glanced at Sir Augustus interrogatively, but Sir Augustus, who had not nown about the Pucklehammer episode, was at a slight oss as to how to cross-examine, so he merely shook his head nournfully.

"Call," said Sir Magnus, "Emily Nelly Delilah Trickle-rot."

"Who the hell's that?" whispered Adrian.

"Black Nell," said Sir Magnus.

Black Nell, like a chirpy moth-eaten little bird, climbed nto the witness-box and peered over the edge of it with ome difficulty.

"I understand," said Sir Magnus, "that you encountered he defendant Rookwhistle and his elephant when you vere on your way to Tuttlepenny Fair."

"That's right," said Black Nell.

"Now, you are by trade a fortune-teller?" enquired Sir Magnus.

"Witch," said Black Nell.

A rustle immediately ran through the court. The jury gave her their absolutely undivided attention.

"Witch?" said the judge.

"Yes, your honour," said Black Nell. "I am a white witch. Black Nell's me name."

"I find this very confusing," said the judge, looking at Sir Magnus. "Would you like to elucidate?"

"Certainly, my lord. There are apparently two forms of witches. The black kind who do evil deeds or are reputed to do evil deeds, and the white ones who do good deeds. This lady is a white witch and during the course of her witchcraft she also tells fortunes."

"Do you use a crystal ball?" enquired the judge.

"Sometimes," said Black Nell. "Not always though."

"I had one once," said the judge musingly, "but I could never see anything in it."

"It's a question of concentration," said Black Nell. "You should try it in a diamond ring some time."

"Diamond ring? Really?" said the judge. "I must try that."

"May I continue, my lord?" enquired Sir Magnus with a long-suffering air.

"By all means, by all means," said the judge.

"Now, when you met the defendant and his elephant, what happened?"

"I was asleep, see," said Black Nell, "and suddenly my whole caravan started to shake."

"We now appear to be suffering from a surfeit of wheeled vehicles," said the judge. "This caravan has not appeared before, has it?"

"No," said Sir Magnus. "It is the caravan belonging to the witness."

"Why was it shaking?" enquired the judge.

"Because the elephant was scratching herself against it," said Black Nell.

"Do elephants scratch themselves against caravans?" the judge asked Sir Magnus.

"I believe, my lord, that all pachyderms, if they find a suitably abrasive surface, will ease any minor skin irritation by rubbing themselves against it," said Sir Magnus.

"We are certainly learning a lot about elephants," said the judge with satisfaction. "Well, go on."

"When you finally came out of your caravan," said Sir Magnus, "did the elephant attack you?"

"Lord bless us, no," said Black Nell. "Tame as a rabbit she was. We all sat down and had breakfast together."

"So she did no damage to your caravan, nor did she attempt in any way to harm you?"

"No," said Black Nell. "That creature wouldn't harm a fly."

"Thank you," said Sir Magnus, and again glanced at Sir Augustus.

But Sir Augustus was feeling that he was liable to get bogged down in a lot of irrelevant details about witchcraft and again refused to cross-examine.

"Will you now call," said Sir Magnus, "Peregrine Filigree."

Mr. Filigree, wreathed in smiles, undulated his way into the court and wedged himself with a certain amount of difficulty into the witness-box.

"Hello, Adrian," he shouted, waving a fat hand. "How's it going?"

The judge peered at him.

"Mr. Filigree," he said, "I would be grateful if you would confine yourself to giving evidence and not carry on an exchange of saucy badinage with the defendant."

"I am sorry, your lordship," said Mr. Filigree, chastened.

The clerk of the court held out the Bible for him to take the oath.

"You haven't by any chance got a prayer wheel, have you?"

"What's that?" said the judge.

"A prayer wheel, my lord," said Sir Magnus. "I believe

it to be something that is used quite extensively in Tib
and similar places where Buddhism is the basic religion.

"What do you want a prayer wheel for?" asked th
judge.

"Because," said Mr. Filigree, "I am a Buddhist."

"I don't really think, Sir Magnus," said the judge
"that we can expect the clerk of the court to go runnin
around at this late date in order to find a prayer wheel.
am not altogether sure that it would be legal either."

"Perhaps, Mr. Filigree," said Sir Magnus, "you woul
be kind enough to take the oath on the Bible, and preten
that it is a prayer wheel."

"Very well," said Mr. Filigree. "If it's going to be o
any help to you."

"Now," said the judge, "perhaps we can proceed."

"Mr. Filigree," said Sir Magnus, "on the night of th
29th April the defendant, Adrian Rookwhistle, and h
elephant arrived at the *Unicorn and Harp*, a hostelry whic.
you and your daughter run?"

"That's right," said Mr. Filigree, beaming. "It was
most lovely surprise."

"Would you like to tell his lordship and the jury, i
your own words, exactly what happened."

"I'd love to," said Mr. Filigree.

He clasped his fat hands together as though in praye
and fixed his round eyes on the judge.

"You see," he said, "I haven't had an elephant for years.'

"Do you mind elaborating that extraordinary state
ment?" said the judge.

"Well, you see," said Mr. Filigree, "I once had one hun
dred and one of them; the chief one, of course, was Poo
Ting. But that was some considerable time ago."

"Am I correct in believing, Sir Magnus, that the witnes
is saying on oath that he had one hundred and one ele
phants?"

"Yes, my lord."

"It seems to me," said the judge, "and please d
correct me, Sir Magnus, if I am wrong, that the defendan
had considerable trouble with one elephant. How is i

at this gentleman managed successfully to keep one
undred and one?"

"I believe, my lord, that he kept them while in India
ı a previous incarnation," said Sir Magnus suavely.
Though that is not the really important point at all. I
ıerely brought this witness into the box as he has had
ıch considerable experience with elephants."

The judge was now even more confused than the jury.

"I suppose," he said, "he is what you might call an
xpert witness."

"Exactly so, my lord."

The jury had been nodding and whispering like a barn-
ıl of hens and the foreman got to his feet.

"Excuse me, my lord," he said, "but could we have one
oint made clear?"

"Yes, I think so," said the judge doubtfully. "There are
everal points which I would like to get clear. What is it
ou wish to know?"

"Well, we're a bit puzzled like with this incarnation
hing."

"A good question," said the judge, and looked hopefully
t Sir Magnus.

"In parts of the world," said Sir Magnus oratorically,
where they believe in Buddhism as opposed to Christian-
ty, one of the beliefs is that you live a whole series of
ves."

"Quite right," said Mr. Filigree.

"Therefore, in calling Mr. Filigree as a witness, we are
xceedingly lucky. Nay, I would go further and say that
his is probably the most extraordinary piece of evidence
ver to have been put in front of a jury. You are having
he benefit of Mr. Filigree's expert knowledge of elephants,
athered over the course of years, and as you have gleaned,
entlemen of the jury, not just one elephant, not even a
ıassing acquaintance with a pachyderm, but he had in
ıis possession one hundred and one of them. Now you
vill all instantly perceive that a man who has possessed
ıo less than one hundred and one elephants is in a much
ıetter position to advise us more humble mortals, who

have not even had the privilege of keeping one elephant

The foreman of the jury looked faintly stunned. H opened his mouth once or twice like an exhausted gol fish and then sat down.

"Mr. Filigree," said Sir Magnus, "I have pointed o to the jury your expertise on all matters appertaining elephants. I would now like you to tell the jury wh your impression of the elephant in question, Rosy, was

"Rosy," squeaked Mr. Filigree, his face growing ev pinker, "is one of the sweetest, most adorable elephants have ever met in my life. If she had a fault at all, it w the minor one of not having any tusks."

"Why is the lack of tusks a fault?" enquired the judg

"You cannot bore holes in them," said Mr. Filigree.

"Sir Magnus," said the judge, "I do wish you wou' exercise a little control over your witnesses. It seems to m they are dragging in a lot of extraneous matter which ha nothing to do with the case in question."

"Of course, my lord," said Sir Magnus.

"I had no wish to appear harsh towards Rosy," said M Filigree earnestly, waving his fingers at the judge.

"Would you have said, then that she was a viciou creature?" enquired Sir Magnus.

"Vicious!" said Mr. Filigree, his face growing deep re at the mere thought. "Rosy vicious! She's one of th nicest elephants I have ever met."

"Thank you," said Sir Magnus. "And you speak, course, as we all know, from a vast experience of keepin elephants."

Sir Augustus did not really want to cross-examine bu since he had been forced to let two witnesses slip throug his fingers, he felt he ought to put up some sort of shov He rose to his feet and glared at Mr. Filigree.

"Mr. Filigree," he said, cuttingly, "would you not sa that if we do not share your beliefs in reincarnation, tha the evidence you have given is null and void?"

"No, no," fluted Mr. Filigree earnestly. "You canno help it if you don't believe. You see, I have positive ev dence. I was telling Adrian about my cat. That is a very good example."

"Sir Augustus," said the judge, "I don't know why it is, but every time you get up to examine a witness, you manage to introduce a new animal of some sort. I find this very confusing."

"My lord," said Sir Augustus, "I was merely trying to make clear . . ."

"Well, you are not making it clear," snapped the judge. "We have now got a cat mixed up in it."

"It was a beautiful cat," said Mr. Filigree. "He recognised me instantly."

"The cat has absolutely nothing whatsoever to do with the case," said the judge. "I find your line of questioning, Sir Augustus, most irrelevant."

"As your lordship pleases," said Sir Augustus with restraint. "Then I have no further questions." He sat down and glowered at Sir Magnus, who was lying back with his eyes closed and a beatific smile on his face.

"The witness may stand down," said the judge. He shuffled through his notes and then looked at Sir Magnus.

"Do you intend to call any more witnesses, Sir Magnus?" he asked.

"Yes, my lord. I have several more."

The judge looked at his watch.

"Well, I would be glad if you would make it as rapid as possible," he said.

The next witness that Sir Magnus introduced was Honoria, and to Adrian's astonishment, for his heart had sunk when her name was called, she proved to be an admirable witness. It was not until afterwards that Adrian learned that a bottle and a half of gin had gone into the making of her performance, but she stood in the witness-box, her magnificent bosom heaving in a low-cut dress that had every juryman's eye fixed longingly upon it. She was in turn soulful and vibrant. Her eulogy on Rosy and on her own friendship with her was a masterpiece. She stood heaving and panting in the witness-box, her head held up proudly while tears trickled in vast quantities down her cheeks as she described how she and she alone had been responsible for the wrecking of the theatre by her introduction of gin into Rosy's diet. By the time she had finished there was not an unmoistened eye among the jury and even the judge had to blow his nose vigorously before dismissing Honoria.

The next witness to enter the box was Ethelbert. He corroborated Honoria's story and even added a few embellishments of his own. He was reprimanded at one point for calling the judge "darling boy", but nevertheless it was obvious to everyone in court that he was an honest and enthusiastic witness.

Sir Magnus had wanted to call Samantha, but Adrian had put his foot down. He was not going to have Samantha standing in a witness-box, being bombarded with questions from Sir Augustus. As it turned out, he need not really have worried, because Sir Augustus, after his futile attempt to cross-examine Mr. Filigree, sat hunched like a depressed crow, and shook his head every time he was asked to cross-examine.

"Now, my lord," said Sir Magnus after Ethelbert had left the box, "we are starting to get a clear picture in our minds."

"I suppose you are right, Sir Magnus," said the judge doubtfully.

"I think I have shown beyond a shadow of a doubt that the elephant in question is one of the most charming and tractable animals of its kind. On the occasions when it caused a certain amount of damage it is quite obvious that this was inadvertent and the animal can be in no way blamed for it, nor indeed can its owner."

"Well, that point may have been cleared up to your satisfaction, Sir Magnus," said the judge, "but not as yet to mine."

"Very well, my lord," said Sir Magnus, "then if I may crave the court's indulgence, I will recall Lord Fennel tree."

Lord Fenneltree drifted amiably back into the box

polished his monocle, inserted it in his eye and beamed round.

"This is jolly," he remarked. "I didn't think I'd be up here twice."

"Lord Fenneltree," said Sir Magnus, "will you kindly take your mind back to the night of 28th April. The night of your daughter's birthday ball."

"Yes, yes," said Lord Fenneltree. "I have it clearly in mind."

"Now, you had arranged for yourself and for the defendant to ride into the ballroom with the elephant, had you not?"

"Indubitably," said his lordship.

"Did the elephant prior to that display any evil characteristics?"

"What, old Rosy?" said his lordship. "Of course not. Wonderful animal."

Sir Magnus smiled with quiet satisfaction.

"But on the night of the ball," he continued, "did the defendant display any qualms about the projected adventure?"

"Qualms," said his lordship chuckling. "He was a quivering mass of nerves. He worries too much, that boy, you know. That's half his trouble. I keep telling him it's very fatiguing."

"In other words," said Sir Magnus, "he did suggest to you that it might be an unwise manoeuvre to introduce the elephant into the ballroom."

"Frequently," said his lordship. "About ten times a day on an average."

"For what reason?" enquired Sir Magnus.

"Well, he didn't think my wife would like it," said Lord Fenneltree. "My wife has that effect on some people."

"I can well imagine," said Sir Magnus dryly. "So before the actual night of the ball, he had made several endeavours to stop the plan."

"That is quite correct."

"Was he still alarmed on the evening of the ball itself?"

"Alarmed is a mild way of putting it," said his lordship.

"And of course when he found that she was drunk it was all I could do to persuade him to go ahead with the plan."

"I see," said Sir Magnus silkily. "Then the defendant in actual fact wanted to call the whole thing off prior to the ball, and on the evening of the ball, finding the animal was intoxicated, he again made serious attempts to persuade you to abandon the project."

"Yes," said Lord Fenneltree.

"So, in other words," said Sir Magnus, "one could really say that the havoc created at the ball was neither the fault of the animal, who was under the influence of alcohol, nor the defendant, since you were directly responsible."

There was a pause while Lord Fenneltree mused on this for a moment. It was an original approach that had escaped him hitherto.

"Come to think of it," he said at last, breathing on his monocle, polishing it and screwing it back into his eye, "come to think of it, you are quite right. The whole thing was my fault."

"Rupert," came the bugle-like call of Lady Fenneltree from the body of the court. "Watch what you are saying."

"Who is creating this interruption?" enquired the judge, peering round myopically.

"I think it's the witness's wife," said Sir Magnus with satisfaction.

"My lord," boomed Lady Fenneltree, "my husband is being led astray."

"Madam, do you mind being quiet?" enquired the judge.

"I will not be quiet," shouted Lady Fenneltree. "I have never met such an inane judge in all my life. I will not stand by and see a miscarriage of justice sliding under your nose."

"Now, now, dear," shouted Lord Fenneltree, waving at her in a placating manner, "just keep calm."

"I will not keep calm," shouted Lady Fenneltree.

"Lady Fenneltree," said the judge, "this case is quite confused enough without your adding to it."

"You're the one who's confused it," shouted Lady Fenneltree.

"Madam," said the judge icily, "if you do not be quiet and sit down, I shall have you removed from the court."

Lady Fenneltree grasped her parasol in front of her like a spear.

"You will do so at your peril," she said.

"Remove that woman," said the judge excitedly.

Two large constables moved in on Lady Fenneltree who, displaying a remarkable agility for her bulk, danced back three paces and then lunged with her parasol. The point of it caught the largest constable a shade north of his umbilical and he doubled up, completely winded. Lady Fenneltree then wheeled and hit the other constable over the back of the neck. It took the two constables several minutes to subdue her and drag her ignominiously from the court, and the jury watched breathless and fascinated. As she was dragged out, her last despairing cry was carried down. "Rupert, don't you dare say anything."

"Lord Fenneltree," said the judge, "I apologise to you for the necessity of having to deal with your wife in that fashion."

"My dear chap, don't mention it," said Lord Fenneltree. "I am lost in admiration. Would it be possible for me to have the names of those two constables before I leave?"

"After that unfortunate incident, may I proceed, my lord?" enquired Sir Magnus.

"Pray do so," said the judge.

So we now know," said Sir Magnus looking at Lord Fenneltree, "that you are directly responsible for all the damage caused by the elephant at your ball."

"Yes," said Lord Fenneltree, "I don't think you can put it fairer than that and I for one am only sorry poor old Adrian has ended up in this way. He's a charming young man and it was a most delightful elephant."

"Thank you, Lord Fenneltree," said Sir Magnus. "I have no more questions to ask you."

He sat down and with an air of triumph took out his snuff-box, plugged some snuff up his nose and then gave an enormous and triumphant sneeze and smiled winningly at Sir Augustus.

"Well, um, yes," said the judge. "Have you anything to say, Sir Augustus?"

Sir Augustus, who had been looking more and more miserable, rose to his feet, quivering with ill-suppressed indignation.

"My lord," he said shakily, "I have little to add to my previous summary of the case. I can only say at this juncture that I hope that my learned friend's introduction of so many dubious witnesses has not in any way damaged his case in the eyes of the jury. The introduction of white witches, strolling players of doubtful background and people who believe in reincarnation should, I would think, undermine rather than buttress the case for the defence."

Sir Magnus rose to his feet. "If I may interrupt for a moment," he said, "I would also like to point out to my learned friend that among white witches, strolling players and believers in reincarnation, there was Lord Fenneltree."

He sat down and Sir Augustus gave him a look of such scorching ferocity that Adrian was surprised not to see Sir Magnus disappear in a tiny puff of black smoke.

"It seems to me," said Sir Augustus, "that the jury can only bring in one verdict, and that is that the defendant, Adrian Rookwhistle, is guilty."

Sir Magnus got to his feet.

"I think, my lord, gentlemen of the jury, that I have made my side of things more than clear. I feel from the evidence that we have heard that I have more than vindicated the good character of the defendant and of the noble creature who is his companion."

The foreman of the jury had been opening and shutting his mouth for some considerable time. He now got to his feet.

"What is it, what is it?" said the judge testily.

"Excuse me, your honour," said the foreman, "but is the elephant in question the one what's been down on the beach for the last week?"

"Yes," said Sir Magnus, "she enjoys going down there and playing with the little children."

The foreman sat down and had a whispered conclave

with the rest of the jury. Sir Magnus watched them with a beaming, paternal smile.

"I think, my lord," he said smoothly, "that I can rely on the good sense of the jury to bring in the right verdict."

"Yes, yes, well," said the judge. He shuffled his notes in a rather flustered fashion. "I would be glad if you would stop whispering among yourselves and pay attention to me," he said to the jury.

The foreman of the jury got up once more.

"Excuse me, my lord," he said, "but we have already reached a verdict."

"You what?" said the judge petulantly. "I've got to sum up."

"Very well, sir," said the foreman and sat down again.

The judge cleared his throat, peered at his notes and then sat back in his chair and closed his eyes.

"Basically, what you have got to decide," he said, "is whether or not the defendant, Adrian Rookwhistle, is guilty." He opened his eyes and cast a glance of triumph at the jury. "That," he continued, "might be described as the crux of the whole case. However, there are certain things that you have to consider before you say definitely one way or the other that he is guilty or not guilty. We have heard a lot of evidence." He shuffled his notes in a rather hopeless way. "A lot of evidence," he repeated, "some of it for, and some of it against. Now it is not my job to tell you what to think, only to guide you along the right lines. You are perfectly free to think that the defendant is guilty even if he is not guilty. On the other hand, you can equally well think him not guilty, if he is guilty. That is the beauty of our legal system. I am merely here to act as a guide through the intricacies of the law." He paused and coughed gently to himself for several seconds, shuffling again through his notes, many of which slipped off his desk to the floor.

"Now, we have heard evidence which proves conclusively that Adrian Rookwhistle, being in possession of the elephant and therefore, presumably, in control of it, allowed it to do considerable damage both to human beings and to property.

But your astuteness will make you perceive that this evidence can be counteracted by other evidence which proves conclusively that the animal in question was not evilly disposed and that the defendant was forced into these invidious situations."

The judge paused and cast a sharp look at the foreman of the jury.

"You are following my line of reasoning?" he inquired. The jury nodded as one man.

"Now, it is incumbent upon you," said the judge waving a finger at them, "to bring in a verdict of not guilty should you think that the defendant, Adrian Rookwhistle, was in fact, er, um, erum, not guilty. On the other hand, should you think him guilty, you must show no fear or favour and bring in a verdict of guilty, taking into consideration, as I have said, every aspect of the case. There are many points which you should consider and consider carefully, for example there is the point, on which I am not at all clear, as to whether or not elephants like gin. Again you might like to consider what I consider to be the vital evidence about the elephant sliding on the parquet. Now we have been assured by no lesser legal authority than Sir Magnus that elephants can slide on parquet. Therefore, if we accept this as a fact, we are driven to the conclusion that the elephant in question did slide on the parquet and as Sir Augustus has so penetratingly pointed out, caused considerable damage.

"Then there is the evidence of the caravan. You might say to yourselves, either individually or collectively, did the elephant really scratch itself against the caravan, or was this an unprovoked attack? The fact that the witness who was in the caravan at the time suffered no damage should in no way influence you. She may indeed have been the victim of an unprovoked attack which she did not recognise or, as has been suggested by the defence, the elephant was merely scratching itself. Now you, gentlemen of the jury, have a solemn duty ahead of you. You have heard both the case for the prosecution and for the defence and it is up to you to gather up all the details that have been vouchsafed to you and weave them into a whole. My job is merely to clarify things for you. So I will now ask you to go away and quietly consider all the facts of the case and if you bring in a verdict of guilty, who is to blame you? On the other hand, if you decide in your wisdom, and being in possession of the full facts, to bring in a verdict of not guilty, no finger of condemnation can be pointed at you. In closing I can only say that I hope I have been of some help to you in forming the right decision. You may now retire to consider your verdict."

The foreman of the jury got to his feet.

"We have decided not to retire, your lordship," he said.

"Most irregular," said the judge. "You should have time for consultation and consideration."

"We have considered, my lord," said the foreman.

"Well," said the judge reluctantly, "what is your verdict?"

"Well sir, we would like to get one thing quite clear in our minds before announcing our verdict. Is the elephant in question definitely the one that has been playing with my kids on the beach?"

"I think, Sir Magnus," said the judge, "that you are best qualified to answer that question."

"Yes," said Sir Magnus. "If you possess children who have been playing on the beach recently, then assuredly they will have been playing with the elephant in question."

"In that case," said the foreman of the jury, "our verdict is not guilty."

There was an outburst of clapping in the court in which the judge joined absent-mindedly. When the noise had died down, the judge cleared his throat and peered at Adrian.

"Adrian Rookwhistle," he said. "You have been found guilty of the charges brought against you."

"Beg pardon, my lord," said the foreman of the jury, "but we have found him not guilty."

"Oh," said the judge, "did you? Well you have been found not guilty of the charges brought against you and so I find it my bounden duty to sentence you," he paused and collected his thoughts, "so I find it my bounden duty to discharge you without a stain on your character."

The judge peered at the jury.

"You have been an honest and upright jury," he said, "and have carried out your duties extremely well. I therefore discharge you and absolve you from jury duties for the next year."

He shuffled his papers in an abstracted sort of way and then leant forward to the clerk of the court.

"Are there any more cases on the list?" he asked in a hoarse whisper.

"No, my lord," said the clerk of the court. "This is the last of them."

"Good," said the judge. He sat up and peered at Adrian. "There is just one more thing," he said. "I wonder if you could see your way to accede me a minor request?"

"Certainly, my lord," said Adrian.

"I would very much like to see the elephant in question," said the judge, adding shyly, "you see I have never seen an elephant."

"Certainly, my lord," said Adrian. "I am going to go and tell her the good news now, if your lordship would like to join me."

"Splendid," squeaked the judge. "I will meet you outside in a few minutes, Mr. Rookwhistle."

He leapt out of his chair as the court rose, and scuttled out of his door.

21 THE VERDICT

Adrian stepped out of the dock feeling slightly dazed and was ushered out of the court on a wave of good-will, Sir Magnus holding him by one arm and Lord Fenneltree holding him by the other, while Mr. Filigree and Ethelbert danced about getting in everybody's way. They all ended up on the pavement outside the court and there was Samantha. She smiled at Adrian.

"I'm delighted you got off," she said.

"Are you really?" said Adrian.

"Yes," she said.

Adrian stood staring at her great, green, gold-flecked eyes and felt himself going red to the roots of his hair.

"I . . . I'm very glad that you're glad," he said inanely.

For some reason Samantha was blushing too.

"Yes, I'm very glad," she said.

"When you have driven that point home sufficiently," said Sir Magnus, "I would suggest that we all repair to my place to have a celebratory drink."

"Sir Magnus," said Samantha, "we are really most grateful to you for having got Adrian and Rosy off like that."

"Nonsense," said Sir Magnus. "A mere bagatelle."

"You know," said Lord Fenneltree, "I cannot help feeling that I didn't contribute very much to your defence."

Ethelbert was convulsed with laughter to such an extent that he had to be held up by Honoria.

"I think, dear boy," said Lord Fenneltree, "I think, if you don't mind, I will come along with you for a few days, wherever you are going. It will give my wife a little time to collect her thoughts."

"Well, I know where *I'm* going," said Adrian suddenly, with decision, "I am going back to the *Unicorn and Harp*— if the owners will have me."

"And Rosy?" said Mr. Filigree anxiously. "You will bring Rosy, won't you?"

"If I may," said Adrian, looking at Samantha.

"I think we can find room for you," said Samantha.

"I suppose it isn't possible that you would have a small inglenook that I could occupy for a brief period?" said Lord Fenneltree, staring at Samantha earnestly through his monocle.

"I tell you what," said Mr. Filigree, squeaking with excitement at the thought. "Why don't we all go back there? There's plenty of room for everyone and we could have a *party*."

"What a very excellent idea," said Sir Magnus.

"The *Sploshport Queen* is leaving soon," said Lord Fenneltree. "We'll cross on her and then I will take the ladies in my landau while you all go by train."

"I don't think a train's going to carry Rosy," said Adrian. "No, you all go on ahead and I'll walk Rosy there."

"Rubbish, my boy," said Sir Magnus waving his cane. "I am on intimate terms with the station master. I'm quite sure we can get Rosy fitted up, if not in a first-class carriage, at least in some portion of the train."

At this point the judge, wearing to Adrian's amazement a loud check suit and looking as though he had got into it by mistake, joined them. Adrian explained what the plan was and the judge blinked wistfully at Samantha.

"I suppose, Lord Turvey," said Samantha tactfully, "you wouldn't like to come to the *Unicorn and Harp* as well?"

"My dear child," said the judge, "I would be absolutely enchanted. It so happens that I have not got to dispense justice for several days and a little rest in the country would do me a world of good."

"Excellent," said Sir Magnus. "It will give me an opportunity to discuss the next case with you."

"I don't know whether that would be very ethical," said the judge.

"Well, there's scarcely any point in your coming unless you are going to discuss the case with me," said Sir Magnus.

"Well, in that case," said the judge, "I suppose it will be all right."

Reluctantly leaving Honoria, Black Nell and Samantha with Lord Fenneltree, Adrian, accompanied by Sir Magnus, Lord Turvey, Mr. Pucklehammer, Ethelbert and Mr. Filigree, went back to Sir Magnus's house.

As soon as they arrived Adrian rushed to the stable and was greeted by a delighted squeal from Rosy.

"Well, you miserable, destructive, drunken creature," he shouted affectionately, throwing his arms around her trunk and giving her a hug, "we've got off scot free."

Rosy, who had not been particularly worried about the outcome of the case, nevertheless realised that Adrian was in good spirits and so she flapped her ears and squeaked again.

"Fascinating," said the judge, who had followed Adrian into the stable and was standing at Rosy's rear end gazing up at her. "Sir Magnus was quite right about that trunk never being able to reach the chandelier."

"That's the tail," said Adrian. "The trunk's this end."

"Oh," said the judge. He fumbled in his pocket and produced a pair of lorgnettes which he put up to his eyes and peered through them with considerable interest at Rosy's backside.

"You're absolutely right," he said. "It's got hairs on the end."

He walked round to the front and peered at Rosy through his lorgnettes.

"Fascinating," he said. "Absolutely fascinating."

"Well, come along," said Sir Magnus impatiently bustling into the stable. "If we don't get going we'll miss the boat."

So Adrian grasped Rosy's ear and, followed by his retinue, led Rosy down to the docks. The voyage was uneventful except for sea shanties sung by Sir Magnus and the judge. When they landed at the other side the ladies were left with Lord Fenneltree and the others made haste to the station.

Here, by dint of much roaring and cajoling on the part of Sir Magnus, they eventually hitched an open wagon to the three forty-five to Monkspepper. Rosy entered it without any fuss whatsoever.

"Now," said Sir Magnus, looking at the station master, "chairs, Bert, chairs."

"Chairs, Sir Magnus?" said the station master, bewildered. "What sort of chairs?"

"Chairs, man. Out of the waiting-room," said Sir Magnus. "Something to sit on."

"But aren't you travelling in a compartment, Sir Magnus?" asked the station master.

"Of course not," said Sir Magnus. "If this truck is good enough for Rosy, it's good enough for me. All I want is a chair to sit on."

The flurried station master procured a bench and two chairs from the waiting-room and these were installed alongside Rosy in the truck. Then Ethelbert, Mr. Pucklehammer and Adrian sat themselves down on the bench and Sir Magnus perched scowling on one chair and the judge on the other. Sir Magnus took a gigantic pinch of snuff, sneezed and said to the station master, "All right, Bert, you can let her go now."

The fact that the train was already twenty minutes overdue and most of the passengers exceedingly restive had apparently escaped his attention. The station master, mopping his brow, blew a tremulous blast on his whistle, waved his green flag and the train shuffled and clanked and swayed its way out into the countryside.

It was a beautiful hot summer's day and everywhere was green and gold and the sky was as blue as a Siamese cat's eye. It amazed Adrian that they could, in the short space of a couple of hours, whisk themselves across the many tedious miles of countryside that he had tramped with Rosy. They got out at the little country station for the village of Parson's Farthing, and walked a mile and a half down the dusty road to the *Unicorn and Harp*.

"Darling boy," said Ethelbert, round-eyed, "I had never realised the countryside was so big, and simply hundreds of leaves."

"The leaves are much bigger in Papua," said Mr. Filigree. "Very much bigger." He stretched out his fat little arms in order to show how enormous the leaves had been.

"I don't know about you," said Sir Magnus to Mr. Pucklehammer, "but I feel a flagon of ale would come in very handy."

"It always does," said Mr. Pucklehammer. "It has been my experience in life that some things are handy and some aren't, but you can't go wrong with a flagon of ale."

"Do you know," said the judge, peering at Rosy, "without my glasses I still have difficulty in telling which end I'm looking at."

"Which end of what?" asked Sir Magnus.

"Rosy," said the judge.

"I do hope," fluted Mr. Filigree, dancing up the road, pigeon-toed, "that Samantha's got something to eat. I know we have plenty to drink."

"Well, as long as we've got plenty to drink," said Sir Magnus, "I don't see that it really matters. You don't by any chance keep cherry brandy, do you?"

"Oh yes," said Mr. Filigree. "As a matter of fact we have got rather a lot of it. I ordered three barrels once, but unfortunately nobody seemed to like it."

"Just shows," said Sir Magnus, taking snuff and sneezing, "people nowadays are lacking in good taste."

At last they rounded the final corner and there was the *Unicorn and Harp*, like a friendly black and white cat squatting under its golden hat of thatch.

"Hurrah!" yelled Ethelbert exuberantly, the country air obviously having gone to his head. "We've arrived."

At the sound of Ethelbert's shrill cry, the door of the *Unicorn and Harp* opened and Lord Fenneltree and Samantha appeared.

"Have a good journey?" shouted his lordship.

"Splendid," bellowed Sir Magnus waving his stick in greeting. "I have decided that it is more comfortable to travel in an open truck with an elephant than in a first-class carriage with a lot of bores."

"Or *sows*, for that matter," said the judge, and was convulsed with laughter.

"Sam, dear," panted Mr. Filigree anxiously, "what about food?"

"Oh, you don't have to worry about that," said Samantha. "Lord Fenneltree has been exceptionally kind. We stopped on the way and he insisted on buying a lot of things for us to eat."

She led the way round to the meadow at the back of the house and there they saw a long trestle-table that had been set up and covered with a snow-white cloth. It was groaning under the weight of food. There was a small platoon of cold roast pheasants, a dish full of plovers' eggs, piles of scaly oysters, a gigantic sugar-cured ham, whose flesh was as delicately tender and pink as a sunset cloud, and a great saddle of cold roast beef which must have come from the biggest bullock in the country.

"This is extremely kind of you, Lord Fenneltree," said Adrian. "Considering that I won the case."

"Dear boy," said his lordship earnestly. "I wouldn't have provided it if you had lost the case, but I thought a light snack would help us all to recover from the journey."

"My joy would be complete," said Sir Magnus indistinctly through a mouthful of oysters and plover eggs, "if I could have a tiny splash of the cherry brandy which Mr. Filigree told us about."

"Certainly, certainly," said Mr. Filigree, wiping pie crumbs from his mouth, and he danced into the house and reappeared with a small barrel. This was soon set up and Sir Magnus took up sentry duty beside it.

The shadows were lengthening across the emerald green grass and a sense of peace and goodwill settled over the whole company. Mr. Pucklehammer, waving a large tankard of ale in time, was humming softly to himself. Black Nell, who had just recovered from an acute attack of hiccups, was reading Honoria's palm and predicting a future career for her that even Sarah Bernhardt would have envied. Lord Fenneltree was lying on the grass apparently in a trance, staring up at the sky and listening to a long and complicated lecture on the law by the judge. Adrian sat opposite Samantha and watched the sunlight scattering itself through the leaves of the tree and dappling her copper-coloured hair. Presently the sight of her beauty was too much for him and he got up under the pretext of seeing how Rosy was doing, and went down to the barn.

Rosy had joined the party for a brief period, but when she found that the delicacies on the table did not appeal to her palate and that Adrian would not allow her to have more than three pints of beer, she had wandered down to

the barn to console herself with a pile of carrots and mangolds. Adrian marched into the barn and stood staring
at his great, grey protégée. She flashed him a quick
look from her tiny twinkling eyes, flapped her ears and gave
a small squeak of greeting.

"It's all very well for you," said Adrian bitterly, and
started to pace up and down the barn feverishly. "You're
all right as long as you get enough to eat and all the
booze you want. You are quite happy. But what about me?
Have you ever considered me?"

He paused dramatically and looked at Rosy. Rosy's
stomach rumbled in a musical fashion and she put out her
trunk and delicately touched Adrian's hair.

"There she is, out there," said Adrian, "as callous as
anything. She gives me no encouragement at all. I really
don't think that we can stay here after all."

Rosy gave a long sigh. Adrian resumed his pacing.

"Well, perhaps we could stay here for a day or so," he
said, the thought of being apart from Samantha again
making him feel slightly sick. "What I cannot understand is what is the *matter* with her? One would think *I*
had got *you* into all this trouble, instead of the other way
round; and anyway, we are free now, so what's all the
fuss about?"

Rosy had placed a large mangold on the floor and was
delicately rolling it to and fro with her forefoot, but she
gave a small squeak just to show Adrian that she was
paying attention.

"No," said Adrian, firmly, "if we stay here, there must
be a clear understanding. I am not going to be hounded
by that ungrateful creature."

Rosy sensed Adrian's annoyance, but she realised that
it was not directed at her, so she was quite content.

"I shall be firm with her," continued Adrian, drawing
himself up and sticking his chin out commandingly. "I shall
tell her that she is behaving like a child. *That's* what I'll
do." He glared at Rosy triumphantly and Rosy gave another small squeak by way of applause.

"You have to be firm with women," said Adrian. "Look

at Lady Fenneltree. *That* was the way to deal with *her*. They get above themselves." Even in his distraught condition, Adrian could not see a single point of resemblance between Lady Fenneltree and Samantha.

"I shall go now, Rosy," he said, wagging his finger at her, "and get our position quite clear. Otherwise I don't intend to spend another night under this roof."

This sudden determination which had overcome him was due principally to the fact that he had been so captivated watching Samantha's face and the way she laughed and flirted with Sir Magnus, the way her teeth gleamed white as milk when she smiled, the warm colour of her hair, that he had inadvertently drunk a pint of ale belonging to Sir Magnus, which had been heavily laced with cherry brandy.

"I will," he said, striding to the door and turning to glare at Rosy, "return with my decision soon."

Endeavouring to look as fierce and implacable as Sir Magnus cross-examining a hostile witness, Adrian strode back to the table. Black Nell was just telling Honoria that she could see her married to a very rich man with fourteen children. Mr. Filigree was down on hands and knees conducting a whispered conversation with a stag beetle. Sir Magnus, his arm round Mr. Pucklehammer's shoulders, was joining him in a spirited rendering of "Soldiers of the Queen", to which Ethelbert was doing what he fondly imagined to be an oriental belly dance, and Lord Fenneltree was still lying in a trance on the grass, listening to Lord Turvey.

"Where's Samantha?" barked Adrian. At least he had meant to bark but he had to clear his throat several times before he could articulate the words.

"Samantha," said Honoria in surprise, looking round. "I expect she's gone into the house."

"Good," snarled Adrian. He somewhat spoiled the effect of this by almost tripping over Mr. Filigree as he marched towards the *Unicorn and Harp*. He strode into the big stone-flagged kitchen with its dark beams and its friendly row of gleaming pots. Samantha was standing at one end looking out of the window. Adrian made his way down the length of the room and stood just behind her. He cleared his throat.

"Samantha," he said trenchantly, "I have got to talk to you."

"Why don't you *shut up*?" said Samantha fiercely.

"Now, it's no good adopting that high-handed attitude with me," said Adrian, taken aback. He stuck his hand inside his coat in a Napoleonic gesture.

"If you don't shut up and go away," said Samantha wheeling on him, her face flushed, her eyes glittering dangerously, "I won't be responsible for my actions."

"Come, come," said Adrian backing away a bit, "you're behaving like a child."

"And you," snapped Samantha, "are drunk."

"I am not drunk," said Adrian, stunned. "I am as sober as anyone else."

"You're drunk," said Samantha cuttingly, "otherwise you wouldn't have had the courage to adopt that high-handed tone with me, as though . . . as though you were speaking to a *horse*."

"A horse," said Adrian aghast, "I never spoke to you as though you were a horse."

"Exactly," said Samantha, "as though I was a very old and very badly trained horse."

And to Adrian's intense consternation she burst into tears.

"Oh, don't do that," said Adrian in agony. "I'm sorry . . . I apologise . . . only please don't cry."

"I'm *not* crying," said Samantha, the tears pouring down her cheeks.

"Well, what are you doing," said Adrian with desperate joviality, "having a bath?"

Samantha looked slightly taken aback and then, astonishingly, chuckled through her tears.

"You *are* a fool," she said affectionately.

Adrian felt as though somebody had driven a red hot skewer through his heart and twisted it.

"Oh, Samantha," he said, "I do love you so."

Samantha looked at him. "Well, that's good," she said at last, "it makes the feeling mutual."

"You mean," said Adrian incredulously, feeling as though he had been lifted into the stratosphere by a balloon, "you mean that I . . . that you . . . that you and I . . . that you . . ."

"Well, you've taken long enough about telling me," said Samantha.

"Do you mean to say," said Adrian, "that I . . . that you . . ."

"You know," said Samantha, looking up at him, "if you go on stammering like that, we are never even going to get to the honeymoon."

Adrian pulled her into his arms and kissed her warm mouth. Then he kissed the tears (which were surely the largest and finest tears that any woman had ever shed) from her cheeks, and then he kissed her mouth again because he couldn't really believe that it had felt and tasted like rose petals.

"You mean to say that you'll marry me?" he said huskily.

"Well, it may be new information to *you*," said Samantha, "but I made up my mind to marry you the moment I saw you lying on that sofa the night you arrived after the train accident."

Adrian looked at her incredulously—then he kissed her again.

"I must tell somebody," he said.

He rushed through the kitchen and out of the back door of the *Unicorn and Harp*.

"Hoy!" he bellowed.

The tranquil and slightly inebriated scene under the oak trees was galvanised. Even Lord Fenneltree sat up.

"I am going to marry Samantha!" shouted Adrian.

"Do you mean to say you've only just discovered *that*," said Sir Magnus, with disgust.

"But . . . how did you know?" said Adrian puzzled.

"I'm not going to divulge," said Sir Magnus. "There are some trade secrets which one doesn't bruit about."

"You're going to marry Sam?" said Mr. Filigree, getting to his feet with a start, and completely forgetting about his conversation with the stag beetle.

"If you approve," said Adrian.

"Approve," said Mr. Filigree. "Why, it's simply marvellous news. It means that Rosy will be an *in-law*."

"You don't by any chance have any champagne, do you?" said Adrian, light-headedly.

"An excellent thing," said Sir Magnus. "Champagne and cherry brandy are the perfect things for a toast."

They all trooped into the big kitchen and, while Mr. Filigree got out the champagne, which was slightly warm but none the less welcome for that, Honoria and Black Nell kissed Samantha enthusiastically and then Honoria burst into tears.

"What are you crying about?" asked Ethelbert.

"I always cry at weddings," sobbed Honoria with dignity.

"But this isn't a wedding," Ethelbert pointed out.

"It's *almost* a wedding," she said.

The glasses were filled and Sir Magnus proposed a toast to the happy couple, which was drunk with great enthusiasm. Adrian was just about to kiss Samantha for the fortieth time when he suddenly remembered Rosy.

"Good heavens," he said. "I've completely forgotten about Rosy. She must have a celebratory drink."

"I'll get her," fluted Mr. Filigree, "the poor dear."

He billowed his way out of the room.

"I hope," said Lord Fenneltree to Samantha, "that you will allow me the privilege of calling here occasionally when you are married?"

"You will always be one of our most welcome guests," said Samantha. "In fact, all of you will be."

"Yes, of course," said Adrian.

It was at this point that Mr. Filigree reappeared, running as fast as his bulk would allow him. He was pink, panting and perspiring.

"Adrian," he shrilled, "Adrian, come *quickly*."

"Whatever's the matter?" said Adrian startled.

"It's Rosy," squeaked Mr. Filigree. "When we weren't

looking she pinched the barrel of cherry brandy and she's gone running off with it."

Oh God, thought Adrian, it's starting all over again.

"Quick," said Sir Magnus organising things, "we must surround her before she gets too far away. Forward!"

And he rushed out, the tails of his coat flapping behind him, closely pursued by Honoria, Black Nell, Ethelbert, Mr. Pucklehammer and the judge, with Mr. Filigree wobbling in their wake.

Adrian turned and looked at Samantha.

"Are you *sure* you want to marry me?" he said.

"Quite sure," she said.

"Even in spite of Rosy?" he asked.

"Principally because of Rosy," she said smiling.

Adrian kissed her swiftly.

"Well then, excuse me a minute," he said, "I must go and catch my only living relative."

And he ran out into the sunlight in the wake of the others.

FAMOUS ANIMAL BOOKS IN FONTANA

Joy Adamson
"BORN FREE", "LIVING FREE", "FOREVER FREE".

The three classic best-sellers about Elsa the lioness, and her cubs. "Deeply moving and absorbing". *Gavin Maxwell*

George Adamson
"BWANA GAME"

The fascinating autobiography of a man totally dedicated to the preservation of wild animals. "A remarkable man—and a remarkable book." *Guardian*

Gerald Durrell
"TWO IN THE BUSH"

The story of his tour of New Zealand, Australia and Malaya in search of rare animals. "Will delight his fans and armchair naturalists everywhere." *Evening Standard*

Jacquie Durrell
"BEASTS IN MY BED"

The delights and difficulties of a life shared with her famous husband, writer and animal-lover Gerald Durrell. "An enchanting and very funny book." *Sunday Times*

E. P. Gee
"THE WILD LIFE OF INDIA"

A plea for the preservation of wild animals and birds in India. "Absolutely splendid. The photographs and text are of a very high quality." *Peter Scott*

Bernard and Michael Grzimek
"SERENGETI SHALL NOT DIE"

The famous story of the Serengeti National Park and the plight of its animals. "A remarkable book . . . Should be read by everyone." *Gerald Durrell*